The
Christmas Tea Shoppe

Jaclyn E. Robinson

The Christmas Tea Shoppe
First Edition, 2022
Copyright © 2022 by Jaclyn E. Robinson

Scripture quotations and words of Jesus taken or adapted from or adapted from the New American Standard Bible, ® Copyright ©1960,1962,1963, 1968, 1971, 1973, 1975, 1977, 1995 by the Lockman Foundation. Used by permission.

This novel is a work of fiction. Names, characters, and incidents are either the product of the author's imagination or are used fictitiously. Any resemblance to actual events, locales, organizations, or persons living or dead is entirely coincidental and beyond the intent of either the author or publisher.

To order additional books: *www.jaclynerobinson.com*

ISBN: 978-1-952943-17-1

E-book also available.

Editorial: Inspira Literary Solutions, Gig Harbor, WA, www.inspiralit.com
Book Cover Design, Inside Art, & Layout: Brianna Showalter
Printed in the USA.

For Mama, who loves me
with the grace of God every single day.

Contents

Prologue

"Bring it in, sunshine," said Sara, drawing her sister Grace in for a hug. "I wish I didn't have to go back tonight, but my ride has a date tomorrow and I couldn't convince her Homecoming in Homily would be more fun."

Sara's eye roll only partially conveyed her frustration. She always looked forward to coming home from school, especially the time spent with her little sister. Too many milestones had come and gone in her absence. Sometimes she wished they were closer in age, but she was hopeful the five years between them wouldn't matter as much in the future.

"Did you convince Nana and Papaw to let me go with Craig to the bonfire at the beach after the dance?" Grace asked, practically bouncing with excitement, her light blonde ponytail swinging with the movement and hope shining in her large, blue eyes.

"I did, on two conditions: First, you stay with Craig the entire time—"

"And second, no drinking. I know, I know."

Sara chuckled. "Yeah, I'm sure you do. But you forget, I've been to a few of those bonfires myself." A peachy blush crept into her high cheekbones.

"Spill it, sissy," demanded Grace, raising her eyebrows.

"Let's just say I made some personal choices I hope you'll avoid, for your own good."

"Fine. Keep your secrets this time, but eventually you'll have to tell me," retorted Grace, her lips mewed in a full pout.

Sara smirked and pulled her all-time favorite person close for one last hug, whispering into the shell of Grace's ear, "You make me happy when skies are gray; you'll never know, dear, how much I love you."

Grace stepped back with a smile, eyes exuding contagious joy, and sang the rest of words back to her sister. "Please don't take my sunshine away."

With a shiver, Sara Hart tried to shake the memory that clung to her thoughts and skin like cobwebs. She shifted from side to side for the umpteenth time on the uncomfortable metal chair.

It wasn't until Grace's junior year in high school that the behavior considered by most to be normal teenage rebellion escalated to a real cry for help. By the time her sister left home at the tender age of seventeen, she was drunk or high more often than not, and stealing from the people who had lovingly raised her in order to keep herself that way.

When Grace left town without a note or any indication of where she was going, it was as though she'd disappeared into the ether. Not even her best friend, Craig, knew where she had gone. Without a diploma or skills to feasibly support herself, everyone assumed Grace would eventually come back or reach out for help. But as weeks turned into months followed by years of waiting, they were left to assume the worst had finally happened. Life carried on nonetheless; seasons changed, folks married, families were started, her grandparents passed, and acceptance set in while Sara's grief morphed into guilt. She had failed to save the one person who needed her the most.

Without a phone call from Child Protective Services, she might never have known Grace was alive, let alone that she'd borne a child. Still in shock from the previous night's late night phone call, Sara looked at the little girl who was now her responsibility.

What am I getting myself into? she asked herself for the millionth time.

Across the room, her niece sat quietly coloring and trying to blend in with the shadows forming on the wall from the sun's slow descent outside the decrepit building. No child should endure the things she had. Physical abuse, neglect—God only knew what else her young mind had been exposed to.

Guilt sat heavy on Sara's shoulders once again as she thought of Grace, but it would seem her erstwhile companion had come to collect its debt in the form of her niece. A demanding master, guilt wasn't the only emotion riding her hard. In fact, it was a small drop in the large ocean her feelings had become since yesterday.

Though Sara was slightly petrified of becoming an impromptu mother, she liked to think any sane person would be. Reasoning with herself that fear was meant to be overcome, not gotten into bed with, she decided to simply put her ducks in a row.

Surely being a parent can't be any harder than running a successful business, right?

Glancing through the file folder sitting front and center on the social worker's institutional desk, Sara tried to reign in her grief. The ugly photographs documented the physical abuse endured by mother and daughter at the hand of Grace's boyfriend, the only piece of information Sara had to go on as she tried to piece together the sad story.

The social worker only added to Sara's misery when she said, "Your sister's relationship with the man appeared to be more of a business transaction. I don't think they'd been together very long, if you get my meaning."

Sara sat up straighter at the woman's implication, looked the social worker directly in the eye, and with a lift of her left eyebrow dared her to say the actual word out loud. Even if her sister was a prostitute, it was none of this stranger's business. The woman knew nothing about her sunshine. If anything, the information before them should produce compassion, not judgment. Wisely, the social worker chose to take the discussion in a more productive direction.

Ms. Adams cleared her throat and straightened the already tidy polyester bow at the bottom of her slender, brown neck. Her chicory eyes bored into Sara's.

"Apparently, a neighbor had the good sense to report a domestic dispute when the argument spilled onto your sister's front lawn. Unfortunately for your sister, it meant being charged with drug use and possession, in addition to child neglect. If convicted, she'll most likely serve time at a women's penitentiary. Rather than wait for her parental rights to be terminated or have the child put into the system, Ms. Hart signed her parental rights over to you, her only stipulation being no further contact with y'all."

The request elicited only mild surprise from Sara. Shame could strike a mighty blow better than any weapon. It sought to keep a person laid low and hiding, slithering in the dark crevices of a lonely heart, poking and prodding until a person felt they no longer deserved to be loved. She would give her sister space for the time being, but she had no intention of following through with such a ridiculous notion long term. Family was family, after all, and shame was no match for an overbearing sister. Sara didn't believe in letting go, and she only knew one way to love: fiercely.

Please watch over Grace and show her how much you love her, even behind prison bars, Sara prayed silently.

"If you'll just sign here, here, and here, you can take temporary custody of your niece. The judge assigned to the case will determine permanence based on your in-home visits and the child advocate's recommendation."

Sara reached for the pen Ms. Adams waved in her general direction. With a heavy sigh, she signed the paperwork and marched over to the corner where the little girl still sat.

"I'm your Aunt Sara. You're going to live with me now."

Even to her own ears the words sounded gruff. Too little, too late to cry over spilled tea. Better to brew a whole new pot and start fresh.

Her niece ducked her small, blonde head to avoid eye contact and held her breath while Sara took her by the hand. No tears or arguments sprang forth as they stepped outside into early twilight, and what Sara desperately hoped would be a new beginning for all of them.

She buckled her niece into the booster seat she'd bought from Walmart only that morning, along with a handful of other items for the immediate future and assured herself she was up to the challenge of being a single parent. A little self-bolstering never hurt anyone, least of all the person in need of it. She placed her key in the ignition, turning it over until the car's engine roared to life.

Normally a short drive from Mobile to the small town of Homily on Alabama's Gulf Coast, time kept its own counsel and slowly crept into dusk, her precious cargo resolutely mute in the back seat. Every glance made in the rear-view mirror was yet another reminder of Sara's newfound responsibilities.

....

"Let's get you settled in, sweet pea. This is the house your mama and I grew up in. You get to have your own room and we can paint it any color you want. Would you like that?"

When her question garnered no response, she tried again.

"Do you like macaroni and cheese casserole with bacon?" She waited another beat, and said, "It was your mama's favorite, so I thought it might be yours too."

Defeated by the continued silence, Sara led her charge inside the bungalow full of memories, her sister a ghostly companion to their every step.

Dinner was the quiet affair she feared it would be, and neither of them ate more than a few bites. A half hour later, Sara dipped her elbow into the hip-height water to check the temperature and helped her niece into the small, claw-foot tub, afraid she would slip on the slick surface.

I should add an anti-slip mat to the shopping list.

Sara worried at her bottom lip with her teeth as she took in the bruises on the little girl's back and forbade herself to cry. A fist pressed to her lips, she swallowed the sob threatening to choke her, desperate to keep herself under wraps in the child's presence.

Is this my life now? A constant barrage of worries and overwhelming emotions? Striving for perfection but already certain I'll fail spectacularly?

Startled by the intrusive sound of Sara's sobs, her niece turned from the bubbles she splashed in, cropped curls bouncing this way and that with her movements. She looked so much like her mama that Sara hurt with the loss of Grace all over again. Helpless to keep her feelings dammed any longer, she didn't lean away as tiny hands reached out to cup her face. Tentatively, she covered those small ones with her own as bath water mixed with salty tears. Almond-shaped eyes the color of cornflowers met her gray ones directly for the first time.

"It's okay, Aunt Saywa. I'm here now."

One

Dear Sunshine,

I just found out the sister I lost is found. You are no longer dead but alive! Do with my letter what you will, but with it I send hope for your future. The gentleman is Mr. Daniel Montgomery, and he's the best defense attorney in the state of Alabama. Please, let him do what he can to help. Don't worry about the cost. Love you, to the stars and back.

Always, Sissy

Matt

Matthew Dixon rolled over to answer the phone vibrating on his nightstand. Through bleary eyes, he squinted at the time, ran a hand through his short, brown hair, and turned off his alarm. With only the faintest light shining through the blinds of his bedroom window, he desperately wanted to hit snooze, but it wouldn't be fair to the attending physician on duty to be late. In addition to his usual daytime shift, he'd been on call the previous few nights and spent more hours at the hospital than sleeping. Unfortunately, this fact did not make for a good excuse among doctors.

Though no longer a resident, Matt had yet to figure out how to enjoy much of a life outside his profession; it was probably his own fault for choosing emergency medicine as his specialty. In life, there are endless emergencies but never enough hands on deck, or so he'd been told numerous times during his residency.

He took a quick shower, neglecting yesterday's dark growth on his jaw, and rushed through the rest of his usual routine. Matt reached for his phone, which he'd left on the bed in a mound of disheveled sheets and comforter, and was almost to the staircase when he remembered his watch and beeper. With a quick turnabout, he quickly grabbed the forgotten items and caught a whiff of his favorite smell trailing up the stairs from the kitchen.

Gran was listening to the local morning show on the radio while she pulled homemade biscuits from the oven, the space almost entirely covered in the tools of her trade. Flour lay scattered over the wood-block counters, a rolling pin tossed to the side, and cake tins were stacked in any leftover nook or cranny. Of course, Matt also knew the kitchen would be spic and span by seven a.m. He snatched two biscuits from the cooling racks on the counter before drifting toward the coffee pot—the elixir of life, caffeine.

"Don't you sneak those biscuits as if I won't notice, and leave without a proper goodbye, young man." Gran's tone was stern, but she couldn't fool him. He knew her heart was the gooey center of a toasted marshmallow.

"I would never, and you know it," Matt replied with a wink and dimpled grin.

"I surely do. Now where's my kiss, sweet boy?" she demanded as she presented her soft cheek. The scent of her lotion tickled his nose with a hint of vanilla, but she pulled back to shake her finger in his face before he could follow through.

"And take two more biscuits for the road. Not an ounce of fat on you. No woman will ever want a man with nothing to hold onto."

"I thought it was the reverse of that which was true."

"Well, yes, I suppose so. After all, God gave women curves for a reason. It's just a matter of how much padding we add to them," she chuckled, smiling like a cat who'd stolen the cream, her fair cheeks turning rosy.

He chuckled at her blush before leaning over once more to kiss her cheek and obediently took two more biscuits for the road.

"I think your curves are perfect, Gran."

With his travel mug in hand, Matt headed for the front door.

"Matthew," Gran called from the kitchen doorway. "Sara Hart called yesterday from The Christmas Tea Shoppe to let me know my favorite tea is back in stock. Be an angel and pick some up for me on your way home today?"

"Happy to oblige."

"She also mentioned her niece is coming back to town soon."

"Hopefully they'll have a nice visit together," he responded, shoving his feet into his running shoes. Matt quickly tied them before grabbing his work out bag from under the entry bench. He would need to hit the gym after his shift if he was ever going to keep Gran's cooking from taking up permanent residence on his frame. He knew she meant well, but trying to convince her that his body didn't need the extra weight any more than he needed someone to hold onto in life would only fall on deaf ears.

"Mm-hmm. I've known Abby since she was little bitty. Cutest thing you ever did see, and smart too. Graduated valedictorian from Homily High. I remember how proud Sara was of her."

"She sounds nice, but I have to leave now if I'm not going to be late."

"All right, sweet boy, but don't forget the tea."

Nancy Dixon bottled her frustration away. Her grandson could hear just fine, but he wasn't really listening to what she was telling him.

"I won't, Gran," floated back to her as he turned in the direction of the front door.

Nancy watched her grandson leave, accepting defeat and certain he would do exactly that.

"Oh, well," she grumbled to herself before remembering she wasn't alone in her troubles. "Lord, I could use a little help down here. Point of fact, I think our boy could use some deliberate interference on your behalf."

Happy to have passed along her burden, she made her way back down the hall. After all, those biscuits were not going to make themselves.

....

Wearing light blue scrubs and his favorite baseball cap low over his eyes, Matt pulled up the zipper of his faded hoodie to guard against the early morning chill and stepped into the jasmine- coated spring air. He looked up past the live oak surrounding Gran's yard, taking note of the sky's progression from orange into pink and what would eventually become the perfect azure of a southern coastal day. Not a wisp of cloud in the sky.

He made a beeline for his granddad's 1944 Ford pickup, painted a glossy black and trimmed in chrome, noting the garbage cans lying halfway between the driveway and the road for the second time in as many weeks. He glanced from the cans to Gran's large, four-door sedan parked in the gravel next to his truck and resolved to address the issue with her soon. In the meantime, he righted the plastic bins against the backdrop of the two-story white house with navy shutters.

The house, built in the mid-1800s and designed in the traditional South Carolina Lowcountry style, was slightly elevated off the ground with a broad hip roof and wraparound porch. The architecture was distinct, if a bit unusual for its location. Matt had lived here often growing up—first, during his dad's army career, which moved them from one post to the next at regular two-year intervals, and then after his parents' divorce. Fortunately, his grandparents' house had provided the stability he craved as a child and longed for as an adult.

Once medical school was complete, followed by a residency in emergency medicine at Duke University, Matt had looked for attending positions at hospitals within easy driving distance of his gran. He'd jumped at the opportunity to work at Grant Hospital, located close to the Mobile County line and serving the community of Homily. He nailed the interview and accepted the job a week later, knowing he was exactly where he was meant to be.

When he'd called Gran to share the news, she insisted, "Of course you are where you're supposed to be. God doesn't make mistakes, Matthew Lee Dixon. Besides, there's far too much space in this house for me. You can take your old bedroom. It'll be just like old times."

And to some extent it was. She still went to bed early and got up with the sun, but these days she rested after lunch and spent less time in her prized flower beds. When his granddad passed away ten years earlier, Gran seemed more than capable of taking care of the house and yard, but at eighty years old, he was starting to see how time had taken its toll. Fortunately, her diabetes appeared to be under control for the time being.

Matt made a mental tally of all the house decay that needed to be fixed in the future. He would either need to make time to do the projects himself or hire a contractor. Hopefully someone at work could give him a few recommendations in town. Word of mouth made small towns like Homily go round in more ways than one.

Abby

Abigail Hart caught sight of her reflection in a store window on Main Street as the airport shuttle pulled away from the curb. She stopped to scrunch her pale, blonde ringlets, which only added to the frizz, and tried to arrange them into some semblance of order. In all honesty, she didn't know why she bothered. It would all just wind up in a mess on top of her head by the end of the day anyway. At least the heat wasn't so bad at this time of year. She knew in a few months that wouldn't be the case, even with a breeze coming off the water nearby. Her trip home could not have come at a better time, both for the mild spring weather and for personal reasons.

The bell above The Christmas Tea Shoppe tinkled lightly as she pushed open the wood door, the aroma of baked goods and warm tea instantly enveloping her in the sweet smells of home. Closing her eyes and breathing in deeply, Abby took a moment to soak in the feeling of welcome she always felt upon entering Aunt Sara's tea shop. Some of her earliest memories were of the shop and time spent here with her aunt. She knew there were other memories lurking in the corners of her mind from another time and place before Aunt Sara, but they were murky shadows she could easily push away. She'd made a habit of ignoring anything to do with her mother.

The first time she'd stepped into the Christmas Tea Shoppe had been right before Christmas, and the shop had certainly lived up to its name. While always decorated with a nod to the season, the shop went all out for the holidays with a real tree, and fresh fir and cedar boughs covering every available surface.

That first Christmas, the shop's oak trim had been polished to gleaming with garlands of cranberries and tinsel draped along its understated lines, and scents of pine and cinnamon wafting through the shop. Snow globes balanced precariously on top of a glass case holding all manner of delectable treats, with Aunt Sara's famous southern white cake topped with buttercream frosting and edible hibiscus being the *pièce de résistance*. It was truly a winter wonderland for any child, with glass ornaments, twinkling lights, and an endless flow of hot chocolate topped off with whipped cream and crushed candy cane sprinkles.

Looking around, eyes wide with a child's curiosity and wonder, Abby had watched adults perched in dainty Queen Anne chairs at tables swathed in pristine white cloths topped with silver tea sets. Hints of peppermint, bergamot, and clove had wafted from fine bone china teacups, while ladies delicately lifted bites of cake to their crimson lips with antique silver flatware. It had all seemed like magic to Abby then, just a small child, but every time she walked into the shop, she still remembered what it had been like to walk in for the first time.

"Hi there," a voice rang out through the space, interrupting her walk down memory lane. It was followed up with a drawled, "Just let me know if I can help you with anything."

As she stepped towards the front counter, the hardwood surface creaked under her feet. Abby tacked a smile on her face and looked for any sign of recognition from the young woman who stood sentry. Aunt Sara often hired community college students to help in the shop during the busier times of the year, and school breaks never failed to bring travelers to the coast. Even with hired help during the holidays and summertime, her aunt worked full time as tourism overran the town, much to the delight of every shop owner on Main Street.

When no sign of recognition flashed in the young woman's eyes, and thinking her aunt must be in the kitchen, Abby asked, "Is Sara in today?"

"No, I'm afraid not. She went home early, but I'd be happy to help you or pass along a message."

"Thank you, but I'm sure Sara and I will run into each other soon," said Abby, tongue in cheek.

"Okay, let me know if I can help you with anything else."

17

No doubt repeating a mantra Aunt Sara had drilled into each of her employees, the woman was unfailingly polite.

"There is never an excuse to be rude. Sassy maybe, but never rude," whispered her aunt's voice in her head.

When Abby had the gall to ask the difference between the two at the quarrelsome age of ten, her aunt had simply shaken her head and handed Abby one of many dictionaries kept on the built-in bookshelves that lined the living room wall. Taking a pencil and paper from the telephone drawer in the kitchen, Aunt Sara had then silently sat her down at the dining table to write out each of the definitions ten times apiece. Once completed, her aunt used clothes pins with magnets glued onto the back to hang them on the refrigerator, as though they were works of art instead of punishment. Never again did Abby question her aunt's vocabulary knowledge.

Abby left the shop, her rolling suitcase bumping over the sidewalk behind her. She was glad to have a little more time to herself to mull over her future plans. When she'd broken her engagement a year ago, she had initially thought to make her way home to live with her aunt, but she'd left Homily with good reason after college. The years of whispers and the way folks sometimes looked right through her, as though all they saw was her mother, had taken their toll. Abby wanted them to leave her mama in the past the way she had tried, but failed, to do.

She was almost past the town's square when a Cadillac Seville in candy apple red suddenly pulled up next to her, passenger window rolled down to reveal a woman with rich molasses skin and cropped white hair in tight curls.

"Abby Hart, is that you? Baby girl, I haven't seen you in too long."

"Hey, Mrs. Hanson. It's good to see you."

"Your aunt must be so excited to have you home. It's about time you came back."

"Yes, ma'am. My visit is long overdue."

"You look like you could use a ride. Hop on in, child," Dot said over the air conditioning blowing full blast, the scent of shea butter and coconut wafting out the open window.

"Thank you for the offer, but I could use the walk after sitting so much today. It's only a couple more blocks."

"Suit yourself. Tell Sara hello for me," Dot said, rolling the window up, only to reverse direction halfway. "And before I forget, tell her the Michaelsons have worked themselves into a tizzy over the new awning for the shop. They're complaining to anyone who'll listen that your aunt didn't ask the HHPS first."

Abby kept her amusement to herself. Dot Hanson was one of Aunt Sara's staunchest supporters, and one of only a few people she had genuinely missed in her absence.

"Mm-hmm. Those old biddies are always startin' trouble. As if this town could preserve any more history than it already does— some of it not even worth saving if you ask me, not that anyone does."

"Yes, ma'am. I'll be sure to pass the message on."

"Y'all come by for hushpuppies later this week. Mine were always your favorite."

Without waiting for her reply Dot shot away from the curb, headed west at 90 mph. The words of an old song came to Abby's mind—something about a little old lady from somewhere in California.

TWO

Dear Sunshine,

Thank you for your letter. Per your request, I'll keep our communications brief. To answer your question, I've been living in Homily since completing school. I'm sorry to have to tell you that Nana and Papaw passed away shortly after. With the small inheritance they left me, I opened a shop in our little downtown, off the square on Second and Main. The Christmas Tea Shoppe is Homily's very own tea parlor and importer of fine teas. Love you, to the stars and back.

Always, Sissy

Matt

After checking in with the residents on shift to ensure all moving parts were working with the precision of a well-oiled hinge, Matt made his way to the pediatric wing on the second floor to follow up with Johnny, a patient from the previous week. Airlifted to Grant Hospital from a rural clinic a few counties over, Johnny had suffered second-degree burns to most of the left side of his torso and arm, which meant remaining in the hospital for the duration of his wound care. Matt had been the attending on duty when the energetic little boy came into the ER on an already busy evening.

He took a sharp left off the elevator and walked to the nurses' station, where the charge nurse sat with her gaze on the computer screen in front of her.

Shelby pushed her glasses back up onto the bridge of her nose and pierced him with her all-seeing, amber-colored eyes before greeting him in her alto drawl.

"Morning, Dr. Dixon."

"Morning, Shelby. I like the new glasses. Tangerine is fun. And, dare I say, suits you."

She raised her right eyebrow in response and replied, "They're bifocals, and no amount of sweet talkin' is gonna change the way I feel about them."

"Okay. I'll just put my charming self on the back burner for now, but you know one of my favorite parts of the day is trying to get you to smile. How's our patient in Room 221 doing this morning?"

"Feeling rambunctious as usual. His poor Mama's gonna have a coronary trying to keep him calm and resting so those wounds can heal." Shelby gave him a half smile and continued, "She could probably use a break, and so could I if you want to check his wounds and vitals since you're here."

"Happy to oblige. You know I'd do just about anything for you and your staff." He meant every word too. Matt had made a practice of being observant throughout his residency. Nurses worked long hours and spent more time with patients and their families than the physicians did. Most were a fount of information, and the best ones were both thorough and empathetic to the plight of their patients—which reminded him, "How is George doing, by the way?"

"Back to complaining about everything as usual. Though, after that gallbladder scare last fall, I suppose I can put up with him for a while longer."

Shelby said it in her typical matter-of-fact manner, but Matt heard the relief behind her statement.

"Tell him I said to exercise, eat his greens, and take good care of you. Doctor's orders." He began to pivot in the direction of Johnny's room but stopped. "Oh, and tell him thank you again for helping with the plumbing in Gran's bathroom over the weekend while I was on shift. She wants to know his favorite pie."

"Pecan, but don't you think twice about that. George was more than happy to help. Makes him feel useful and keeps him out of my gray hair. Now go on. I've got work to do and that little boy's Mama has probably pulled out her own hair by now."

Matt entered his young patient's room with a peek over his shoulder at Shelby. Though her straightened black hair was streaked with a few silver strands, it wasn't close to the gray she described, and her mocha skin barely wrinkled at her eyes when she smiled. Matt wondered what it might be like to be with someone through the ups and downs of life for a lifetime like Shelby and George. As much as she fussed about her husband's attitude, Matt knew from watching the two of them together that George adored his wife of forty years. They shared a kind of intimacy with one another that only death could sunder. It was the same kind of relationship his grandparents had achieved, and his parents never could.

He turned back to focus on the little boy running circles around his visibly frazzled mother and smiled at the barely controlled chaos that was Johnny. A person had only to be in his presence for a moment to understand how the rascal had knocked a pot of boiling water onto himself during a game of tag in the kitchen with his older brothers. The wonder was how his injuries couldn't curb his energy.

"Dr. Dixon! Dr. Dixon! Dr. Dixon!" Johnny exclaimed. His childish exuberance so evident in every chant, Matt couldn't help but grin ear to ear in return.

Abby

"Aunt Sara, I'm home," Abby called out.

She took another step into the small entryway of the house she'd grown up in, toed off her espadrilles, and threw them down haphazardly by the front door. She tossed her coral cardigan and matching purse onto the sofa as she walked through the living room—never mind the hooks mounted to the wall at the left of the door, or the shoe basket underneath, near the narrow stairs that led to the bedrooms on the second floor.

She made her way to the back of the house and Aunt Sara's favorite place, knowing the sunroom was where she would most likely find her aunt. Enclosed years earlier, with windows lining three of the four walls, the sunroom could be reached through an open doorway in the corner of the kitchen.

Filled with brightly colored woven rugs and white wicker furniture covered in plush cushions, the room radiated relaxation with lazily spinning fans whirring overhead and afternoon sun dapples from the multiple magnolia trees in the backyard. Guests were formally entertained in the small living room at the front of the house in what was once the parlor before Aunt Sara removed the wall separating it from the dining room and kitchen. But the sunroom remained a place for family and only the closest of friends.

She had not bothered to be quiet when she entered the house, so Abby was surprised to find her aunt asleep on the couch wrapped in a soft throw blanket, a book left open on the small side table next to her aunt's reading glasses. Picking up the book, Abby turned to the page bookmarked with a turned-down corner. As she suspected, it was a regency novel written by one of her aunt's favorite authors.

As much as Aunt Sara loved a good romance though, she had never married. On the rare occasion the topic of marriage came up between them, her aunt repeated the same phrase, "I am as single as a dollar, and I am not looking for change." In her husky voice she'd follow up by saying, "I might be single but that doesn't mean I'm immune to a good romance. After all, isn't that what God does for all of us? He pursues us until we understand just how big and wide his love for us is."

The response always felt a tad bit dramatic to Abby, and though she wanted to roll her eyes, she would never have the audacity to disrespect her aunt's opinions. Besides, when would Aunt Sara have found the time to date? For all intents and purposes, she had been a single mother running a full-time business. Abby couldn't help but wonder if that was the real reason her aunt had never married. Saddled with her irresponsible sister's child, she never got the chance.

Eyes heavy from sleep, Aunt Sara touched Abby's hand lightly.

"Well, don't you look as pretty as a spring day, baby girl."

Abby looked down at the denim wrap dress she'd put on earlier that morning before catching her flight to Mobile.

"Huh. I've worn this dress so much to work the kids have taken to calling it Ms. Hart's lucky blue dress. Or so Lily Sutton made sure to inform me one day while I bandaged her playground knees."

"I've always loved that color on you. It matches your eyes."

Abby shooed away the compliment with a wave of her hand.

"Maybe my students are right, and I put it on this morning with the subconscious hope for luck. Does flying out on schedule count?"

Sara pushed herself upright, a bit of sleep wrapped around her vocal cords, and responded, "If your flight actually left on time, I'd say it's either a miracle or the Almighty thought it was past time for you to come home." It was said with gentleness, but no less rebuke for Abby's absence this last year.

"Now I know you wanted your space, baby girl, but staying away from home is your way of punishing yourself and we both know it."

Blowing out an audible breath, Abby sank into the couch. "Sometimes I hate the way you see through me, Aunt Sara."

"There's no hate in this house, only love. Besides, I don't see through you. I *see* you."

How many times had Abby heard those words growing up? Too many times to count. Her aunt was right, nothing but love resided in her home. With another deep breath, Abby gathered the words that are hard for anyone who isn't perfect.

"I'm sorry, Aunt Sara. I'm sorry for staying away so long. I have no good excuse for it." It was as close to the truth as she could get in the moment.

Aunt Sara wrapped her up tightly and softly spoke the words Abby needed to hear. "It's okay, baby girl. All is forgiven. God's grace makes it so." Drawing back, her aunt looked her in the eye and said with more enthusiasm, "Now, how about we pull out the butter pecan ice cream I bought at the Piggly Wiggly yesterday?"

"Do you even need to ask?"

"No, but we are definitely going to spoil our dinner by eating ice cream so late in the afternoon."

"Well then, we should make sundaes, so we don't need to eat dinner at all."

"I like the way you think. Let's do it, sugar! Let's ruin our dinner!"

Abby laughed loud and full in response, unable to remember the last time she had done so. Like unbuttoning a pair of jeans after a good meal, her relief kept her company while she set about making triple scoop sundaes with extra maraschino cherries on top to celebrate coming home.

....

Once Abby finished unpacking her suitcase, she quickly texted her best friend Maggie to let her know she'd arrived safely at Aunt Sara's. No doubt they would catch up on the phone sometime the next day or the day after. Used to seeing Mags, or at the very least talking to her, on a daily basis made the moment somewhat lonely. Abby missed her friend already and the prospect of moving back home felt more poignant than it should have otherwise.

With a sigh, Abby pushed her melancholy thoughts aside, and tried to focus on the time she would have with Maggie before leaving permanently in a couple of months. Besides, it wasn't fair to Aunt Sara to spend her entire visit in a constant state of trepidation about the future.

By the time she joined her aunt in the living room, Sara was already settled into the needlepoint pillows sewn by their Nana. Together with the beige houndstooth-patterned sofa Sara had found at an estate sale in the next county over, the effect was one of comfort and style. Abby tucked her legs underneath herself in a wingback chair across from her aunt, pushing back into the lumbar cushions she'd bought at a post-Christmas sale a few years ago. The oak hardwood floors were covered by several rugs purchased from a local textile artist. The entire front room of the house seamlessly blended old into new.

As Aunt Sara's hands fluttered over the tea tray in front of her, arranging milk and sugar like soldiers on a battlefield, Abby let her eyes continue to trace around the familiar room. Flanked by white, painted built-ins and lined with jars in varying heights and colors, and an antique oval mirror overhead, the mantel captured center stage over a gas fireplace for the colder months. From there, the formal living area flowed directly into the dining room, centered with a round federal-style table and four matching chairs Aunt Sara had reupholstered in colonial blue velvet when Abby was in high school. Despite the small space and low ceiling, the area was well lit with a delicate, three-light pendant resting flush in a molded crown, pendeloques dripping with feminine delicacy to welcome each guest to dinner.

The kitchen itself wasn't large but removing the breakfast nook had allowed Aunt Sara to add an island for extra counter space. She complained on occasion about the open space, because by default it meant she had to keep her kitchen clean in case a guest popped by unannounced. But this was always quickly followed by a light laugh and the admission that there are worse things in life than a messy house, or friends who care enough to stop in for a visit.

Besides, the kitchen was airy and updated with navy blue cabinets, white marble countertops, and subway tile backsplash. Except for an oversized copper mixer on her counter, a matching teapot on her stainless-steel stove, and canisters for baking supplies, the place looked neat as a pin.

Abby lifted the dainty rose-patterned teacup Aunt Sara handed her and gently sipped the steaming lavender Earl Grey tea that in recent years had become an imported pantry staple. While on a trip to England a few years earlier, for an ethical tea conference, her aunt had taken a day trip to Bee Hill Lavender Farm just outside of London. The small family-run business, which usually sold most of its products directly on site, conceded to send her several boxes as a trial partnership. Three years later, the tea was still one of Aunt Sara's top sellers at The Christmas Tea Shoppe.

Lifting her own cup of the comforting brew, Aunt Sara asked Abby the inevitable. "So, what finally brought you home for spring break, sweet pea?"

Abby could have answered the question any number of ways, but Aunt Sara knew her too well to try and pull one over on her. Not to mention their weekly conversations on the phone. It wasn't as if her aunt didn't know the goings on of her life. Better to keep it straight forward, Abby decided.

"I'm heartsore, and maybe a little lost, too."

Aunt Sara visibly paused in thought for a moment, her lips pursing slightly to the side before responding. "Well, I guess admitting it is always the first step. But have no fear, sugar, because God is in the business of binding up the broken hearted and finding the lost."

Abby tried to digest her aunt's words. She wanted to believe them. Still, she couldn't help but wonder if God really cared about her struggles. Surely, her troubles were insignificant when compared with everything else going on in the world.

Three

Dear Sunshine,

To the question you posed, I ask why not? Christmas is a season for joy. It's a time when the impossible becomes miraculous; when love and redemption came into this world wrapped in the glad tidings of a child's birth. What greater gift could God have given than His only son? The shop is my daily reminder, and maybe for others too, that God so loved the world, He gave us Christmas to prove it. Love you, to the stars and back.

Always, Sissy

Matt

Eight hours after his first shift began, Matt sought out his favorite room in the hospital to help prepare for the second one he'd taken for a colleague with a bout of food poisoning. Even though he loved working in the ER, he knew any room with the right equipment could be used for an emergency. No, his favorite room inside Grant was the chapel.

The chapel had been designed and built with deliberation. It contained a beautiful, stained-glass window rendering Jesus as a shepherd among lambs and overlooking a sturdy altar of acacia wood. Because the chapel sat at the end of the first-floor wing and extended past the rest of the sterile building, sunlight shone through the vivid colors most of the day. The altar held court with carved trumpets and lily of the valley climbing up on either side, while front and center a depiction of a dove with an olive branch sat atop a throne.

Somehow, being in the chapel always brought Matt a sense of peace without displacing all his other emotions. Thankfulness and joy were sometimes present, but more often it was tears of grief and desperate prayers for loved ones in surgery or the final throes of life. Matt took a seat in a pew at the back to give others their privacy, while a resident chaplain kept watch nearby, available day or night to assist patients, families, and staff.

He took out the compact Bible he'd stashed in his hospital locker for moments like this, reading the fine print that calmed his spirit and renewed his strength. Losing a patient was never easy.

His heart broke for the family, even though he'd done everything he could. Sometimes it simply wasn't enough.

Silently he prayed, *Give me wisdom and discernment. Comfort those who grieve. Amen.*

His pager, clipped to his scrubs at the waist, went off as he left the quiet solitude of the chapel. Quickly making his way down the sterile, white corridors, Matt knew it was only a matter of time before it was followed by a voice over the hospital's PA system requesting his presence in the ER.

"So much for getting a little shut-eye," he murmured, increasing his pace while his conscience niggled at him. He may not be interested in having a serious romantic relationship, but if he kept up this pace, he wouldn't be giving himself the opportunity to build a life outside of work any time soon. Gran's voice in his head saying exactly those words didn't help ease his inner thoughts, none of which mattered when he entered the ER a minute later.

"What do we have, Jazmyn?" Matt asked, taking the chart from a petite nurse with floral tattoos for sleeves.

She pushed back the wide headband holding her mahogany afro in place. "Male in his twenties. Severely beaten with a bat. Multiple contusions and possible fractures. His ribs resemble roadkill. Our patient said his girlfriend's brother took a bat to him after he slapped her around."

"How unfortunate," said Matt dryly, clenching his jaw. "Is our patient pressing charges against his girlfriend's brother?" he asked nodding toward the officer posted outside the curtain.

"Police are here for our patient. His girlfriend pressed charges first."

"Well, it appears my granddad was right then."

"How so?" she asked.

"Sometimes a person actually reaps what they sow."

"If that were true, his girlfriend would've been holding the bat. Looks like he got off easy to me," Jazmyn murmured as she pushed back the curtain.

Abby

Abby lay in bed, her eyes staring blankly at various dark spots in the room. Even without a light on, she knew every detail. The walls were painted a light turquoise with accents of lilac gracing the top of her white dresser on the far wall and the nightstand tucked into the corner beside her double bed. A quilt made by the sewing circle at Homily Baptist Church warmly cocooned her in varying shades of the same colors.

Aunt Sara had bought the quilt for Abby's thirteenth birthday, and with her usual fanfare had presented the gift wrapped in bright-pink tissue paper and beribboned with light pink tulle.

"If my baby girl is officially a teenager then she needs a grownup room with grown up bedding," her aunt had declared.

The next day, they drove to Hickam's Toolbox to pick out paint, with a quick stop at the shop for tea and red velvet macarons. Then it was off to Attic Embellishments for treasures to finish the transformation of her bedroom into what Aunt Sara called a *boudoir*—which turned out to be a fancy French word for a lady's bedroom, much to Abby's delight.

Perhaps she'd buy a quilt to send Maggie for Christmas this year, assuming the local churches continued their tradition of an annual bazaar to raise funds for the fire department's holiday toy drive. Pleased with her idea, Abby smiled into the dark. The iron bed frame squeaked as she rolled from one side to the other and her thoughts returned to her earlier conversation with Aunt Sara.

"Shouldn't you be wide awake and ready to chat the night away, what with your afternoon nap?" Abby jokingly chided her aunt.

"I've just been a little fatigued of late. No need to fuss over me. I'm not as young as I used to be, is all."

Abby almost rolled her eyes but caught herself in the nick of time.

"Aunt Sara, you're only fifty-seven." *And a beautiful fifty-seven she is*, Abby thought with another concerned glance in her aunt's direction.

Like a movie star from Hollywood's Golden Age, Aunt Sara had an hourglass figure and wavy, auburn hair that fell to her shoulders. Her fair skin remained mostly unwrinkled except for the laugh lines at the corners of her storm-gray eyes and mouth. She really was stunning, but mostly it was her zest for life and the grace she exuded for everyone that made her aunt stand out in a crowd.

"Not until June. Don't make me any older than I am, child."

With a hint of exasperation Abby laughed in response. "My point exactly."

"Besides, I want to be at the shop early tomorrow. With the month of May just around the corner, I need to make sure I'm prepared for Mother's Day. You know we always have a full house, since it's the only Sunday of the year we're open."

"And sometimes customers even come for second breakfast and elevenses. I have no doubt you are well prepared for the masses on any given day."

"Oh, just listen to my baby girl quote Tolkien and chide me in the same sentence. I've always known how smart you are, but I know I didn't raise you to be rude. You can make it up to me by helping in the shop tomorrow."

"Perfect. It'll give me a chance to spend as much time with you as possible before going back to a classroom full of students eager to be out for the summer."

Despite the imperfect circumstances awaiting her return, Abby was determined to finish out the school year before turning in her resignation. She had every intention of using this spring break to heal and regain her footing so she could leave her failed engagement behind her—Lord willing, with a clear conscience and open heart.

She'd finally drifted off to sleep when the sound of glass shattering on hardwood brought her fully awake again. Her heart lodged in her throat, Abby raced from her room and down the narrow steps, a loud thud reverberating through the floor as she rounded the banister in a sprint for the kitchen.

Aunt Sara lay unconscious in front of the porcelain sink, broken glass strewn in every direction.

Her heart in her throat, Abby tiptoed quickly through the minefield, wincing when a small piece embedded itself in the big toe of her left foot. Her aunt appeared to be bleeding from cuts to her hands and a small gash on her forehead, but her shallow respiration and faint pulse were much more alarming. Reaching up for the old rotary-style phone kept on the kitchen counter, Abby watched in panic as her hands shook and dialed for help. The three numbers went round and round endlessly until a calm monotone voice answered, "9-1-1, what is your emergency?"

....

The ride to Grant Hospital in the car behind the ambulance had felt interminable. Though Aunt Sara was still breathing on her own when the paramedics arrived, they made it clear being unconscious meant any number of things had gone wrong, or still could.

Now the wait in the ER seemed just as endless while Abby paced the floor in front of a muted television hung in the corner broadcasting some late show with celebrity guests. In cotton pajama pants, a ribbed tank top, and a blazer she'd found in her aunt's car, Abby chewed on her bottom lip and alternately pushed back the ringlets escaping the bun she'd fashioned her hair into as part of her nightly routine.

Finally, at the end of her short tether, Abby determined to ask the formidable registration staff, again, if an update would be available in the near future. She spun ungracefully in her flip flops, big toe smarting from the movement, in the direction of the front desk and abruptly halted as her nose smacked into the wall in front of her. Except the arms that steadied her meant there had to be a body attached to them. Once her feet were planted firmly on the ground, her eyes traveled up the clothed wall to meet a pair of green ones, bright as freshly mowed spring grass.

"Ms. Hart, I presume."

"Um, yes?"

"As in, you're not sure if you're the person in question?"

"No. I mean, yes. I mean, I'm sure. I'm her. I'm Abby."

Despite the night's events, she cackled. The jagged sound escaped her lips, and it wouldn't take much to cross the line into hysteria. Helplessness and fear, emotions Abby had buried many years earlier, had risen to the surface when she'd found Aunt Sara unconscious on the kitchen floor. She would give almost anything to stuff those feelings back into the closet they'd come from.

"Good, now that we've established who you are—" the man softly smiled until his cheek popped a dimple on one side.

"I'm Dr. Dixon. The intake desk said you requested an update on Sara Hart?"

"Yes, we're family. Actually, each other's only family. Is she okay?"

"She's stable at the moment and resting comfortably—"

"What's wrong with her? Why did she faint like that?" Abby interrupted in her rush for answers, desperate to put the fear clawing through her body to rest. She had barely survived her mama's leaving when she was little; she might never recover if she lost Aunt Sara now.

Abby felt shaky and slightly breathless as she tried to get a grip on her emotions once more. Fortunately, she'd managed to find her way into a plastic waiting room chair at some point. Dr. Dixon, whom Abby noticed had kind eyes, sat across from her and waited until she was ready to hear what he had to say.

Four

Dear Sunshine,

Yes, folks in town know Abby is your daughter. I always introduce her as my niece, and even though they give me the hairy eyeball while they wait for an explanation, at some point they realize one isn't forthcoming. The rumors are flying about your whereabouts, but I suspect they'll die down when everyone finds something new to gossip about. In the meantime, I do my best to keep Abby from the hearsay. Love you, to the stars and back.

Always, Sissy

Matt

Matt took in the woman's frantic, and somewhat disheveled state, helpless to stop the wave of tenderness that washed over him. Her expressive eyes reminded him of the bachelor buttons growing in his gran's garden, and he could tell the pale, blonde hair pulled up in some fashion of a knot was rather curly. He would bet anything it was just as soft to the touch as it looked too.

Compared with his own six feet, he guessed her height to be slightly above average. Though her bone structure was delicate, and her upper arms had barely filled his hands, she had curves. Her jacket did little to hide that fact as she pulled it in tightly to wrap her arms around herself.

He'd taken one look at her shaky countenance and led her over to the chairs a few steps behind them to continue their conversation. No sense in having another patient on his hands.

"Why don't we start with the answers I can give you. Then I have a few questions of my own, which will hopefully help us get to the bottom of what's happened to your aunt."

Abby nodded her assent and gripped her hands together tightly in her lap, but he still caught their tremble. He debated placing his hand over hers in a gesture of comfort but didn't want it to be misconstrued as inappropriate or even assurance. He honestly didn't know if her aunt would fully recover, though chances were good. Refraining from what felt more like instinct than a decision, he started in, "Most of the cuts on her hands and upper body are superficial, though I did have to stitch a couple of deeper ones. Specifically, the gash on her left thigh and forearm. I'm assuming she fell on top of the glass after it broke?"

"Yes. I was upstairs asleep at the time, but when I heard the glass hit the floor I rushed down. Aunt Sara passed out before I could make it into the room. The sound was so loud it echoed through the house."

She finished in such a quiet voice he almost missed it. Of course, what she didn't say, Matt could hear all the same. The silence that followed had felt final. No longer afraid how it might be perceived, he slowly reached out to cover her clasped hands with his own, giving hers a gentle squeeze, and watched the worry fade from her eyes at the contact.

It brought to mind the words written in his gran's neat penmanship on a three-by-five card taped to the door of her coffee cupboard. The notecard probably took up residence long before he was born, but he had taken to reading it for himself on the rare mornings he made the coffee: "Peace, I leave you; my peace I give you; not as the world gives do I give to you. Do not let your heart be troubled, nor let it be fearful." Simple words, but they had captured his attention, asking him to let the truth of them sink deep into his soul the same way he would invite an old friend in to share a meal.

Once her hands relaxed beneath his, Matt released her, immediately feeling a sense of loss. He forced away the puzzling sensation and pushed ahead with his questions. "Has your aunt complained of any fatigue, shortness of breath, or nausea lately?"

"I only arrived in town earlier today, or I guess it's yesterday now…" Abby trailed off, tucking a wayward curl behind her ear before continuing, "She hasn't said anything during our weekly phone calls. I caught her napping this afternoon, which isn't strange by itself, but I wondered if she was feeling okay when she insisted on going to bed early. My aunt owns The Christmas Tea Shoppe in Homily. She claimed to be worried about getting there early in the morning to do some inventory and other preparations…" Abby shook her head slightly, trying to dispel cloudy thoughts caused by stress and fatigue. "Sorry, I'm rambling."

"I imagine you've had a long day and quite a scare."

She nodded in agreement and said, "I guess she couldn't sleep, though, since she was in the kitchen." Pausing for a moment to find her thoughts, she asked, "Is any of this information helpful, Dr. Dixon?"

Her voice was utterly feminine. In fact, everything about her was, from her pert nose and rosebud lips to the toes peeking out of her flip flops, painted in a lush, cotton-candy pink. Matt bobbed his head in answer to her question and tried to clear his wayward thoughts of what was quickly becoming an attraction.

"I think it's safe to say your aunt was in the early stages of a heart attack." Matt watched as Abby froze at the news. This was the worst part of his job. "Her EKG confirmed this as well, but fortunately, we were able to use clot-dissolving medications to help restore the blood flow." He paused and found himself staring at Abby. "I'll make sure to add the information you provided to her file for the team overseeing her care from here on out," he said, trying to sound professional and hoping she hadn't noticed his lapse in concentration.

"I don't understand...don't heart attacks only happen to people with unhealthy lifestyle habits?"

Matt watched her crumble in on herself, shoulders bent forward, hands to her mouth and tears threatening to spill over. All of it brought out his deepest compassion. As a physician, it never got any easier to tell someone about their loved one's precarious health, but she was putting his own emotions through the wringer. He tried to distance himself and carried on with the information pertinent to her.

"Though a poor diet and lack of exercise can contribute to blocked arteries, sometimes it's hereditary. For instance, high cholesterol or blood pressure can run in families and, if left untreated, eventually lead to heart disease. Your aunt may have had symptoms previously, but they tend to be different in women than men and can easily go undiagnosed. Fortunately, we've been able to stabilize her enough to move your aunt to the Coronary Intensive Care Unit, where they can better monitor what's happening. Visiting hours are over, but I'd be happy to take you up to see her before you head home."

"Thank you."

Matt held his hand out and let her lead the way to the elevator. He watched her play with the wisp of curl by her ear and nibble her lower lip with her teeth. She was obviously worried, and he could practically hear the gears turning as she processed the information and what it might mean for the future. He hit the button for the CICU and gathered his own thoughts before proceeding.

"Ms. Hart?"

"Please, call me Abby."

"Abby, I think I should give you a heads up about what you're going to see when we get to your aunt's room."

After a short pause, she darted her eyes in his direction as they made their way from the elevator down the hall, giving him her full attention. Matt briefly explained that her aunt was under heavy sedation; it was the best way to keep her comfortable until the cardiologist could examine her in the morning, assuming she remained stable throughout the night. She would have a cannula in her nose for oxygen, an IV for medications and other fluids, and a heart monitor.

They came to an abrupt stop in front of Sara's room. "We didn't need to intubate, which can sometimes be more traumatic for people to see their loved ones—" he cut himself short, registering Abby's rapid breathing beside him. Her pale face reflected back at him through the large window; her hands squeezed the sill to keep herself upright. Matt forced her into a seated position on the floor and gently pushed her head between her knees.

"Breathe in, Abby. One-two-three. Slowly breathe back out to the same count. In, one-two-three. Out, one-two-three. There you go, nice and steady."

When her breathing evened out after a minute, he stood and pulled her up until she was standing close enough to embrace. Matt held himself back, but just barely. Something about this woman made him want to physically comfort her. It wasn't his normal reaction when following up with a patient's family. Compassion? Absolutely. But this bone-deep yearning to draw Abby in and take care of her went way beyond his usual boundaries.

Matt forced himself to step back but made sure she was steady before retreating further. When he spotted a nurse at the floor station he asked, "Can you please get Ms. Hart a cup of water? She's feeling a bit unsteady."

A moment later, the nurse returned, pressing a cup directly into Abby's hand. "Here you go, honey. It's always a bit of a shock to see someone we care about in distress, but I promise she's in good hands."

Abby only nodded her appreciation and sighed as she sipped the water.

Catching the name on the nurse's employee badge, Matt said, "Thanks again, Kai."

"Sure thing. Let me know if y'all need anything else."

Matt led Abby to one of the chairs lined up against the opposite wall. After they were both seated and he'd watched her for a few moments, mostly to reassure himself, he filled her in on the phone call he'd made earlier to the hospital's cardiology department. "Dr. Jillian Schultz is one of the best cardiologists in the country. She'll be here to examine your aunt and discuss her options first thing in the morning."

....

An hour after he'd left Abby Hart in the CICU with her aunt, Matt's head finally hit the pillow in his room at Gran's just as the sun began to rise. He inhaled the light perfume of fresh linen from the detergent she'd used for as long as he could remember. She'd done his laundry again despite multiple assurances that he could do it himself.

"I know you can do your own laundry," she'd argued, hands fisted on her hips. "But I'm home all day while you're out there saving lives. It makes me happy to make your life a little easier when you are home."

"Gran, I've been doing my own laundry since I was twelve. I even managed to do it through the insanity of residency. Besides, you make me sound like a superhero. If anything, I'm more of a Clark Kent."

"Farm boy goes to the big city as a reporter?" she'd asked, confused.

"I was thinking more along the lines of intelligent, devilishly handsome boy next door."

"I think you might be thinking of someone else," said Gran with a flick of her wrist as she'd pushed him out of the laundry room.

Some people might assume his gran was old fashioned or just conforming to a mold society had created for her. Neither assumption could be further from the truth. Matt recognized at an early age that Gran went through life with a different perspective than the other grownups in his small sphere. It occurred to his young self she found contentment in the most mundane tasks, and was the first to volunteer when someone needed help. She was generous with both her time and money.

Of course, seven-year-old boys aren't always the most insightful creatures. When he'd asked her why she didn't go to work like his mom did, she replied without a ruffled feather, "Because I work at home. By keeping house and taking care of others, I'm doing what I'm called and able to do. God gives to each of us gifts and talents to be used for a purpose. It just so happens your mom wears different hats than I do. She's a wife, a mother, a homemaker, and an artist. One is no better than the other, and make no mistake, sometimes a body just feels thankful to have enough and whatever else the good Lord provides."

Crickets sang the night into another dawn, lulling Matt toward sleep. His breath deep and even, lids heavy and limbs satiated with a day's labor, he made a vague mental note to thank her for the clean sheets. The last thing he thought of before he went to sleep was the beautiful woman he had met in the ER. Thinking of her, he fell into a deep sleep, his dreamland retreat a garden filled with teacups in every shade of blue.

Five

Dear Sunshine,

You haven't written in a couple of weeks, and I can't help worrying. Is it because I mentioned coming to see you for visitor's day in my last letter? You can ask me not to come, but I think we need to put the past behind us and the best way to do that is to meet in person. I'm off to pick up Abby from ballet class, but I've included a preschool picture of our girl. Love you, to the stars and back.

Always, Sissy

Abby

The Christmas Tea Shoppe closed for two weeks while Abby spent her days with Aunt Sara in the hospital. Speaking with the cardiologist for the first time had been simultaneously reassuring and terrifying. Though Dr. Schultz believed immediate bypass surgery would have the best long-term effects on her aunt's quality of life, the recovery would be more extensive than other options.

Surgery had taken roughly five hours to complete, and Abby was positive they'd been the longest five hours of her life. The twenty-four hours following it weren't much better, but at least her panic attacks hadn't returned. She told herself doctors were used to seeing people at their worst, but her pride had taken a beating for her moment of weakness in front of the handsome doctor with kind green eyes.

After Abby had decided to stay with her aunt instead of returning to her job following spring break, Maggie had generously offered to fly in and sit with her through all of it, but Abby couldn't bring herself to pull her best friend away from her own family.

"Really, I'd be happy to come. Now that the human hoover will take a bottle, Tucker can take care of him for a couple of days so I can be there with you and Sara."

Regardless of her circumstances, Abby chortled. Only Mags would refer to her breastfeeding sweet little boy as a human vacuum. Not that she was wrong. At six months old, he looked like a mini sumo wrestler. She had no doubt her friend would drop everything for her, but with a family and a horse farm to run, Abby felt it was too much to ask.

With Aunt Sara's discharge from the hospital also came her insistence that the shop reopen. "I'm losing money with every day it's closed, sugar. Not to mention the employees who depend on me for their paycheck. If we don't open the shop soon, they'll be forced to find employment elsewhere, and then what will I do during the busy summer season?"

Abby tried to ignore what her aunt was saying as they entered the house and Aunt Sara's temporary bedroom on the first floor. It would be a couple of weeks before her aunt had the stamina to climb stairs. Gently guiding Aunt Sara onto the borrowed twin bed someone from the church had delivered the day before, Abby tried to get a word in edgewise.

"Aunt Sara—"

"If we don't open this week, we might as well hand the keys to the landlord and file for bankruptcy. One of us must be there every day from here on out."

She was sure her aunt was more worked up than someone who'd just had their chest cracked open should be.

"That sounds dramatic, even for you. Are things so tight the shop will go under if we stay closed for one more week?" Abby asked, her forehead bunching in disbelief. "Or maybe your employees could run the shop in your absence? I'm sure you've trained them well and they're more than qualified to handle the day to day running of it."

A perfectly logical solution, or so Abby thought.

"I'm afraid there is just way too much to do at this point, Abigail. One of us has to be on point," Sara stated emphatically, trying to cross her arms to punctuate her declaration. Instead, she winced as the movement stretched staples literally holding her chest together.

It was the use of her given name and Aunt Sara's obvious discomfort that made Abby finally concede the argument. Her aunt only used it when she was serious—or being seriously dramatic, in this instance. Hiring an in-home caregiver for the daytime to help Aunt Sara through her recovery was not ideal, but since she was in no way physically ready to return, it only left Abby to step in. Not that she could ever fill her aunt's shoes.

....

Three days later Abby listened patiently while Aunt Sara chided her for draping a sweater around her shoulders and tucking the blanket under her legs until her aunt resembled a wool mummy lying on the wicker couch in the sunroom. Satisfied her aunt wouldn't succumb to a chill while she was gone, regardless of the seventy-five-degree temperature outside, Abby gave her another patient look and handed her a dainty teacup covered in hand-painted butterflies and filled with healing green tea.

"Baby girl, stop fussing over me. I'll rest easier knowing you're at the shop getting ready for the upcoming tourist season."

Abby looked at her aunt doubtfully. "Are you sure?"

"I know I look a little bit like death warmed over, but I promise I'm in good hands with the gal you hired. Paige seems like she's got just the right mix of coddling and gumption. She'll take good care of me but won't go too easy on me either. After all, I've got to get moving again. Can't leave all the fun to you."

Aunt Sara winked, but Abby still cringed at the idea of leaving her aunt's care to someone else.

Sara pressed on, "Besides, you already turned in your resignation earlier than you wanted to."

"I was planning to leave at the end of the school year anyway. Taking a leave of absence this late in the year would be silly," sighed Abby, disappointed she'd be unable to finish the year with her students. Her principal understood, but she felt guilty knowing she had left the school, her students, and their parents in the lurch. Not to mention leaving Maggie before she had planned to. "I'll say my goodbyes when I go back to pack up my apartment once things have settled down here." It was a consolation prize, but the best she could do in her current circumstance. Aunt Sara needed her; she didn't have time to wallow in her feelings.

"Well, thank goodness for all those years you worked at the shop on school breaks. I have no doubt all the time you put in will make this venture seem like a piece of coconut cake for you."

"I'm happy to help. The shop is as much home as this house is," replied Abby, even though she felt overwhelmed with her new responsibilities. What else could she do though? Aunt Sara had given up her whole life to take care of Abby. It was only fair to do the same for her.

"I don't know what I'd do without you, sugar."

Abby leaned in and kissed her aunt's cheek before gathering up her bag. She waved goodbye to Paige who was prepping a heart-healthy breakfast while she listened to an audiobook on the mating habits of penguins.

Penguins are better parents than mine were. No daddy to speak of and a mama who gave me away the first chance she got. They didn't give up anything for me.

Abby slipped on her go-to converse sneakers and reached for her matching black raincoat. How they'd gotten to the front door was a mystery. She was almost positive she'd left them somewhere in the vicinity of the dining table a few days earlier. Heavy humidity drenched her curls as she stood on the front porch and pulled in the smell of ozone, Aunt Sara's next words lost to the snick of a closed door.

Matt

Coffee at Bean on Main was just what the doctor ordered after a hard run on a Saturday morning. It wasn't the quietest spot in town, but it did make for lively people watching and this morning Abby Hart was sitting a few tables away from him. Matt observed Abby's eyes flutter shut as her lips closed over the straw in her cold and frothy drink. Her enjoyment made his lips spread into a slow, wide smile.

Unlike the last time he saw her, she wore a sundress that revealed just enough of her legs to make him quickly reign in his thoughts before they could travel elsewhere. It wasn't easy, and no, he wasn't a creeper. In fact, he couldn't remember the last time a woman had caught his attention like this. Even dressed in pajamas and worried about her aunt, she'd been a pretty picture, but today's snapshot made his breath hitch and his chest tighten perceptibly. Which is probably why he hadn't noticed sooner the woman shuffling in his direction with a child in tow.

"Well, if it isn't Matthew Dixon, as I live and breathe. How are you, baby?"

Before he could swallow his sip and respond, the plump woman dressed in a tropical muumuu had snatched the coffee cup right out of his hand.

"Put down that coffee, young man, and give me a hug."

"Yes, ma'am," Matt said as he rose to his feet to greet the woman who spoke to him like he was still four years old. He figured she'd earned the right to do so, since she'd known him his whole life. And especially with some of the antics he'd pulled in her sandbox.

Turns out, the size of the skunk does not determine the reach of its spray. His head hung the slightest bit when he thought of the baking soda bath he'd endured, while his granddad laughed from the doorway and his mom threatened to take a switch to his backside for causing so much mischief. Personally, Matt still thought the smell had been punishment enough.

One of Gran's dearest friends, he let Dot Hanson haul him into a hug, though some might compare it to more of a wrestling hold. It was only after she released him that he noticed the little girl half hiding behind Dot's ample hips. She was not more than five or six years old. Braids covered her entire head, the purple beads on the ends of them swishing as she peeked out at him. Her dark chocolate eyes were a perfect match to the doll she held in the crook of one arm.

"Bella, say hello to Dr. Dixon."

Bending down closer to Bella's eye level, Matt held out his hand to introduce himself.

"Go on, child, he won't hurt you. He's Mrs. Dixon's grandson."

Smiling shyly, her missing two front teeth clearly on display, the girl placed her tiny hand in his.

"Miss Bella, I'm delighted to make your acquaintance."

She giggled like any child would in the presence of a grown man attempting to be debonair, and her eyes lit up warmly as she gushed about his gran.

"I just love your granny, Dr. Dixon. We have the best tea parties in her garden! She always less me bring my dolly to the table, and I can have as many cookies as I want. She even helped me build a fairy house in her duh-lah-lee-us!"

"You mean dahlias," corrected Dot gently.

"Thass what I says, Memaw."

The corner of Matt's lip lifted involuntarily. Kids with missing teeth were indisputably cute, but the added lisp was the frosting on a cupcake. He looked back and forth between the two and said, "I have no doubt."

Grinning over Bella's enthusiasm and not at all surprised his gran made this little girl feel at home, Matt met Dot's forthright gaze once more. It didn't take but a moment for Dot to jump in with her tale of familial drama as confirmation.

"She's Charlotte's youngest. They're all staying with me while her husband is on deployment."

"Ah—" Before he could finish his sentence, Dot was off and running again. Only in the south could a simple explanation turn into a full novel faster than quicksand swallows a person whole.

"You're probably wondering why they're not staying with Charlotte's mama."

"Actually, I—"

"Now listen here, I love my daughter dearly, but let's face it: motherhood didn't suit her when Charlotte was little and not much has changed since she became a grandmother. Can't see past herself most days. She spends far too much time worrying about her third marriage, to a younger man no less, if you ask me."

He hadn't, but Matt understood living in a small community meant listening to everyone's story. Gossip was common, and some of it true, but chances were it was mostly hearsay about a neighbor or relative, but never yourself, unless it painted you in a better light. However, some people liked to hang their own dirty laundry on the line from time to time, taking away the power of others to do it for them. Dot was indeed just such a person.

When she'd finished her monologue, Bella looked up at her great-grandmother with a seriousness that belied her years. In turn, Dot gazed into the eyes which mirrored her own and said, "But that's all right, isn't it, baby girl?"

"Thass right, cause we gots you."

"And Memaw has you."

Matt watched the display of spoken affection, reminded once more how relationships, though made of flawed human beings, remained one of life's best gifts. He waved goodbye to Dot and her granddaughter with promises to keep in touch and sauntered over to the woman tucked into a corner booth by the front door.

Six

Dear Sunshine,

I wish I had known how much pain you were in, or that I had been there to intervene sooner. You must know I would do anything to change the path your life has taken. As your big sister it was my job to look out for you, and I am so sorry for failing. Please, forgive me. Love you, to the stars and back.

Always, Sissy

Abby

Abby sat in a four-person booth surrounded by wood panels, her bottom planted in what resembled a church pew. Several original glazed windows dispersed soft light throughout the coffee shop. She relaxed into the bench with contentment and took another blissful sip of her strawberry frappe.

"Ms. Hart, it's nice to see you again."

Startled out of her thoughts, Abby looked up to see a man standing next to her table. It took a few seconds for recognition to kick in.

"Dr. Dixon how are you?" she asked, feeling genuine pleasure at his presence.

"I'm well, but please call me Matt. I think meeting like this outside the hospital means we can be on less formal terms, don't you?"

"Agreed, but I almost didn't recognize you."

"It's the white coat. Or rather the lack thereof," he said.

"I imagine it's the workout attire that really throws people for a loop."

"Not impressive enough, huh?" Matt asked seriously.

"It's not that. I mean, you are impressive. Wait, that's not what I meant either." Her embarrassed laughter rang through the coffee shop, and she could feel the heat in her cheeks.

"May I join you?"

"Of course," she acquiesced with a slight dip of her head.

Taking the seat across from her, he said, "I hear through the grapevine your aunt is going to make a full recovery."

"This is a small town, so people do tend to talk. Though I imagine your information comes from a more reputable source than most."

"Yes, indeed it does. On two counts."

"Two counts? Oh my, you really do know how to make a girl feel special."

"I've been told before, though only by my patients," he chuckled. "I spoke with your aunt's cardiologist last week."

Feeling cheeky, Abby replied, "I'd expect no less from the impressive *Doctor* Dixon."

What are you doing? Abby reprimanded herself. *Stop flirting! Just because he saved the most important person in your life doesn't mean anything.*

"Now you're catching on," he winked.

Was he flirting back? It didn't matter. She had to stop the train before she caused a wreck. Again.

"And who, pray tell, is your second reputable source?"

Matt leaned in as if to share a secret and said, "As it turns out, that source is closer to home. It would seem my gran is a huge fan of your aunt's tea shop. She was sad to hear about her health, but also happened to mention Sara's pretty niece is currently overseeing the daily operations."

"I am indeed. Though I can't say if the pretty part applies."

"Are you fishing for a compliment, *Miss* Hart?" Matt asked in a teasing tone.

"No, I only meant—" Abby stammered, her hands flying to her cheeks, feeling flames infuse them for the umpteenth time since the man sat down. If she wasn't careful, she'd combust all over the table.

"I'm more than happy to agree with my Gran. The woman running the tea shop is lovely."

Lovely? It sounded like a compliment Aunt Sara might dole out when Abby's self-esteem needed a kick in the patootie. So much for worrying about flirting. After she thanked him for the kind words, they spent the next few minutes talking about her new routine, the comings and goings at the shop, and some of his more interesting cases while they finished their drinks.

Abby slapped her hands over her mouth, eyes wide with astonishment. "You have got to be kidding! I had no idea people swallowed so many random objects. Do they need surgery to have them removed?"

He shrugged. "Depends on the object. If it's small and benign, it will usually pass through the digestive system without any complications. If it's too large it could cause a blockage, or if it's sharp...the potential for damage is obvious. Unfortunately, swallowing multiple magnets is a common one for kids and a bad combination that requires surgery."

"That's unsettling, but I admit I still feel a little badly for the couple on their honeymoon. Who knew jewelry could be so dangerous?" she snickered.

Matt smirked and changed the subject, asking, "So, what did you do before taking over the shop for your aunt?"

Abby smiled a bit wistfully and answered, "I taught elementary school."

"A teacher, really?"

"Yes, don't sound so surprised," she scowled in challenge.

He laughed but said, "No, I'm not. It's just that I never had a teacher who looked like you. Ever."

"And exactly what is that supposed to mean?"

Ignoring her question, he asked, "What grade did you teach?"

"Kindergarten."

"Be still my heart." Matt placed his right hand directly over the left side of his chest like he was saying the pledge of allegiance. "Every little boy loves his kindergarten teacher no matter what she looks like. But you make one killer combination."

Abby started to laugh at his exaggerated acting but looked around the quiet cafe to find they were the only ones left after the mid-morning caffeine rush. With a quick glance from her at the vintage watch encircling her wrist, Matt took the cue and said, "Shall we?"

"I wish I didn't have to rush off, but the employee at the shop is only there until noon today."

"Don't worry about it. I'm heading into the hospital this afternoon to catch up on some paperwork anyway."

Matt walked Abby out and held the door for her as they left Bean, saying the usual things acquaintances do when they part ways.

"Thanks again for the chat."

"Maybe we'll run into each other again soon."

Do not look back over your shoulder, Abby commanded herself as she walked away from her charming coffee companion. *Whatever you do, do not to check out the handsome doctor walking away from you.*

Okay, maybe just one casual glance wouldn't hurt.

Turning her head to catch a quick glimpse of Matt walking away, she caught him doing the same, his grin and that ridiculous dimple telling her everything she already knew. Matt Dixon had enough charm to draw a snake from a basket, and he was causing unwanted flutters in the vicinity around her heart.

Matt

Matt was still thinking about his encounter with Abby at the coffee shop when he spied Gran on her knees in the back garden. With a set of small pruners in her hand and the brim of her straw hat flopping low over her forehead, she moved from one plant to another, talking softly to them as she went. The ranunculus bloomed in a riot of color, reaching for the late afternoon April sun, and bees droned with contentment as they collected pollen on their legs. He moved through the screen door onto the back porch, a glass of artificially sweetened sun tea in his hand, the old radio in the garden shed playing Count Basie in the background.

"Gran, I thought you could use something cold to drink and I could use a little time in the company of a beautiful woman."

"Oh, you charmer. Go on with yourself. You know that smile only works on young women, not your old gran."

"And you know I only speak the truth. Besides, I hear true beauty isn't only skin deep."

"Now that's the truth if I've ever heard it, sweet boy. How was your day off?"

Taking a seat in one of the matching rockers painted robin's egg blue, he replied nonchalantly, "Nice."

"Nice, huh?" she asked, choking a troublesome weed in her hand.

"Yes, ma'am."

She finally looked her grandson full in the face. "What did you do with yourself then?"

"The usual. A run, then a stop for coffee, followed by a couple hours' worth of paperwork at the hospital."

Her exasperation clearly proceeded her displeasure. Matt would never learn to enjoy life if he was always working. Just like the stubborn weeds taking over her garden, he was heedless to the kind of destruction such patterns wrought later.

"You know, even the good Lord took a rest on the seventh day."

"Yes, ma'am," he said sincerely, forcing her to let the topic go.

"Dot Hanson stopped by with her granddaughter Bella after lunch to drop off some potato salad she made. She says red spuds make all difference, but I think it's the secret seasoning she puts in it," said Gran.

"That was kind of her."

"Mm-hmm. She also said she saw you at the coffee shop, you know the fancy one on Main."

"Yes, ma'am."

"Matthew Lee Dixon, don't you yes ma'am me one more time. You know exactly what I'm hinting at."

"Do I?" Matt asked blandly, with full knowledge his reluctance to share every detail riled her up. He ought to just tell her what she wanted to know, but for some reason this was more fun.

"Fine. Did you or did you not sit down with a specific pretty woman?"

"Well, I did speak with Mrs. Hanson and her granddaughter. Is that who you mean, Gran?"

"Don't you play obtuse with me, grandson. I know for a fact you had what appeared to be a lively and long conversation with Abby Hart."

"Why didn't you just say so, then?"

"Hmph! Well, I never," she replied with a punch of irritation to her tone.

Matt laughed outright, having managed to fluster her just like he'd hoped.

She smiled reluctantly in response, her eyes glazing over as Matt changed the subject. One moment she was present and the next she'd lost focus, something which was occurring with more frequency.

"Gran, did you hear me?" Matt asked with concern.

"What, sweet boy?"

"I was asking if you knew why the garbage cans keep getting tipped over into the road."

"Oh, that. It's nothing. Sometimes I get too close when I'm turning into the drive."

Matt frowned but kept his thoughts to himself.

"I know what you're thinking," she said sourly.

"I didn't say anything," he drawled, his voice conciliatory. "In fact, I assumed it was raccoons."

"No, you didn't. I can see it all over your face. You're worried about my driving, but I'm telling you my driving is just fine. The problem is with those cans."

"I hear you. Those cans are the devil, and deserve every swipe of the car they get," he said, straight faced. Matt didn't agree with Gran's assessment; however, he also knew when to let sleeping dogs lie. Today wasn't the day to take away her car keys, but he'd use it as a starting point for future conversations. If possible, he would spare her dignity and leave the decision of when to hand them over to her.

Seven

Dear Sunshine,

Abby made a new friend at school, Maggie, the youngest of the Wallace girls, who is already a handful. You might remember, I went to school with their daddy, but bless her mama's heart I don't know what she's going to do with that one. Still, she and Abby are two peas in a pod despite their differences. Love you, to the stars and back.

Always, Sissy

Abby

Abby looked at the list of inventoried goods again, thinking she might go cross eyed from so many little black letters and numbers on a page. Aunt Sara could use a software update, one that would make the entire inventory and accounting system more efficient. And then there was the matter of retrieving her belongings. Her wardrobe was lacking variety, but that could be remedied with a shopping trip to the mall and her aunt's closet.

Not being able to say goodbye to her colleagues, students, and parents had been more difficult than she expected though. Instead of closure, Abby was living with one foot in Homily, and the other in Midwell. Ready to chew off the thumbnail perched at the tip of her teeth, Abby considered taking another break from the shop.

Bean was only a block from Aunt Sara's shop, and though some might assume the town couldn't support such similar businesses, since it only catered to coffee drinkers and her aunt specialized in tea, both shops thrived—almost as if her aunt and the Bean's owner had come to an agreement of sorts not to encroach on one another. Small towns were known for their quaint eccentricities, and Homily fit the category neatly with its motto of, "Where one succeeds, we all succeed."

A strawberry frappe might be just what I need to wade through the rest of this inventory for Mother's Day. Another break couldn't hurt, not that it will be nearly as much fun without Matt Dixon.

Word had spread quickly about Sara's health and replacement at the shop in her absence, both of which made for a steady stream of business from open to close. Whether it was loose leaf, bagged, specially blended, boxed for everyday consumption, or came in a collector's tin accompanied by a fine bone china teapot, The Christmas Tea Shoppe was the place to buy all things tea. Not to mention, the addition of Abby's presence and an assortment of homemade baked goods intended to melt in your mouth. Packaged with the feeling of a Christmas miracle upon every visit, it made for a winning combination. Abby crossed her fingers and hoped she wouldn't mess it up with her own ideas.

With a glance at the clock, she put aside her desire for a break as she waited for two of the more regular employees to arrive. Afternoon tea required a knowledgeable staff with easy smiles and polished manners. Fortunately, Alice and Chloe offered both with minimal drama, due in part to their friendship. They were thick as thieves and reminded Abby how much she missed Mags, who always knew what she needed without her ever having to ask. Aunt Sara was beyond supportive, but it wasn't the same as having her "ride or die" in town.

"Afternoon, Miss Abby. Sorry I'm late," said Alice, rushing inside, her doe eyes apologetic. "Class went long, and then Mama asked me to swing by home to pick up something she'd made for y'all. Hope you like fried okra and catfish," she finished, her lips twisted in disgust.

"The look on your face would suggest otherwise," Abby snickered.

"Don't get me wrong. Mama's an amazing cook, but some things should never be eaten. Ever."

The bell above the door chimed, followed by an exuberant Chloe, her cheeks aglow with the sun's kiss.

"OMG, you are never going to believe what I just heard!" she exclaimed while grabbing Alice by the shoulders. "You know that boy I was telling you about—"

Abby grinned. The girl's enthusiasm was contagious, but she had a full afternoon of office work ahead of her, and afternoon tea began in ten minutes. "I'm sure y'all have a lot to catch up on since you saw each other an hour ago, but I trust you have things in hand out here?"

"Absolutely," they chorused.

"And I love the new decorations," said Chloe.

"Yeah, the April shower's theme is super cute. I love the little umbrellas on the Christmas tree with raindrop garland, and the rainbows on the mantel and wellies underneath the tree are a clever touch," beamed Alice.

Chloe jumped in, "I know, right? My favorite are the strawberry-covered ones."

"I can't decide if I like the duckies or the bees the best," Alice said, a serious expression overtaking her countenance.

Abby smiled and left them to their debate.

....

Abby sat down at the oak secretary's desk in the small office located at the back of the industrial kitchen, retrieving the mail she'd put aside during the morning rush. She briefly considered whether it was a betrayal to open her aunt's mail but decided it would be remiss of her to not sort through it as the shop's current manager. Surely anything that came to the shop was business related, not personal.

The first few pieces of mail held the usual bills from suppliers, including the one from Bee Hill in London. Inside was a personal note signed with kind regards. Additionally, the note acknowledged Ben Galloway had received her aunt's condolences on the passing of his wife, and the brief information that he and his son were faring as well as could be expected.

Leave it to the British to be understated.

At the end was a postscript thanking Aunt Sara for her hummingbird cake recipe.

Doing her best British impersonation Abby read aloud, "My son Henri has a few suggestions for the frosting that I'm sure you'll find amusing, Sara. I apologize up front for any offense, but as you already know I'm at a complete loss as to how to handle such a precocious child. How on earth did you ever manage to raise one by yourself? Any advice is welcome. Please see Henri's additions on the second page."

After reading Henri's advice, Abby closed the slip of paper written in a firm lead print and, with a smile tugging at the corner of her mouth, went in search of her aunt's treasured recipe box.

Twenty minutes later, she finally located a box with the word *Recipes* lettered across the top in the very back of a small cabinet full of random bric-a-brac. It was roughly the size of a shoe box, large for a recipe collection, but Abby figured her aunt had collected a lifetime of recipes. Abby lifted the hinged top and revealed a messy collection of folded scraps of paper. Aunt Sara was usually more organized, but she probably had most of her recipes memorized, which would explain why the box had been tucked away.

Abby smiled as she pulled out a folded sheet of paper, reminiscing the hours she'd spent baking with her aunt in this very kitchen. But the words sprawled across the paper didn't make any sense.

Dear Sissy,

Thank you for the gardening advice, and for the Senior pictures of Abby. I can't believe how grown up she looks. Unfortunately, I can't make it to graduation, but you've done an amazing job of raising her. I made the right decision when I left...

Tears blurred the rest of the words. Abby whimpered and tried to breathe through the tightness in her chest.

"Mama?" Abby said out loud. She didn't need to see the close at the end to know who it was from.

To Abby, her mother might as well have been dead. She knew her mother had given full custody to Aunt Sara, but as far as she knew her mother had disappeared afterward, abandoning her completely. Though Abby had asked about her mother often as a child, Aunt Sara had been vague in her answers. Eventually, she'd given up and pushed the hurt down into a locked part of her chest. Her mother didn't want her, so why would she care? Of course, this calloused, numb approach had never really worked, but if Abby always kept her mother hidden deep away, she could move on.

But did these letters mean Aunt Sara had been in contact with her mama the entire time? She grabbed another letter from the box and read the date in the upper right corner. January 1, 2011. That was only a few months ago. Abby sank to the tile floor, her gut a churning mess and her vision starting to black out around the edges. Even if her mother hadn't chosen to abandon her initially, she had known about Abby all along and still didn't want anything to do with her.

Abby remembered the night before high school graduation, asking herself if her mother even remembered how old she was, or that she would be graduating this year. But now Abby knew her mama had known and chosen to stay away.

Breathe, just breathe. In one-two-three. Out one-two three. Do not pass out.

Shattered by her mother all over again, Abby sobbed into her hands until the tears were spent and only hiccups remained. Standing up, she grabbed the insidious box and shoved it into the nearest cabinet. *Out of sight, out of mind,* was how she consoled herself. No sense crying over spilled tea. She had always known that all her mother would need to do was contact Aunt Sara.

You already knew she didn't want you. Your mama isn't worth the heartache.

....

Several hours later, feet sore from a long day at the shop and shoulders burdened with her aunt's secret letters, Abby slouched in Sara's silver Accord parked in front of her childhood home. If she didn't go in soon, Aunt Sara would start to worry, and Paige would be late for her evening class. Abby finally got out of the car and opted for the front porch swing, and the novel she'd picked up from the hospital gift shop during her aunt's surgery. Much too anxious to read at the time, maybe she could use it now to escape reality for a little while longer.

Abby sent off a quick text.

› *Hola, Paige. I'm on el porche whenever you need to vámanos.*

› *LOL. You mean dejas. The other is more like, let's go! Just a reminder, the day's events are logged into the notebook on the kitchen counter.*

Paige kindly indulged Abby's efforts to practice what little Spanish she knew from some of her former students' *las familias*. When had her whole life become a designation of before and after Aunt Sara's heart attack in only a month's time?

Abby sent back a thumbs up and waited for the dots pulsing on her phone to become words.

> *Your tía is taking a siesta in el solárium. She won't be ready to eat for another hour. Adios, chica.*

> *Gracias,* Abby shot back, and settled onto the swing.

> *De Nada* :)

....

A few minutes later she heard the familiar rumble of a Harley in the drive at the rear of the house. It was classic, gold, and flashy enough for a woman who worked wonders to ride. Paige had a penchant for using the back door, and it put Abby in mind of the phrase "backdoor friends are best." Paige's easy-going personality had smoothed away any wrinkles caused by the folds of change, and she had inserted herself seamlessly into their daily routine. She made it possible for Abby to oversee the shop without constantly worrying about Aunt Sara, and in a few short weeks she'd managed to transform the older woman's diet into a heart-healthy one. She also assisted Sara with the daily exercise regimen prescribed by her cardiologist, which Abby didn't envy at all. Honestly, Paige was a godsend for the Hart family.

While her aunt slept, Abby settled in with her book. The story centered around a young woman's talent for bringing love and happiness to those who visited her bakery, even though she couldn't seem to capture the magic for herself. Then, one day, a stranger walked in and asked for an apple hand pie to go with his latte. Suddenly, everything culminated in a universal happily ever after.

But Abby couldn't help but think the real world didn't work that way. Her own life had taught her that. Sometimes, mothers abandoned their children. Sometimes, engagements had to be broken. And sometimes, the person you love most in the world got sick.

Logically, Abby knew worse things happened in life. The nightly news provided proof on a regular basis. Others suffered so much more than she did, every day, all over the world. For all intents and purposes, her life was already a happily ever after despite her love life being dead on arrival.

So, why am I surprised that my aunt lied to me all these years? Why am I still surprised that my mother doesn't want me? Why do I long for something different? she asked herself, staring at the cover of her book as though it held the answer.

Shaking her head at her melancholy thoughts, Abby put the book aside and brought her feet up beside her. The porch was a little too small for the big swing, but Aunt Sara insisted everyone needed a spot to sit and watch the world go by. According to her, it was a perch from which to gain a little perspective.

"Do you know what perspective is, baby girl?" Sara had asked a concerned eleven-year-old Abby.

"If I say no, will I have to look it up in the dictionary?" Abby had asked in return, her face scrunched up in distaste at the prospect.

Aunt Sara's right eyebrow lifted to join its companion in response to the impertinent question. "Not this time, sugar. Mostly because the dictionary forgot to include this definition as a side note. Perspective means acknowledging God is our creator. And, as such, he cares for his creation. His purpose for us is still in motion even when we can't see the whole picture."

Of course, Aunt Sara's proclamation only led to a multitude of other questions from Abby. "What if someone makes the wrong choice though? And what about the bad things that happen to good people?"

"Those are great questions with complicated answers. But still, I have faith God can do all things and use all situations, even when we mess up or our fellow human beings let us down."

"But what about tornadoes and earthquakes, or cancer and—"

"Hold up just a minute. Something tells me there are a lot of ands, ors, and buts on the tip of your tongue."

"That's 'cause there is, Aunt Sara," said Abby, her foot tapping with impatience to match the arms she'd crossed over her chest.

With a laugh under her breath, her aunt pressed forward before Abby could start in again.

"In light of your curiosity and the need to make my point before the good Lord's second coming, let's just say, God is bigger than we can possibly fathom. Which also means he's capable of overcoming big things. Whether it's mother nature, our health, or even our grief. He does require a little bit of faith in the bargain though. But make no mistake, faith is for *our* benefit not God's. Faith gives us x-ray vision to see the work he's doing, often behind the scenes."

"Why does he act behind the scenes where we can't see?" asked a doubtful Abby.

"Sometimes we get to be a part of his plans by extending a helping hand to others. Whether it's financial, emotional, or physical, God helps us love one another by caring for each other and taking on another's burden as though it were our own."

At the time, Abby found the answer anything but satisfying. However, considering the day's discovery, she fervently hoped God was still in the business of being big enough. In the previous year and a half, she'd watched Maggie get married to Tucker, the love of her life, who also happened to be Abby's ex-fiancé's best friend. This had complicated her relationship with Mags and Tuck when all she wanted to do was be happy for them. Instead, she felt an unjustified sense of loneliness at being left behind. To top it all off, she had to quit her job early to move back into her childhood home, only to find out her mother had known about her all along and chose to abandon her anyway. There didn't seem to be any room for God in her heavy heart.

Abby looked to the late afternoon sky, watching as sunset began to paint the evening horizon in a wash of yellow, orange, and red. The fragrance from the front flower beds rose to tickle her nose while the hum of cicadas filled the air of the otherwise sedate neighborhood. She soaked in the life around her and let some of Aunt Sara's front porch wisdom seep in alongside it.

Eight

Dear Sunshine

Abby is performing in the children's Christmas pageant this year. I might be able to go the rest of my life without hearing "All I Want for Christmas Is My Two Front Teeth." Our girl recently tried to convince me that if the tooth fairy is wealthy enough to buy everyone's teeth, then why doesn't she bring more than a dollar a tooth. I told her the tooth fairy didn't calculate inflation. Love you, to the stars and back.

Always, Sissy

Abby

Sensibly, May flowers follow April showers, so in addition to the usual tea offerings, Abby added White Peony to the menu along with salad options for those who preferred something other than finger sandwiches and truffles from a chocolatier in Mobile. It was a simple but promising business collaboration. Bourbon & Bon Bon's provided a limited amount of product and, in exchange, Abby gave them ample advertising. It meant no overhead for the shop while allowing her to treat her customers at no extra cost to them.

When Abby had spoken with her aunt about some of the changes she wanted to make to the usual menu, and how she wanted to decorate according to the seasons in addition to Christmas, she'd worried Aunt Sara's feelings might be hurt. As it turned out, though, her aunt had been eager to let Abby take the reins.

"Sugar, I think it's a wonderful idea to spice things up a bit. In fact, I probably should've made some changes years ago, but sometimes it's more convenient to stick with what you know. Change can be as uncomfortable as a hair suit, but your vision is the breath of fresh air the shop needs. And the spirit of Christmas, God's grace, will always be at the heart of the shop no matter how it's decorated."

Unlike the rest of Main Street, which opened after church services, The Christmas Tea Shoppe remained closed on Sundays, except for Mother's Day. Traditionally, Aunt Sara made it a special affair with a dress code for gentlemen and hats for ladies. Afternoon tea was held twice, once at noon and again at three o'clock. Both reservations slots were always full, and Abby was determined to make sure this year was no exception in her aunt's absence.

Mother's Day came and went without a sneeze, and Abby thought the touch of spring flowers woven into garlands with floral teacups hung beside faerie ornaments on the tree was a nice substitution for the usual decor. Abby had always decorated her classroom for the seasons, and put all her effort into the shop to push aside how much she missed her students and the guilt of leaving the school in a lurch at the end of the school year. Also, if she stayed busy and kept her conversations with her aunt around the tea shop, she didn't have time to address the lies and betrayal she had found in the recipe box.

For the most part, her risk appeared to pay off. Though a few of the regulars had expressed disappointment, most were delighted with the expanded repertoire, and several had even asked if they could schedule private events with a birthday or anniversary theme. Abby was thrilled with the outcome of her efforts, if not the increased workload, and remained hopeful her disgruntled customers would come around soon.

....

June moseyed in three weeks later with warmer temperatures. Abby tore through the bathroom cabinets in a fervent search for a hair product to contain her frizz before church. Aunt Sara had settled onto the couch in the sunroom and, though she was gussied up, the throw over her lap suggested she wasn't going anywhere anytime soon.

"I thought we could go to church together today," Abby said, a pinch disappointed.

"You go on ahead, baby girl. I'll be fine by myself for a few hours. I'd rather stay home and listen to a podcast instead."

Abby's forehead wrinkled in response, a small frown of concern forming between her brows.

Sara chuckled and said, "I've seen that expression a multitude of times over the last couple of months. You wear it when you're fretting over something, or someone, in this case. I feel fine. I'm just not ready for all the pomp and circumstance that comes with a church service. Besides, I kind of like the sound of the preacher's voice in this series I'm listening to."

Abby's mouth fell wide open, while Aunt Sara stared back at her without an ounce of apology on her face, except for a faint shade of peach on her cheekbones.

"Abigail, please close your mouth before you start catching flies."

Audibly snapping her mouth shut with a click of her teeth, Abby found her words. "Aunt Sara, you can't possibly be crushing on this man…he's a stranger, not to mention a preacher." She spit out the last part like the man had leprosy instead of a spiritual calling.

"I know he's a preacher, sugar. That's why I'm listening to this podcast to begin with."

Abby almost rolled her eyes at her aunt's dry reply. "As I was saying, you can't crush on a preacher. What if he's married?"

"Oh please, people have crushes on celebrities all the time. It doesn't mean anything. Besides, he's not married."

"And how exactly do you know that?"

"Because his status on Facebook says he's single. It really is amazing how you can hop on at any time to see what other people are doing."

"I'm aware—"

"Oh, and the photographs! I don't know if I'm jealous over how busy everyone else seems to be, or thankful I was raised to know better than to post some of those selfies other people do."

"Your posting photos?" asked Abby, calculating the number of potentially awkward childhood photos now circulating online.

"I just don't know what this world is coming to when people publicize their cellulite for everyone to see."

Abby belly laughed almost hard enough to bust the seams of her turquoise sheath dress. "Seriously, you need to stop. I'm gonna pee my pants."

"What's so funny, young lady?"

Abby tried to calm what had become uncontrollable giggling. "*You,* trying to deflect from your stalker tendencies by talkin' about dimpled thighs."

"Well, it was worth a try. Besides, it has you laughing like a hyena which always brings joy to my poor defective heart."

Aunt Sara batted her lashes, looking like she had mascara stuck in her eye. When Abby didn't take the guilt trip bait, her aunt finally stopped her thwarted efforts at distraction.

"I know, I know. It was petty to throw others under the bus in order to save myself. Anyway, I'm not really stalking him. His Facebook page is mentioned on the podcast, and I just wanted to make sure he is who he seems."

"Fair enough. So, in addition to being single, is he good looking too?

"He's so handsome he's almost dreamy," Sara gushed. "A little bit Robert Redford or Brad Pitt. You know, swoon worthy, and only getting better with age." Her eyes twinkled with her confession, while her mouth leaned toward a smirk.

"Well, it's good to know God's word still holds your interest these days."

"That's enough sass out of you, missy," Sara reprimanded, adding begrudgingly, "I just don't want everyone fussin' over me at church. It tires me out when I have too much excitement in one day. Besides, if I hear, 'Bless your poor little heart,' one more time, the ability to be gracious might abandon me."

Taking her aunt's admission for a white flag of truce, Abby changed the subject. "And how are all of the belles of Homily?"

"Fine. I know they mean well. The ladies from Bible study stopped by to visit on Wednesday, and I received a card of encouragement from everyone on the business association board.

Speaking of which, how are your preparations coming? The Fourth of July is around the corner and the summer tourist season will be in full swing by then," her aunt said, as if Abby weren't fully aware of what the upcoming calendar months held.

"So far so good. I finished the inventory and placed the order for supplies. I've located most of the recipes we talked about. Well, all of them except for the hummingbird cake. I searched high and low through the shop but still haven't found it."

Abby blanched, slightly nauseated by the thought of the letters she'd found instead and hoped Aunt Sara didn't notice her strange reaction.

"Oh, it's probably tucked into a cookbook on the lowest shelf to the left of the fireplace. Let me get it for you, sugar."

Now she tells me.

This was it, the perfect opening to ask about the box of letters she'd found weeks ago. But just like the day she'd found it, she stayed quiet, too afraid to hear the answers she desperately wanted. Abby's jaw clamped shut so tightly it was painful. She turned away and briskly walked to the front door, saying a hurried goodbye with the excuse she would be late for church. The door slammed shut with a bump to her rear end, and a rock settled in the pit of Abby's stomach.

Sara raised her eyes to Heaven with a prayer for patience. That girl of hers still couldn't walk through a room without it feeling like a tornado had whipped through. A book lay discarded on the dining table, a sweater left over the sofa in lieu of a raincoat, and silver earrings sat next to a ceramic trinket bowl as though the effort to put them inside were one step too far. Some folks might perceive it as messy or disorganized, but Sara knew Abby could scrub a bathroom until it sparkled, and the shop ran smooth as Devonshire cream under the changes she'd made. Her niece was simply busy moving on from one moment to the next. There was no time to clean up the current one because there was so much else to see and do around the corner to remain a minute longer in the present. Abby was constantly in motion.

Just like her mama, Sara mused. Grace could never enter a room unnoticed. Attracted to her natural beauty, vibrant laughter, and bubbly personality, everyone wanted to be in Grace's orbit, including Sara. Blonde and blue eyed just like her daughter, she'd had a way of drawing people in with only a smile.

Sara moved across the room to stand in front of the bookshelf with a mind to find the cake recipe Abby wanted and removed her favorite cookbook from exactly where she told her niece it would be. Seated on the couch, she flipped to the back and took the three-by-five notecard between her dainty fingers right before the thought niggling at the back of her mind slipped free like shortening on a greased pan.

"Dear Lord!" Sara gasped, dropping the cookbook to the floor, and clutching her blouse over the new scar between her breasts. She pulled in shallow breaths and tried to calm her racing heart.

Surely Abby would have said something if she'd found the box with Grace's letters. But her self-assurance was poor comfort in the end. Only a conversation with the Almighty would bring her any peace.

Heavenly Father, I put my trust in you. Guide me through the conversations ahead. Let them be in your timing, but I wouldn't complain if it matched up with mine. Amen.

....

Abby snuck into the last row of Homily Baptist Church, admitting she'd rather be anywhere else. She and Aunt Sara were keeping secrets from each other, and she wasn't exactly on speaking terms with God. It was hard to be honest with him when she could hardly be honest with herself. Her prayers were lukewarm at best, and she couldn't remember the last time she poured out her heart to him.

The worship band played up front, the voices in the sanctuary blending in an awkward harmony, beautiful and flawed all at once. Abby tried to give in to the pull within her soul, the place where deep called to deep, and God drew near without her having to take a baby step in his direction. She stumbled over the words crowding her mind, all the while afraid they fell on deaf ears.

"God's Word tells us in Romans 12 to 'be devoted to one another in brotherly love; give preference to one another in honor, not lagging in diligence, fervent in the spirit, serving the Lord;

rejoicing in hope, persevering in tribulation, devoted to prayer, contributing to the needs of the saints, practicing hospitality.' But what does this mean for our relationships here in Homily?" asked Pastor Kirk from the pulpit.

A challenging concept on my best day, let alone under current circumstances.

A broken engagement? *Check.*

Aunt Sara's health? *Check.*

The letters from her mama? *Check.*

Even the shop, which had been such a happy part of her childhood, felt like far too much responsibility today. On the cusp of what Abby had desperately hoped would be a carefree summer, she found herself mired in responsibility and guilt. She didn't know if she was ready for so many life changes if they were only going to saturate her life with burdens.

At least I can say I have the hospitality part down. Score one for The Christmas Tea Shoppe.

Abby followed the other congregants to the fellowship hall where everyone gathered around coffee and cookie tables to catch up on the week's events. Though they celebrated each other's success and gossiped about their failures all in the same breath, like people in most small towns, folks could depend on one another when times were lean. Church helped create that sense of community, but Abby felt exposed without the bustle of the shop around her, a deer paralyzed in the hunter's line of sight.

"Yoo-hoo, Abby, over here!" waived Florence and Faunella Michaelson from the cookie table closest to her.

Abby looked around for a quick exit but, to her immense dismay, found none. With a smile pasted in place, she walked their way, wishing she'd worn armor instead of accessories. Earrings would never deflect a well-intended complaint, let alone a barrage of them.

"Well, don't y'all look... matching in your stoles."

Someone ought to tell them about faux, if only to have the dusty, moth-eaten wraps laid to rest, thought Abby.

"And your sunhats, my oh my. The flowers are so...lifelike," Abby improvised, giving herself mental props for coming up with a compliment. "What a good word by the pastor today, don't y'all think?" she added, hopeful the reminder would keep the two of them from launching a tirade about, well, pretty much anything. Sometimes there was no pleasing a person, or people in this instance.

"Well, it wasn't Pastor Kirk's best, but—" one twin began

"He's got a lot going on at home," said the other, all benevolence.

"You know his wife got the breast cancer again. Bless her kind heart," finished the first, brimming with empathy as she squeezed her sister's veined, sun-spotted hand.

The sisters lived together in the Michaelson Mansion, a crumbling masterpiece of Georgian architecture, despite multiple attempts to move them elsewhere. Half the town speculated the spinsters were wealthy, hording their millions amidst the plaster and a rather famous cantilever staircase. But Abby thought they were simply clinging to a time when the Michaelson family counted for more than a prominent name. They were also the fireplace poker in Aunt Sara's side, as president and vice president of Homily's Historical Preservation Society. How a new awning for the shop diminished the town's historic district Abby couldn't fathom.

Something her aunt once said slid over her memory, sticky as syrup. "History has the potential to be a good teacher, but you should always ask yourself how objective the telling of it is. Because painting the past in anything other than the truth will only lead to reaping a nostalgia that may have been sowed in someone else's blood. My treasure might very well be someone else's junk." Abby knew there was no changing the Michaelson twins' attitude without a real conversation.

"We hope Sara is feeling better, bless her heart," they said simultaneously, and continued as one accord, "and we're thrilled you've stepped in to take over."

"But——" said one.

Abby saw her chance to run and grabbed onto it for dear life. "I'm really sorry, but I need to get home to Aunt Sara and see how she's fairing."

"Of course, you do! We'll come by the shop soon to catch you up on HHPS," chimed the sister in mink and plastic hydrangeas.

"Great! I can't wait," Abby declared, her fingers crossed behind her back. Did it count as a lie if she was trying to be polite?

Probably, but she'd more than make up for it when she had them over for tea.

She stepped out into the light of late morning where a few faces she recognized from the shop waved and spoke hellos, asking after her aunt.

Abby left the church building, but instead of heading to her car, she walked to the playground at the edge of the square. Sitting on a bench next to the swings, she listened to the church bells from First Pres peal loudly as everyone left worship. People made their way down the front steps to parked cars or Bean for coffee, their chatter flitting through the warm air. It framed a happy family picture, one to which she wished she belonged.

Nine

Dear Sunshine

I'm so pleased you joined the women's Bible study. It sounds like a wonderful ministry. I'm sending another care package with the items you requested. I wish you would let me do more, but I content myself with the knowledge you might be home soon. Abby is a voracious reader and shows promise in the kitchen, not that I'm surprised. She was bound to inherit something from me. I've included her recent gingersnap success in the package. Love you, to the stars and back.

Always, Sissy

Matt

Matt let his brown leather oxfords enter her line of sight first, watching as her eyes followed his shoes up his khaki-covered legs to an untucked white, button-down shirt rolled at the elbows. Her eyes met his at the same time and he asked, "May I?"

"Why is it you're always asking to sit next to me, Matt?"

Squinting at the sun in his eyes, a bashful smile teased the corners of his lips and he said, "I just want to make sure I haven't worn out my welcome."

"By all means, then, please share the public bench with me," she replied, sweeping her hand to the side, and returning his smile with a small one.

He sat down, but not too close. Instead, he put his arm along the back of the bench and tipped his head down to look at her. Matt watched her in expectation, sure she must have something on her mind from the way she'd been lost in thought. He had spotted her sitting on the bench and watched for a few minutes before deciding to head over. She'd looked like she could use come company. Finding the silence between them comfortable, he chose not to rush in, positive she would tell him soon enough.

After a good five minutes passed in utter silence, he realized his mistake. Abby wasn't a patient eager to share her symptoms. If he was going to get to know this woman, he would have to be willing to jump in the deep end first.

"How come one of the sweetest girls I know is sitting on this bench under the blue Bama sky, looking for all the world like someone just told her the tooth fairy doesn't exist?"

"What do you mean, she doesn't exist?" Abby deadpanned.

He kept his grin to himself, but he liked her sense of humor. It was smoky and spicy, reminding him of his favorite rye.

"Oh, you're good. So good, I almost forgot about that downcast look on your face."

"Not going to let it go, are you?"

"Not a chance, so you might as well spill it."

"I'm stuck."

"That was enlightening," he replied sardonically.

"Really, that's just it. I'm stuck. I came back to Homily thinking it would help me move toward a finish line of sorts, but instead I've garnered more responsibility and inadvertently moved backward to the start."

Matt nodded his head, his lips flattening into a straight line with serious consideration. Abby hadn't given him much to go on, but maybe he could ease her burden with distraction.

"Well, I don't think we're going to solve your conundrum today, but maybe we can put those thoughts chasing one another in your head to rest for a short while."

Matt had an idea and took her hand the way he would Gran's, as though it was an everyday occurrence between the two of them. Tingles shot up his arm, causing goose bumps despite the pleasant weather. And though he'd never felt the same way about holding another woman's hand before, he sensed a feeling of rightness settle within. Not wanting to look too deeply at what it might imply for the future, Matt told himself Abby needed a friend more than his unsolicited attention.

He led her from the bench and into the small playground in front of them. He held out a swing for her, gallantly bowed and attempted to give her his most charming smile. Matt's only goal became easing the weight of her thoughts and earning the laugh that made his pulse increase.

"Take a seat, princess. Your throne awaits."

Abby laughed like he hoped she would, presenting him with a curtsy and taking a seat on the swing. He pushed her gently and then took a seat on the swing next to her. They swung together for a few moments, the swing's steady motion soothing, before Matt broke the silence they'd eased into.

"Did you come from church this morning?" He assumed so by the dress she wore, but it made for a segue.

"I did. Homily Baptist, just across the way. And you?"

"Of course. First Presbyterian, also just across the way."

She cocked an eyebrow at him as if to say, *Isn't that an interesting and telling tidbit of information.*

"Now, don't give me that look. I'm not opposed to your church, but First Pres is where my gran attends. Me too, I guess, now that I live here."

"That explains why I'd never seen you before Aunt Sara's trip to the ER. You're not from around here."

"No ma'am. My dad was in the military, so we moved around a lot for his job. When my parents divorced, my mom settled us near some of her family in Charleston. But my favorite place to be, hands down, has always been with Gran in Homily."

"If you usually attend with your gran, where is she now?"

"She opted to stay home this morning. She's got a mild cold and doesn't want to pass it on to the other blue hairs in her Sunday school class."

At her raised eyebrows and wide eyes, Matt threw his hands up in a gesture of innocence. "Her words, not mine. She insisted I go on without her. So, after making sure she was resting comfortably, I managed to slide into the front pew with two minutes to spare."

"The first pew, huh?"

"Yes, we staunch Presbyterians know that if you aren't at least ten minutes early, then you're late. Which also means the only seats left open are directly in front of the pulpit, because you must desire up close and personal time with God if you can't make it to church on time."

"Can I get an amen?"

"Amen, sister. And we should probably throw in a hallelujah just to be sure," Matt grinned so wide his cheeks hurt, heart bouncing around in his chest at the sound of her laughter as they bantered back and forth, swinging in unison.

"We really shouldn't be laughing about this. My aunt would be appalled."

"Maybe, but I like to think God has a sense of humor. Especially about all the little things we get our socks twisted over."

"You mean like the way our respective churches once fought over what time services got out, and therefore became the first to ring their bells each Sunday?"

"That story is practically an urban legend around here, but not entirely true. Don't tell me you've been listening to tawdry rumors all these years, Miss Hart."

"I take offense, Doctor Dixon. Don't you know that the local gossip mill provides only the most reliable rumors."

Bowing his head in mock apology he said, "My deepest apologies, madam. I didn't mean to besmirch the good name of Homily's *reliable* gossip mill."

"Well then, on behalf of small-town gossip mills everywhere, I accept." It was said with such benevolence and a straight face he almost believed her sincerity. That is, until she burst into a fit of giggling.

"However, it just so happens I love our small town's history. You might say it's become a hobby of mine in recent years."

"Do tell, the suspense is killing me."

He eyeballed her. "Really, you sure you're interested?"

"I've lived here most of my life and I have a feeling I've never heard the story the way you're about to tell it."

"Well, it just so happens I have an inside source."

"Let me guess. Hmm, is it your gran?"

"Exactly. Are you always such a good guesser?" He asked only to see what she would say in response.

"Ha ha," she said, rolling her eyes. "More like you're predictable. Now, don't keep a girl waiting. Let's hear it."

"You wound me, but as it turns out, my great, great, great-granddad—"

"That's a lot of greats," she interjected under her breath.

"Yes, it is. Now, are you going to let me tell the story or not?"

Flushing slightly, she nodded in the affirmative.

He thoroughly enjoyed her reaction and hoped the tease in his tone removed the sting of his words. "As I was saying—"

"Before I so rudely interrupted you."

"Exactly." Oh man, did he love her feisty attitude. Regardless of those pink cheeks, she wasn't going to let him back her into a corner for anything.

"For real now?" Matt asked, watching her blush deepen when his dimple escaped with a chuckle.

"Yes," she acquiesced quickly.

"Once upon a time—"

"Seriously?"

"Shh," Matt said and leaned over in his swing to place a finger on top of her perfectly kissable lips. "Every good story starts with those four words," he remarked, his voice sounding like gravel in his ears. He removed his finger while his eyes never left her mouth. Their swings had stopped moving. Abby had his full attention even if he didn't have hers.

Lassoing his wandering thoughts, he started, "Once upon a time, just after the Civil War, droves of people looking for a fresh start and available land moved into the area faster than you can say dixie. Shops went in on Main Street and Homily's first school was under construction. They even had a doctor in residence, but not a church in sight. It wasn't long before two of the town's founders set out to rectify the problem. Each went in search of his own denomination's governing body, hoping to bring a church building to the square.

"Unbeknownst to the other founders of the town, both were granted building permits before a town council vote could be called. I guess you might say a sort of backdoor deal was made. Everyone went on their merry way having decided there was no harm done with a church to anchor both the east and west sides of the square while Town Hall oversaw the north. That is, until both churches wanted to hold services at the exact same time on Sunday mornings. It quickly became obvious this was a decision with catastrophic consequences."

"The bells?"

"Yes, indeed. The bells were so loud the first morning when both church services ended simultaneously, the local paper reported that the town's doctor treated folks for hearing loss. In all reality, it was probably just a coincidence and more than likely wouldn't happen on a regular basis. However, to ensure it didn't, the town council asked the two trouble-making founders to flip a coin to see who would let out first, and therefore be the first to ring their church bells across the square each Sunday."

"The Presbyterians lost, did they?"

"No, they did not. It turns out the pastor of each church took matters into his own hands. They decided since Homily Baptist was listed before First Pres in the town's registry of completed buildings, they'd ring their bells first."

"Well, that makes sense to me."

"And, it means I don't have to be to service as early as you do." He winked, receiving a wide smile that reached all the way to her beautiful eyes in return for his efforts. His heart rate continued to beat a quick staccato and endorphins filled his blood stream. Pride swelled within him for putting a smile on her face. It seemed the only thing he wanted to do.

Abby

Abby left Aunt Sara sitting on a blanket in the backyard underneath a weeping willow with a book and a few gardening tools for some "easy" weed pulling. With a chicken salad sandwich for the road, she planned to go to the beach for some sunshine, and to stick her toes in the sand. Usually, Abby spent all the time she could with her aunt when she visited, but as she had practically moved back in, she no longer felt like a visitor. Even though most of her clothes and belongings were still lying abandoned where she had left them when she departed for spring break all those months ago.

Abby needed some time to herself. While nothing perceptible had changed, she felt a distance between herself and her aunt that permeated the house. Avoidance had become her new game plan. So long as her aunt didn't bring up her mother, neither would she. It was obvious the woman still didn't want anything to do with her, otherwise she would have reached out.

It's not as if mama doesn't know where to find me, and leaving me is her loss, not mine. I can do this. I can take care of Aunt Sara. I can make the shop relevant. I can leave my past behind. She said the words to herself over and over, the mantra failing to form the concrete barrier around her heart she longed for.

Distracted by her thoughts she'd parked outside The Christmas Tea Shoppe instead of her intended destination, and watched as a giant peeked through the shop's windows.

"Can I help you, sir?" Abby asked, getting out of the car.

The man jumped and hit his head on the troublesome awning.

"Yes, 'am," he stammered, looking sheepish.

"Mr. Wilson?"

He smiled kindly and removed his hat.

"Miss Abby, look at you, all grown up. I hardly recognized you, you got so big," he rushed to say.

Abernathy Wilson, or Abe as everyone in town called him, was a man as tall as he was wide, muscles bulging from the physical labor he did on his farm. A gentle soul, everyone in Homily knew he was shyer than the perception his impressive size gave off.

"Aunt Sara told me your wife passed last year. I'm sorry for your loss, Mr. Wilson."

He hung his head, his heart on his sleeve for her to see. "Yes 'am. Miss my Etta Lynn every day."

"Did you need something from the shop? We're usually closed on Sunday, but since I'm here, I'd be happy to help you."

"I came into town for church, and thought I'd get a gift for my grandbaby's first birthday while I'm here."

"Why don't we step inside?" Abby said kindly, unlocking the door.

Abe followed behind her at a respectable distance, dressed in a dapper, navy, pinstriped three-piece suit, the door left wide open in his wake.

She looked at him, a question in her eyes.

"Sorry, Miss Abby. Old habits are hard to break...me being a black man and nobody but us in here."

The words he didn't say resonated through her head. Abby sometimes forgot the last lynching in Alabama had only happened thirty years earlier. She swallowed hard and nodded with understanding, but his words seared her heart. The system was broken if good men lived in fear of reprisal.

"I was glad to hear your aunt's feeling better. Problems of the heart are no laughin' matter."

In more ways than one, thought Abby. "How long have you known Aunt Sara?"

"Only since high school. I was supposed to attend the county school, but Homily recruited me for football on account of my size. Daddy hoped I'd get a college scholarship, but he passed my senior year, so I stayed home to take care of the farm and Mama instead."

"So, y'all were friends in school?" Abby asked, curious about a teenage Aunt Sara.

"Somethin' like that. She was always wavin' at me in the halls and tryin' to get me to talk with her. I can still picture her long red braids and plaid skirts, handin' out flyers for one cause or another. Until the day she caught me walkin' home from practice with a small mob following behind me, tossin' rocks and slurs at my back. I had taken someone else's spot on the team, to their way of thinking."

"What happened next?" she inquired when he stopped as though the ending were obvious or didn't matter.

"She got outta her car, shook a fist in those boys' faces, and told them if they ever bothered me again, her Papaw was gonna have a word with his good friend, Coach Cochran. Gave me ride home every day from then on."

When he didn't continue, she assumed he'd said all he was going to say on the subject and decided to move on to the quest at hand.

"Are you interested in a teapot or a cup?"

"Etta left her tea set to Jazmyn. Figured I'd start a new one for her daughter. What you think, Miss Abby?" he asked, wringing his hands in indecision.

"I think you can't go wrong with either choice."

"Do you have anything with birds? My baby girl sure does love birdies, always chirpin' right along with them," Abe bragged like a proud grandparent.

"Yes, sir, I know just the one," she said, reaching for the top shelf of the hutch to the left of the mantel. He extended his long arm above her to pluck the piece off.

"Thank you," she laughed. "I could use a few of your inches."

"Yes, 'am. Comes in handy every now and then."

"I'll wrap it for you. Pink or purple ribbon?"

"Both, please."

Abby pulled out a brown paper box and lined it with tissue paper, gently placing the teapot in a cocoon of gold while Abe looked around the shop.

"I sure do like the new decorations, Miss Abby. Folks in town been talkin' 'bout the changes. Makes the place feel brand new and reminds me miracles happen every season, not just Christmas. That baby Jesus sure changed everything though, didn't he? He brought grace for everyone, every day of the week."

It was probably the most she'd ever heard him say, she was glad she had this moment alone in the shop with him.

Five minutes later, Abby saw Mr. Wilson out of the shop. "Thank you. Your visit was the highlight of my day," she said and watched as a lazy smile spread across his handsome countenance.

The shop was the last place she'd expected to find herself today, but it turned out to be the only place she needed to be.

Ten

Dear Sunshine,

Abby looks more and more like you with every passing day. Except for the curls, I almost can't tell the difference between her second-grade picture and yours. She's shyer than I remember you being, but she's the same brand of sunshine and sass. And I understand why you don't want to move back home, but I don't have to like it. Promise me you'll keep in touch. Love you, to the stars and back.

Always, Sissy

Matt

After walking Abby to her car, Matt went home to check on Gran. Finding her in front of a movie, he fixed her a lunch of chicken noodle soup he'd made the night before, some homemade biscuits on the side, and a cup of chamomile-lemon tea.

Since his shift at the hospital didn't begin until later, he decided to start on his list of house projects and repairs. He'd picked up most of the supplies at Hickam's Toolbox earlier in the week so he could work on things when he had a few hours to spare. The store was small in comparison to Home Depot, but he liked to support local businesses whenever he could.

Going around the side of the house, he struck out for his granddad's workshop tucked into the corner of his grandparents' property, just shy of the creek marking the property line. The property was one of the largest plots in the neighborhood, with most of the other houses on smaller plots dotting the road.

Most people never realized how much land the house sat on. The view from the road was deceptively narrow, but both the house and land were originally part of a large cotton plantation. In the years following the Civil War, the owner sold off parcels of land to pay his debts, and eventually the surrounding neighborhood had been incorporated into the town of Homily.

As Matt drew closer to the workshop, he passed the carefully marked pile of wood that lay near the edge of the property. It was simply a pile of dilapidated boards, but it was all that remained of what had once been a slave cabin. Matt remembered asking his grandfather about it when he was young.

"Why do you keep it, Granddad? You can't even tell what it used to be!"

"Because, son, it's an important part of history that needs to be preserved. Besides, some people in this town would rather forget this pile of wood, and what it once was, ever existed. Never forget, Matthew, the family who owned this property before us enslaved people and forced men, women, and children to work the land, in the house, and what used to be a detached kitchen. We have a little bit of the history from what was left behind, but not enough to return the land to those who worked it, or to name those forced to live in that slave cabin."

His granddad continued, "No wrong is ever made right with denial, Matthew. You can't sweep it out the door with the rest of the dirt and dust."

"How come some people want to forget? Why do they have so much hate in their hearts?" Matt had asked, trying to keep up. He loved spending time with his granddad, but the man talked more than his gran sometimes.

"I think hate takes root when people let ignorance, fear, and jealousy run amok. Do you understand, son?"

"Yes, sir, I think so. Gran says we should only ever love one another and treat people the way we want to be treated. Um…and lies are sneaky stinkers hiding in plain sight."

"May the good Lord help us; hopefully someday we'll remember those lessons," said Beaux Dixon with a tug on the bill of Matt's cap.

As an adult, Matt understood life was little more complicated than love or hate. People were rarely made up of one or the other. Good folks make bad decisions sometimes, and a blind chicken catches a kernel every now and then. Still, he wondered what the town, and their family land, would look like if America had kept its promise of forty acres and a mule.

His grandparents had bought the house in a dilapidated state with the intent to restore it to its former glory. Beaux Dixon had served in World War II, and upon his return promptly married his high school sweetheart, Gran. They hoped to fill its rooms with children, but as Gran was fond of saying, if you want to make God laugh tell him your plans. Matt's dad was born ten years to the day of his grandparents' wedding. They fondly referred to him as their tenth anniversary gift.

Unfortunately, he was the only child they would have. For some mysterious reason, his grandparents were unable to conceive after that. Regardless, they painted a happy portrait of a family. His dad joined the military just after his eighteenth birthday, not because he didn't love his parents, but because his wanderlust was too much to stay. He once told Matt his hometown would be perfect if it weren't so small. Even now, he took off somewhere new every few months.

Matt didn't feel his father's pull to leave. Homily contained one of his favorite people in the whole world, which made it the perfect town for him.

Let's face it, it's only getting better now that Abby Hart has made an appearance.

Meeting a woman like Abby made a man evaluate how he spent his time. His dad tended to put his job before family and, though he had more time for Matt since retirement, it still wasn't the same. Hindsight allowed Matt to acknowledge his father had been a hard worker and good provider, but it didn't mean he missed him any less growing up. These days they settled for a weekend of camping and deep-sea fishing together a couple of times a year.

Matt's mom had remarried a few years earlier. She stayed busy with her new family, a loud bunch who'd welcomed her with open arms. She made weekly phone calls to catch up, but when he had a holiday free, he usually chose to spend it with Gran.

Pulling his thoughts back to the job at hand, he put on a pair of safety goggles and earmuffs, picking out pieces of reclaimed longleaf pine from a pile he'd found at an estate sale a few years before. Estate sales were like treasure troves of history, and he liked to explore them for reclaim possibilities while his gran waded through the jewelry and knickknacks. A few of Gran's porch boards had rotted, and he hoped to try his hand at a little carpentry on the house, thankful his granddad had taught him enough to be useful.

The steady sound of the table saw hummed low beneath the muffs while he focused his attention on pushing the boards slowly through the blades. It was a strangely hypnotic rhythm established between man and machine. Finished with his cuts, Matt ran them through the router to create tongue and groove joints before putting a first coat of stain on the replacement boards. With a glance at his phone, he tidied the workshop and went to clean up for his shift.

Poking his head into the den to check on Gran, he found her snoring softly on the overstuffed couch. Not that she would ever admit to it if he brought it up.

"Gently bred southern women don't snore, Matthew Lee Dixon. We breathe deeply with gusto. One might even say we do it wholeheartedly, like we do everything else."

"You mean just like southern women don't sweat; they glow?"

"Exactly, sweet boy. We glisten with purpose."

As if men and women didn't have the same bodily functions.

He stuck a post it on the stack of books resting beside the coffee table where she couldn't miss it, grabbed his keys and a hoodie in the front entry, and closed the door quietly behind him.

....

A few hours into his shift at the hospital, Matt got the call. It was the one he dreaded most days, especially the days he left Gran by herself for an extended amount of time. Up until then, it had been a slow night in the ER, so he'd decided to grab a granola bar and a cup of coffee to tide him over through the rest of his shift. At the last minute, he snatched a banana from the fruit basket by the register. That was when his beeper and cell phone went off at the same time.

He abandoned his items to the checkout clerk in the cafeteria with an apology, and answered his phone on the third ring, breaking into a run. One of the triage nurses he worked with regularly quickly and calmly relayed the information he'd need on arrival. The nurse had no doubt been thorough, but when he pushed through the double doors and entered the space which had become his second home, he couldn't recall a single detail. Only the words telling him Nancy Dixon had been admitted.

By the time Gran was settled into a room for the night and resting relatively comfortably, thanks to a morphine drip in her IV, visiting hours were over. Matt ignored the clock in the room ticking away the hours of life and settled into a chair next to Gran's bed. The nursing staff understood the rules of time did not apply to the current situation, not that it would have mattered if they had. One look at his face told everyone all they needed to know. The doctor they worked with in proximity everyday wouldn't leave the premises until his grandmother had been discharged into his care. He'd already called his parents to let them know about the accident. There was nothing left to do but settle in to watch over the woman who'd always watched over him.

He planned out her recovery while he waited for morning, letting guilt slide in close next to his thoughts. Matt could only blame himself for her injuries.

If I had taken her keys away the other day, neither of us would be here.

There would be no need for worry or prayer. He tried to turn his thoughts away from himself and toward the only one who could offer him any comfort, thanking God for his gran's life and seeking her healing. Matt had foolishly let himself believe her pride was more important than her safety. He needed to ask her forgiveness as well as God's for his mistake. With that thought, he laid his head on the bed beside her, tucking her frail hand within his, and promptly fell asleep.

He awoke with a start to find light streaming through the crack in the curtains, and Gran's eyes upon him. They looked bleary with pain, but not confused, and he released a sigh of relief. He held out a glass of water from the tray next to the bed, speaking in the soft tone he saved for his younger patients. "Gran, do you know why you're here?"

She nodded in return, and spoke in a hoarse voice, "I'm so sorry—"

Matt held the cup to her lips until she reached up to take it from him. When she was done, she tried again. "Did anyone else get hurt?"

"You mean besides the light pole in the Walmart parking lot?" He tried to inflect humor into his voice but knew he hadn't fooled her when she frowned back at him.

"Thank the good Lord I didn't hit the minivan. I swerved to miss it, but I must have misjudged how close I was to the pole," she said shamefully.

"I'm afraid I might be as much to blame as you. I knew you were having trouble with your eyesight, and instead of telling you what any doctor would, I told myself I was sparing your dignity. I should have been honest with you when I realized what was happening. I'm lucky you weren't killed." He choked on his last few words, tears shining in his eyes. He quickly and discreetly wiped them away when the nurse on duty entered the room.

"Morning, Dr. Dixon. Mrs. Dixon, I imagine you're feeling a little worse for wear. How's your pain on a scale of one to five, five being high?"

"Well, it's not as bad as childbirth, but I'm not exactly looking to get out of this bed any time soon."

"Sounds like a middle of the road three to me. I can increase your drip once you've seen the doctor and we've taken care of your catheter. It's going to make you sleepy, and though the rest is good for healing, we need to check a few priorities off the list first."

Nancy looked to Matt for direction, but even though he agreed with the assessment, he wanted Gran to make her own decisions when given the opportunity. Just because she shouldn't be driving didn't mean she couldn't oversee her healthcare.

"I'll just step out to give you some privacy then. Want me to confiscate anything from the cafeteria for you?" he asked. She gave him a wobbly smile and shook her head before giving the nurse her full attention.

Eleven

Dear Sunshine,

Which Halloween costume should I make for Abby this year? She really wants to be a knight or a pirate, but I was thinking something more along the lines of a princess. I know, I know, I should let her pick for herself. How is the recovery house? Do you like your roommates? Call me, for anything, anytime. Love you, to the stars and back.

Always, Sissy

Abby

June came and went in a flurry of tourists and locals alike. The Christmas Tea Shoppe hosted multiple graduation, birthday, and anniversary parties, clearing more than the previous two summers. Abby decorated with sea glass beads for garland, paper waves across the mantle, and mermaids hung from the tree in hues of blue, green, and coral. Beneath the tree, various plastic sea creatures climbed felt sand and invited young customers to get hands-on while parents ordered or simply caught their breath from all the family fun.

The seagull in place of an angel received mixed reviews but the summer tea menu was a worthy five stars. Combined with peach scones and mango *crème fraiche*, most were willing to overlook the odd bird perched at the top of the tree.

Unfortunately, she had yet to see Matt in the throng of summer business. For someone she hardly knew, she sure did miss running into him. But Abby knew better than most, the shop had a way of bringing people together inside its sturdy walls, if and when the time was right.

....

Abby bent over to pull out more paper plates, plastic ware, and takeaway cups for the strawberry shortcake with whipped cream and blackberry sweet tea the shop would be serving at Homily's Fourth of July on the Square Festival. Like every celebration in her hometown, the name itself was a mouthful, let alone the number of festivities. The morning began with a parade around the town's square, followed by the Miss Fourth of July pageant. Much to every gossip's delight, the mayor's daughter had won the past three years in a row.

In years past, The Christmas Tea Shoppe stayed open for the festival but didn't provide a booth in the square. After a lively debate with Aunt Sara about the pros and cons and too many logistics to count, they decided it might be fun to be in the center of things with the other businesses. Though simplifying the menu meant giving people a taste of what they had to offer instead of the whole menu, being in the square gave them an opportunity to show their town spirit.

Aunt Sara managed to help Abby for a few hours at the stand before going home to rest. If she felt up to it, she said, she'd join Abby for a picnic and fireworks in the evening. For now, Abby needed to restock her supply of takeaway items because the shortcake and sweet tea were flying off the proverbial shelves.

"I'll take one shortcake, an iced tea, and a smile, please."

Abby whirled around at the request to find herself staring into a set of twinkling green eyes. An instant smile stretched across her tan face at the site. It was a welcome surprise.

"How are you? How's your gran?" she asked.

"I see word has gotten around."

"Of course, it has. We live in Homily, where any tidbit is a welcome distraction from our own troubles. Mrs. Hanson comes in weekly for a special blend of tea, and she happened to mention her good friend, Nancy, was recovering from a car accident. To her credit she was very concerned and bought an extra tin for her friend. She also mentioned that I knew her friend's grandson, which caught my attention since I haven't seen or heard from you in a few weeks."

"That sounds suspiciously like you might have missed me."

"Aren't you a presumptuous one. I simply meant I was concerned for my new acquaintance. After all, this is a small town where people run into each other daily, and you practically went and disappeared overnight. For all I knew, someone had kidnapped you."

He burst out laughing, not that she could blame him. It was a preposterous excuse.

"Kidnapped me? That's a good one. How about you just admit you like my company."

"Perhaps."

"Okay, well *perhaps* you can let me make up for my sudden absence by joining me for a picnic tonight before the fireworks. I'll bring dinner if you bring dessert."

Without skipping a beat and forgetting about the plans she had already tentatively made with her aunt, Abby blurted out, "Works for me."

His eyes lit up with surprise and possibly a hint of pride at her quick concession.

"I'll meet you in front of the bandstand at six sharp."

A line had begun to form behind him, so Matt gave Abby a salute and another smile, disappearing into the throngs of people gathered in the square despite the sultry summer heat. The breeze blew in gently off the water, ruffling her curls and cooling the sheen of perspiration along her skin while she passed out endless amounts of shortcake and tea.

"Thanks for supporting The Christmas Tea Shoppe. Be sure to visit us downtown, folks."

Her mouth had gone as dry as school paste by the time five o'clock rolled around. Families began to arrive with blankets and picnic baskets to prepare for the evening's activities while Abby packed up the booth. It was always a nice surprise how easy packing up was compared to set up. Besides, Abby didn't have much time if she was going to drop off the leftovers and supplies at the shop, get a little dolled up, and still meet Matt at the bandstand by six.

....

"Mags, this isn't a date," Abby said, putting her phone on speaker while she checked her appearance once more in the bathroom mirror at the shop.

Cheeks pinched for a hint of color. *Perfect.*

A little cherry lip gloss for shine. *Delightful.*

Lashes bathed in a light coat of dark mascara, and her new red sundress with navy peep-toe wedges. *Hello, Fourth of July.*

Her hair was a riot of undisciplined curls, but the silver headband kept it off her face. All in all, she felt the effect was natural and not overdone for a summer night's picnic with a friend. Granted, a handsome friend who made her heart flutter.

Just the teensiest bit, she told herself with more conviction than she felt.

"Yes, it is, sweetie. That man is not interested in only being your friend if he asked you to join him for a public meal. He knows exactly what's going to follow."

"Contrary to yourself, girlfriend, I am not a first-date kisser. No insult intended."

"None taken. Besides, I'm not talkin' about kissing, not that it would hurt for you to get a little action. I mean all the tongues that are gonna wag when everyone in town sees you together tonight."

"Still not a date, but I do need to leave for my nondate with my friend the doctor soon."

"It is too a date—"

"Tell Tuck hello, and kiss Caleb's sweet sumo cheeks for me. Bye Mags, miss you!"

"Okay, but it's still a date—" Maggie yelled into the phone as Abby hung up.

Grumbling to herself about how Mags always needed the last word, she put away the rest of the supplies from the booth and locked the shop door behind her. On her way to the bandstand, she passed the bench and playground where she'd spent a Sunday morning talking with Matt, the two of them chatting her worries away. Abby smiled and walked a little faster, anticipation nipping at her heels.

Children ran through the square, sparklers fisted in their hands, parents yelling to be careful, and children doing their best to ignore them. In the distance, musicians set up for the night in the bandstand, a great monstrosity of a gazebo, with white gingerbread trim and twinkling lights wrapped around and strung from every piece of wood. It reminded Abby of an oversized wedding cake, but without the bride and groom standing on top.

A mandolin and dobro held court in the center along with the usual fanfare of guitars and a keyboard. She pictured the band playing while couples danced in the grass and idly wondered if a slow dance could be in her own future. Except tonight was a non-date. Matt was kind and a lot of fun to be around, but he had never implied he was interested in anything more than friendship. Do friends dance together? *Yes. Yes, they do,* she decided.

Except he did ask you out tonight, a little voice in her head argued. Maggie's, to be sure. She could practically hear her best friend's cackle of glee.

Maybe, she volleyed back. *But maybe not.*

With a look around, Abby stopped short at the sight of Matt seated with his back to her and engaged in conversation with Homily's beloved mayor, one blanket over. Unlike Mayor Thorne's red and blue plaid, though, her friend sat on a quilt that looked well loved, and if she wasn't mistaken, made in the traditional double wedding ring design. Groaning softly to herself, she shook her head over his colossal and very public mistake. He probably had no idea what those rings symbolized, which meant he didn't have a clue what fodder they were about to provide for the gossip mill by having dinner together on top of them.

She came up behind Matt, the mayor glancing at her with a tight-lipped smile. He acknowledged her presence, albeit with polite indifference, as though he knew she hadn't voted for him in the previous election. "Mayor, it's nice to see you this evening."

Matt turned around and stood up in one smooth movement. With a grin wide enough to showcase his dimple, Matt's eyes lit from within, and he reached to take her hand to help her take a seat on the blanket. He paused as his eyes traveled the length of her from her navy peep-toe wedges all the way up to her sparkling headband, his amiable smile much more to her liking than the mayor's, who still watched them from the corner of his eye.

Abby wondered where the mayor's typically congenial personality had disappeared to when the answer to her question appeared at the man's elbow. Anna Mae Thorne kissed her daddy's cheek and with a distinctly feline smile greeted Matt.

"Dr. Dixon," she practically purred, refusing to even greet Abby. "Don't you look just as handsome tonight as you do in your white coat. I'm sure all the single ladies of Homily are swooning with you in our midst. I was just telling Daddy this morning how blessed we are to have a doctor such as yourself working at our little hospital. One devoted not only to his work, but his family, and this town too."

Abby watched Matt squirm under the woman's praise, never mind that Grant Hospital was large enough to serve the entire county.

"Thank you, but really I'm only—"

Without even taking a breath, Anna Mae steamrolled right over whatever he was going to say. "Daddy said you're interested in joining the Homily Historical Preservation Society. I'd be happy to introduce you to the board. Maybe we could get a drink beforehand, you know, to go over some of the *expectations* for membership."

Abby almost gagged over the woman's saccharine voice and not-so-subtle invitation, but then remembered Aunt Sara's advice about dealing with catty women. "Never let them see you back down, sugar. Kill 'em with kindness if you have too. And for heaven's sake, do not stoop to their basement-level behavior."

Sara had done her best to raise Abby to take the high road, but she couldn't take one more second of Anna Mae's poorly hidden attempts to latch onto Matt, even if it meant stooping just a smidge. Maybe she could admit her own motivations weren't entirely selfless either. Anna Mae's lush figure, chest thrust forward for all the world to admire in a strapless cocktail dress, makeup done to perfection, and highlighted hair straight as a pin made Abby feel a little insecure about her own attempts to look nice after working the booth in the heat all day.

Honestly though, who wears a cocktail dress and stiletto heels to a picnic?!

Abby accepted Matt's proffered hand and slipped her hand far enough into his to interlace their fingers. She smiled sweetly at the woman standing across from her and looked up at Matt, who in turn was staring down at her like she was a mirage in the desert.

Oh, dear Lord, let me be the water. Wait, what? I did not just think that.

Abby's thoughts began to run hither and yon. With a quick grab for the reins of reason, she tried to drag them in. There was some kicking and screaming along the way.

"Honey, I'm absolutely famished after working at the booth all day. Why don't we take a seat and dig into that delicious meal you packed?" She may or may not have batted her eyelashes at him. Either way, she was in it to win it now.

Matt returned her smile like he knew exactly what game she was playing and was more than happy to play along. "I think you'll find I packed all your favorites."

"Perfect, because I brought dessert." She didn't lift the bag still clutched in her unoccupied hand, letting Anna Mae imply what she would from her words.

He dropped his voice to a sultry murmur and said, "And here I thought spending time with you was the sweetest part of tonight."

Abby blushed. The heat started in the bottom of her stomach and moved through her entire body. She tried to tell her heart, along with the rest of herself, to calm down. Matt was simply acting the part she had created for him, nothing else. Unable to hold his gaze any longer, she swallowed hard and sought out her opponent to assess the damage.

The look on the other woman's face surpassed her expectations. Abby considered taking a photo for posterity's sake, especially as Anna Mae's eyes followed the two of them as they sat with one accord on the quilt. Tongues were going to wag tomorrow, but Abby didn't care one iota as she listened to this year's pageant winner pout loudly and stomp off in the direction of what could only be her next victim, her daddy following quickly at her heels.

Matt waited all of ten seconds before bellowing a laugh, the sound causing goose bumps up and down her arms as it carried across the square, catching the attention of several onlookers.

Get a hold of yourself, girl. It's only laughter.

But being the person to make him laugh so uproariously made her feel light enough to fly.

Abby grinned broadly and quietly said, "I hope you don't mind."

"Mind? Of course, I don't mind. I'm happy to hold your hand anytime you want, especially in front of that woman."

"Not a fan, huh?"

"Not particularly. I get the feeling I would only be another trophy for her mantel, so I think I'll pass. Besides, I'm pretty sure she grows fangs and claws once she's got a person in her clutches."

"Well, I'm glad I could rescue you from any unwanted advances then."

"So am I. Though, if you were feeling a little jealous, I wouldn't blame you."

"Oh really, and why is that?" she asked, annoyed at the implication.

"Because it means you might like me as much as I like you, Miss Hart."

It took the wind right out of her sails when she realized he wasn't being arrogant. Not knowing what to do with his words, Abby glanced down at her hands in her lap and promptly changed the subject.

"How is your gran doing? You didn't say when I asked this afternoon."

Twelve

Dear Sunshine,

Our girl spends every school break at the shop with me. She's helpful in the kitchen and courteous to the customers, most of whom she knows from town. Still, I worry Abby needs more time with other kids her age. So, she and Maggie are going to sleepaway camp for two whole weeks this summer. I feel lonely just thinking about it. Love you, to the stars and back.

Always, Sissy

Matt

Matt hesitated for a moment, caught off guard from the rapid change in topic, and if he was honest with himself, he was disappointed that Abby had ignored his declaration. It was a blow to his pride, but one he'd weather without making a donkey out of himself.

"I think I was too preoccupied asking you to dinner at the time. Gran is on the mend. The car accident left her with a couple of bruised ribs and knee trauma. She stayed in an inpatient physical rehabilitation center for a couple of weeks, and now that she's at home, I take her to physical therapy weekly. With her age, the progress is slow but she's resilient. I admire her determination to remain independent, even if it is what got her into this mess to begin with."

"What happened?"

"She swerved to avoid an oncoming minivan in the Walmart parking lot and drove her car into a light post." Matt sighed at the thought. "Her depth perception is deteriorating, which is not an uncommon occurrence as people age, but her diabetes probably accelerated the problem. The hardest part for me is that I knew it was becoming an issue, but I was so concerned with her independence I kept putting it off. I should have taken away her keys instead of waiting for her to hand them over."

Abby placed her hand on his arm, a gesture of comfort. "It's a hard realization when the people we love and look up to need to be taken care of. It's not easy to have those kinds of conversations, but I'm sure you did the best you could by trying to preserve her dignity."

"No, I should have taken them away, even at the expense of her pride. I'm a doctor; I know better. If she'd been a patient, I wouldn't have thought twice. I recently found out her own doctor made the recommendation more than a year ago, which Gran promptly discarded and kept to herself."

"You're also human and this isn't a patient we're talking about. It's your gran, and that makes it complicated. Nobody gets it right every single time. Trust me, I should know."

She said the last part under her breath, and he watched her in expectation. At her continued silence he said, "You are quite the mystery, Abigail Hart."

"Really, I'm not. What you see is what you get."

"Fair enough, but something tells me you have more of a story to tell than you ever let on. I guess it's a good thing I'm not going anywhere. We've got time to get to know each other."

"That sounds like a challenge, Matthew Lee Dixon."

His eyes widened at the sound of his full name on her tongue. "Maybe it is, but I'm perfectly happy to wait until you're ready to spill your secrets."

With a dismissive wave of her hand she prompted, "In the meantime, we should probably eat because I am starving!"

"Sounds good. While I pull out the sandwiches and potato salad, why don't you tell me how you found out my middle name."

"That was easy. It's listed on the hospital's provider website I found when I was doing research on Aunt Sara's cardiologist."

He chuckled and said, "That seems a little unfair. How am I supposed to find your middle name without being a total creeper?"

"You could just ask."

"Seriously, you're going to make it that easy for me?"

"Not at all. Where would be the fun in that? All you have to do is guess correctly." Abby gave Matt a sly smile and a sidelong glance.

"What do I get if I do? Wait, don't answer that. *When* I guess it, you owe me a dance before the end of the evening."

Nodding, she said, "Agreed."

With a worried look she put her hand out to shake on it. He met her stare and shook her proffered hand gently, holding on a moment longer than necessary before reaching for his sandwich.

They ate in companionable silence for a while, listening to the band warming up under the lights of the bandstand. Matt had been throwing out guesses here and there for the last half hour when he blurted out, "I can't believe I didn't think of it before now. It almost seems too obvious."

"You sound pretty sure of yourself," Abby said nervously.

"Jane. Abigail Jane Hart."

Abby grimaced enough for Matt to throw back his head and chuckle before asking, "Either I'm way off base, or the idea of dancing with me is that bad, huh? I'll have you know, I'm actually a pretty good dancer."

"And humble too," she said and lightly poked him in the ribs with her elbow.

"At least I can promise not to step on your toes. So, which is it?"

"Neither."

That was it, no further explanation left the glossy lips he'd been admiring most of the night.

"I see. So, you get that look every time someone says Jane?"

She grimaced again, and he laughed once more in response. "Well, Abigail Jane Hart," he said, her name a caress across his lips. "I happen to like your full name very much."

When the band started to play a slow song, Matt stood up and held his hand out to her. Abby let him pull her into his arms where he tucked her right hand next to his heart and placed his other hand on her lower back. The sky shifted toward a pink and lavender dusk, the first stars of the night popping in the distance. He noticed Abby's bare feet in the grass, her head barely coming to his chin with a few soft curls catching in the five o'clock shadow on his face. All in all, the moment felt as perfect as he'd imagined.

Matt moved them side to side in time with the music he recognized from the radio. Abby was humming in key, a little breathless, but present. He committed it to memory for the potential future. Too soon it came to an end, and he released her, if somewhat regretfully. The fireworks weren't scheduled to start for another half an hour, but he had only asked her to dinner, and it appeared their time was up.

Not surprisingly, when he met her back at the quilt, she was already folding up the quilt Gran had sent with him, in a hurry to move on, but she finally looked him in the eye as she placed it into his waiting hands.

With a serious note to her tone, Abby said, "You do realize tongues will be wagging, what with our little performance earlier, this quilt, and a slow dance."

They started walking in unison, though where they were going, he couldn't say. Not that it mattered if it meant he could spend more time with Abby.

"Don't get me wrong, I don't pay much attention to rumors in the first place, because I usually find the real story more interesting. However, if people want to assume we're headed for the altar just because we like to hold hands, slow dance in public, and sit on quilts with wedding ring patterns, I'm not too sure I'd put up much of a fuss," he said, goading her on purpose.

Her mouth popped open into the sweetest shape of an "oh" he had ever seen.

Abby was speechless for all of three seconds before she demanded, "You knew about the quilt this entire time?"

"Of course, it's my gran's favorite pattern. She has at least three or four of them around the house. Gran likes to buy them at estate sales and insists each one brings along its own love story."

"Your gran sounds like a hopeless romantic."

"Assuredly. I've never met a couple so devoted to one another as my grandparents were."

"I imagine having a great love story of her own makes it easier for her to see love through rose-colored glasses."

"Hold on there, I didn't say she's unrealistic. My gran has always said she and my granddad loved each other with as much forgiveness as they did with endearments and the words, 'I love you.'"

"And your own folks?"

"I once asked Gran why she thought my parents' marriage crashed and burned." He could feel Abby grow embarrassed beside him for asking a question with such a sad answer. Matt did his best to put her at ease by sharing Gran's wisdom with the empathetic woman next to him. "She said the best marriages are made of equal parts fire, laughter, and acceptance. Then you wrap it all up in God's grace to remember the gift that it is."

"Huh. I think your gran might be onto something," Abby mentioned as though she were really pondering the words.

They continued on in silence for a few minutes, and when they reached a tree-lined street a couple of blocks from downtown, he asked, "Where are we?"

"Home. My home, in any case. This is the neighborhood I grew up in. Aunt Sara and I live in the same house my great grandparents owned. Aunt Sara's parents—my grandparents— died in a car accident when she was young."

"So, Sara's grandparents raised her and your mom? Or was it your dad?"

They came to a stop in front of the Craftsman bungalow on the corner, enclosed by a short, white picket fence. Matt reached for the gate before Abby could open it for herself. The house was painted a warm butter yellow with white trim, and dark shutters of an indeterminate color framed either side of the windows. Matt followed her down the cobblestone walkway to the front porch, which was lit up by a single carriage lantern,

The sky had finally given in to the night's call, and the two of them gazed at one another under the glow from the porch light. Matt leaned in and gave Abby a kiss on the cheek. He said quietly and respectfully, "Thank you for having dinner with me. This is by far the best holiday I've had in a long time."

"Me too."

Matt waited to leave until Abby closed the door behind her. A serenade of fireworks over Homily's waterfront sounded in the distance as he walked back into the center of town where he'd parked for the evening. Three things had occurred to him by the time he spotted the familiar shiny black pick up.

First, Abby had never said anything about her own parents, even when the conversation naturally went there. Second, in the aftermath of kissing her cheek, he'd forgotten to ask for her phone number, again. It would be unethical to call the number listed in her aunt's chart, not that he couldn't just look her aunt's number up in the phone book or call The Christmas Tea Shoppe, but Matt thought it fundamental to ask for a woman's phone number.

He didn't want to assume she wanted to hear from him; he wanted to know she did. Maybe it was ridiculous considering the number of times they had talked, but he didn't want to leave her with any doubt that he was interested in pursuing whatever this was between them.

And third, he was in over his head and more than happy to tread water with Abby, even if it meant drowning.

Abby

Abby leaned against the closed door and melted like butter on hot toast. Her hand rested on her cheek, savoring the feeling of his warm lips, and not wanting the heat to fade.

"Baby girl, is that you?" Aunt Sara called from the sunroom.

"I'm home, Aunt Sara," Abby called back.

"Well, come on in here and have a cup of tea while you tell me about your date then, sugar."

She found Aunt Sara on the couch, a full tea set and baking magazines filled with unfriendly recipes for her heart laid out in front of her. She grabbed the pillow from the opposite end and tucked one leg underneath her, placing the pillow in her lap. The inquisition could officially commence. Though her aunt had been happy to claim exhaustion when Abby extended Matt's invitation to join him for a picnic, she still expected to hear the finer points of the evening.

Always one for manners, Aunt Sara filled two cups with white strawberry tea, stirring in a spoonful of honey before handing it to Abby. "So, how was your time with Matt?" she asked.

"Good."

"Uh-huh. So that's how this is going to go, is it?"

"Pretty much."

"Abigail Hart, don't you dare hold out on me."

"I'm not; there isn't a lot to tell."

"You do realize I have a meeting with the LLS tomorrow."

"Remind me what that stands for again?"

"Ladies' Literary Society. They raise funds for the libraries in the schools.

"That's nice; are you going over the menu we put together for the fundraiser in September?"

"Yes, but only as a courtesy. They're fully aware I'll serve what I want, but it's nice to at least appear cooperative. Now, quit stalling, sugar. The ladies will just tell me anyway. I'd rather have the upper hand to fend them off."

Abby rolled her eyes, and then winced. "Sorry, I didn't mean it. I'm just flustered."

"What could have you so flustered you've stooped to rudeness, missy?"

"Matt Dixon, that's what, or I guess who, in this instance."

"I knew it, I just knew it," Aunt Sara crowed. "That man has got you all aflutter."

"Aflutter?"

"Don't play coy with me; you know what it means."

Abby unabashedly grinned and told her aunt everything. She didn't leave any of the details out, even when it made her flush to relive them. Besides, keeping the discovery of her mama's letters a secret still felt like too much baggage between them, and became a heavier burden to bear the longer she kept it. No need to add any more to the pile.

"I wish I could have seen the look on Anna Mae's face," Sara crowed with delight.

"I have a feeling my little act is going to come back to bite me in the butt, but it sure felt good to wipe the smirk off her face at the time."

"It certainly says a lot about Matt. He's man enough not to worry about what others will say, but something tells me he's already decided tongues can wag all they want." When Abby looked as though she were going to refute her, her aunt shook her index finger in her face.

"No, no, no. Absolutely not, young lady. He could've chosen not to play along with you even at the risk of embarrassment. Or he could've flipped the quilt over so the pattern wouldn't show. And the good Lord knows he didn't have to dance with you in front of the whole town."

Abby admitted reluctantly, "Dancing with him was perfect. The crowd on the square almost faded away, the two of us swaying to the music in the background. I've never experienced anything like it before."

"It sounds magical. I'm so glad you had a good time, baby girl."

"He kissed me goodbye on the cheek but didn't suggest we get together again. Maybe I'm wrong, and he's only interested in being friends."

"Maybe, or maybe he's taking it slow, letting things unfold between you as they will. There's no reason to rush, Abby."

"I know, it's just…" she halted, unsure how to continue. Was it the timing, the person, or her past holding her back? She didn't have an answer.

"That you almost married another man?" Abby nodded. It was nice talking to the person who knew her best.

"I really thought Lon was the one, until I didn't. How does anyone know for sure?"

"Nana used to say it was part magic and yet as natural as breathing but counted herself lucky to have married her best friend. I always thought I'd marry the one person I could be entirely myself with…he'd be someone who would challenge me to be a better person but love me at my worst. Personally, I think it's rare to find someone with those qualities."

"Is that the only reason you never married?" Abby asked, knowing it wasn't. Why she felt the need to torture herself when she already knew part of the reason her aunt never had enough time to date was because she'd been saddled with her sister's child.

"Part of it. Don't get me wrong, I've dated here and there over the years in hopes of finding someone to share life with. But I only felt the spark Nana talked about once when I was too young to understand the complications a relationship with a certain boy would bring. We had more hurdles to jump than we were prepared for at the time. And some might say I'm too independent for my own good, but I don't pay them any mind. If a man can be single, then why can't a woman?

"Furthermore, while I can't say I have any wisdom to offer on the subject, I don't think it hurts to pray about it. Listen for the small voice buried deep within your heart. Not the one saying, 'This looks like everything I want,' or, 'One of us will change in order to make it work.' Every relationship takes work, but doing the work with the right person usually makes it easier.

"I don't think marriage should start with the idea that you can make it work if you have to, but rather, who do I want beside me when the hard times come? God never promised this life would be easy, but I don't doubt that his grace is sufficient."

Another rock settled in the pit of Abby's stomach. She had certainly loved the idea of Lon, but never felt the spark Aunt Sara talked about. She'd held herself back from him, happy to support his hopes and dreams but never willing to share hers in return. The relationship ended the only way it could because they were never on equal footing. Abby struggled to be honest with herself, and in turn him. Lon Howard deserved better than her half-truths.

"I can see you have a lot to think over, so I think I'll head to bed. And don't be surprised if your young man comes calling at the shop tomorrow. You know, in case you want to put forth an extra effort in your morning routine." Sara snickered, a smirk not far behind as she exited the sunroom.

"He's not my young man. He's a friend," Abby called after her aunt, but all she gained for her effort was her aunt's familiar husky laugh.

Abby yawned and stretched. Unfortunately, Aunt Sara was right. Sleep wouldn't come until she settled her thoughts. She turned on the television. The old black-and-white movie her aunt had been watching wrapped up with a kiss and a happily ever after. Abby wasn't prone to cynicism, but disappointment was another story. She wanted to find her own happy ending someday. Figuring out how to make it happen was a whole other story. She shoved her face into the pillow in her lap, a muffled scream breaking free as she fell back into the couch and promptly started another cheesy rom com.

....

Abby woke up hours later with a wicker imprint on one side of her face, a kink in her neck, and a missed alarm. She had no time to primp as she brushed her teeth while squeezing herself into a pair of skinny capris, a short-sleeve button up, and black ballet flats. Thank goodness she'd over packed for her spring break trip three months earlier. She quickly twisted her hair into some version of a knot at the nape of her neck and, without even a glance in the hall mirror, rushed out the door.

Thirteen

Dear Sunshine,

Congratulations! I knew you could complete your GED. That being said, your job as the night janitor of a high school sounds abhorrent. I can't believe some of the stuff you have to clean up. At least it means you can finally put aside some money for classes at the community college. Or you could let me pay for them like I offered to. Abby made the honor roll again. She's so smart, and creative. Brilliant, just like her mama. You can do anything you set your mind to. Love you, to the stars and back.

Always, Sissy

Matt

Matt looked at his watch for the dozenth time and wondered when exactly The Christmas Tea Shoppe opened the morning after a holiday while he and Gran ate breakfast on the back porch. Though the temperature was moderate for the time of day, he could already feel the heat settling in with a layer of moisture on his skin.

"You look a little flustered this morning, Matthew. How'd you sleep last night?"

"I slept great, and what do you mean I look flustered?"

"Well, you've been bouncing that knee of yours since we sat down to eat, and if you don't slow down and actually chew your food, your old gran is going to have to try and perform the Heimlich maneuver. I don't picture it going very well, do you?"

Matt almost choked on his bite of biscuit with ham and eggs when he laughed and forced himself to slow down with an audible gulp. He really had slept like a baby, once he'd come up with a plan to track Abby down that morning. Now he was in a hurry to follow through.

"Do you know what time the tea shop opens?" He tried for nonchalance but failed when his knee started bobbing all over again.

Gran's smile rose to meet her eyes as she watched his disloyal appendage keep time like the metronome on top of her piano. More than happy to tell him exactly what time the shop opened, she followed it with the information Abby would probably still be managing the shop in Sara's place.

To which he replied, "I know, Gran. And I also know you tried to send me on those errands to the tea shop in the spring as part of a sneaky little plan of yours. But it turns out I didn't need you; I met her at the hospital instead."

"God does work in mysterious ways," she replied demurely, only to ruin it with an *I told you so* stare.

Laughing good naturedly at both the spoken and unspoken sentiment, Matt acknowledged the truth. "He certainly does."

Matt gave himself an extra five minutes so as not to appear too eager, more for Abby's sake than his own. He pushed open the etched glass door of the shop at five after eight. Bells softly chimed above the door when he entered, causing Abby to look over her shoulder at him, her arms laden with red and blue tinsel stars. He quickly stepped forward to offer help and received a tired smile in return. Not quite the enthusiastic greeting he'd been hoping for after the way things ended last night, but a man had to work with what he got when it came to the woman he liked.

Hopeful his charm would win her over, he relieved her of half of her burden and trailed after her to the boxes resting on a nearby table. Some were already filled with silver star ornaments of varying sizes, and he placed the blue tinsel ones he carried into the appropriate box. Abby moved to the mantel to remove what looked like a garland of flags tied together with strips of alternating navy, white, and crimson cloth. It was obvious why the shop was popular with locals and tourists alike—the perfect combination of tradition and history served with an updated twist.

Matt watched Abby as she flitted from one pile of decorations to another, the space she occupied brimming with life and making his chest tighten with want. It wasn't an altogether unpleasant sensation but work usually filled the space where relationships belonged in his life, the exceptions being his parents, Gran, and colleagues. He generally avoided the complications and expectations which came with anything more intimate.

Up to now, it had been easier to keep connections simple while focusing on his career. He wasn't a hook-up kind of guy, and anything more required an investment he'd been unwilling to make. Until Abby, that is. Matt knew he could choose to settle for a friendship with her, certainly less risky than putting himself out there, but he would only be kidding himself if he acted like that was all he wanted with her.

"Looks like it's time to redecorate." Matt wanted Abby talking to him even if it was about the mundane. He'd pull her from her task one way or another, and hopefully into his arms.

"Yep. And thankfully, this is the last of the Fourth's decorations."

She blew out a breath, momentarily lifting the ringlet stubbornly staying put in front of her eyes. Her attempt to contain it at the nape of her neck was all for naught. Matt could hardly wait to get his hands in it. But first he had to get her to go out with him—for real this time, no chance of her misunderstanding his intent. Last night had been an opportunity to get to know each other without all of the pressure. It had also reinforced the notion that no man in his right mind would pass up the chance to call Abby his own. And though Gran thought him foolish on occasion, no one had ever accused him of being stupid.

"So, what's next?" he asked, taking the unruly box of decorations from her arms, and quelling her protest with a dimpled smile.

She gave him a genuine grin this time and explained, "School doesn't start for another month and a half, so I thought I'd do a beach theme, maybe remind folks to get out and enjoy the rest of summer."

"Sounds fun. Tell me how I can help."

"Only if you're sure you don't have anything better to do."

"I definitely have nothing better to do than spend time with a pretty girl. It's any smart man's idea of a perfect day. Now, tell me where I can find those beach decorations for Christmas in July."

"They're in the office at the back, which is a total disaster, by the way."

Abby pointed in the general direction of a door located behind the polished wood countertop holding an old-fashioned brass cash register, and two large, glass display cabinets with cakes, scones, and what appeared to be egg tarts.

Nope. On second thought, Gran calls those "quiches."

"I'm sure I'll manage." Matt glanced at Abby once more before heading through the swinging door behind the counter that led to an immaculately clean, organized kitchen.

Unlike the dining area, which appeared to be a holdover from the Victorian era, only without the clutter, the kitchen was white and stainless with a minimal amount of fuss on the counters. Copper molds and pans hung on hooks attached to a wrought iron rod mounted over a professional cooking range, while glass bowls and cake plates in varying shades of color and size sat on several open shelves on one side of the room. Teapots, cups, and stacked plates took up the remaining space on the opposite wall next to the open doorway of a walk-in pantry. Tucked into the corner was the only other door in the room—one he assumed led to a bathroom or office, and the decorations Abby wanted.

I'll take door number one, for a date with the pretty girl, please.

Disaster might have been an understatement. Other than the oak secretary desk positioned against the wall, every bit of space was filled with cardboard boxes. Most of them were still taped shut and stacked one on top of another. The desk held various stacks of paper weighted with large objects intended as paper weights, no doubt, but not of the usual form. A rather oddly shaped rock painted to look like a butterfly, a small, shiny black dress shoe—like a little girl might wear to church—a jar full of buttons, and his personal favorite, a framed picture of a drawing with a woman and girl holding hands. One small head with yellow curls going in every direction, and the other with long hair colored brown and red.

A soft voice spoke from behind him. "You were taking so long I thought maybe you'd gotten lost in the debris back here."

"No such luck. I was just admiring your organization technique."

Not the least bit offended, she said, "The summer is a busy time for the shop. Between the tourists and my idea to decorate more often...well, I'll get to it eventually. Besides, I know where everything is."

"And the interesting paper weight collection?"

"That is all Aunt Sara's doing. I was looking for file folders and found a drawer full of those instead. There's more where they came from if you can believe that."

"Items from your childhood, from the looks of it."

"I'm assuming they're things I gave Aunt Sara or left behind in the hours upon hours I spent here growing up."

"You must have been young when you came to live with your aunt." It was a passive statement, but one he hoped would open the door for real conversation. Somehow Matt knew asking directly about Abby's parents again would feel intrusive, if the previous night's lack of response was any indication, and he wasn't interested in pushing her away.

"Four, but since I don't remember much before that time, my aunt, Homily and the shop are all I knew before I moved away after college."

When she didn't bring up her parents, he decided to roll with the new direction. At least for the time being. "Must have been somewhere far from here, otherwise I'm willing to bet our paths would have crossed before now. Especially since I moved to Homily a couple of years ago."

"I'm surprised you don't know everything about me already, the way people talk in this town."

"Ah, but I only want to talk with *you* to find out what I want to know."

"Well, that's a refreshing change." She started looking at the boxes, all labeled with their respective contents. When she appeared to find what she was looking for, Matt removed the packages sitting on top while Abby moved the bottom one toward the door with her foot. He put his pile back on the stack and reached around her to pick up the box Abby was shoving along the floor. It was heavy and an awkward size, which gave him the chance to be the gentlemen he had been raised to be. Of course, it always felt good to be needed.

They worked in solitude, taking turns placing ornaments and wrapping the tree in gold beads with miniature suns and sunglasses. "I can't believe you can actually buy tinsel like this," he mentioned as she came up beside him.

"I couldn't believe it either, but apparently you really can find just about anything online."

"Well, I find myself strangely curious regarding anything you've found, Miss Hart," he said with a teasing gleam and a waggle of his eyebrows.

"What do you mean...oh my goodness, you're incorrigible," she chided, following up with a light swat to his upper arm. But he surprised her, catching her hand instead and turning her in a half pirouette until she looked directly at him.

"Three things. First, you have tinsel in your hair," he said while gently removing it from the curl it had gotten tangled up with. "Second, I was only teasing. I promise I didn't mean *anything* by it. And more importantly, are you ever going to tell me where you were hiding before you came back home?"

Abby

If only he knew how close to the truth he is, thought Abby. Because that was exactly what she'd been doing when she followed her best friend to Midwell, Virginia. Maggie wanted an adventure away from Homily and Abby wanted nothing more than to leave the folks who thought they knew everything about her.

Aunt Sara had done her best to protect her from the gossip mill, but when the town's infamous wild child sent her daughter to live with Sara and never came home, jaws had flapped, and telephone wires worked overtime.

Abby's phone vibrated on the counter with an incoming call, but she knew without looking who it would be. What was that saying? "Speak of the devil and he shall appear?" Or was it better to say "she" in this instance?

Matt looked between Abby and her phone, and said patiently, "Go ahead and get it, I'll wait."

"It's not important. I already know who's calling, and she can wait." She knew Mags was only calling to follow up on last night's "it's a date; it's not a date" conversation. She could hear her best friend's excited chatter already. Nope, she definitely was not in a hurry to talk to her in front of Matt.

Of course, it only left the alternative, which was telling Matt about her time in Midwell. And she did, but she left out a few pertinent details she no longer deemed relevant. Mainly, her broken engagement.

He laughed deeply while she regaled him with tales about Mags.

"Your best friend sounds like a hoot! I can't believe it took you five whole days to do a trip that, in theory, should only have taken one."

"What can I say? Maggie likes to stay hydrated, and up until then I had never been out of Alabama. With so much to see along the way, and Mags insisting we see it all so long as there was a restroom within a quarter mile, what other choice did I have?" Abby asked with a shrug.

"Well, I can tell you, guys road trip different from girls."

"How so?" she asked, curious. Without a father figure, brothers, or even a male cousin, she often wondered why men behaved the way they did sometimes.

"For starters, we don't stop unless we have to or it's a place we planned to stop and see anyway. And when we do stop, we don't necessarily need a bathroom.

"Exactly why is that? The latter part, I mean."

"There's a reason for the plastic two-liter bottle you find in a guy's truck, but the side of the road works fine too."

"Ew. Overshare, Matthew Dixon. Besides, haven't you ever heard of ticks in the tall grass? No, thank you." Abby's whole body shuddered, and he chuckled at her reaction. Returning his smile with one of her own, she had to admit she enjoyed spending time with Matt.

"You must miss Maggie. Even though you haven't said so, I get the feeling your time in town last spring was supposed to be temporary. Since you're a teacher, I'm guessing you were home for a short visit when your aunt came into the hospital." He stopped and looked at her expectantly.

"Originally, I was only supposed to be home for spring break, though I intended to resign at the end of the school year and move back home sometime this summer. I'd been away from home for a few years and didn't visit at all the previous summer. Don't get me wrong; I missed Aunt Sara terribly, and Homily…kind of," Abby tacked on the last part belatedly and contemplated whether her feelings about her hometown had changed in the months since she'd come home.

"Why'd you stay away?"

"You know, chasing the illusive dream of freedom and independence all young people think they need in order to be happy." A kernel of truth, if not the whole of it. More like a chance to start fresh without the constraints of her mama's past, and the fear that maybe her mama had somehow rubbed off on her. "At first, I was too busy facing the realities of life in a new place, with a new job, to come home often. It was exciting to have new experiences. I stayed busy, and Aunt Sara was her usual understanding self."

Also true, and her aunt loved her enough to let her make her own decisions, even when they weren't very considerate ones.

"Then Maggie met a hometown Midwell boy after we settled in, got married, and had her first child a year later. I wanted to be there for her, support her through all of the rather sudden change."

She gave a snort through her nose, thinking of her best friend's dive-right-in approach to life, the complete opposite of her own. Mags was brave and Abby was more of a watch-from-the sidelines girl, even though Aunt Sara repeatedly told her otherwise. They were kind words wrapped in her aunt's love for her, but they were false.

"Turns out she didn't need my help. In true Maggie fashion, she took to being a wife and mother like a duck does a pond."

"Sounds like your friend is happy."

"Yeah, I really think she is. And I'm happy for her." She said it wistfully, and even though she wanted to snatch it back, she had neither the energy nor the inclination to keep holding all of her emotions in check.

"I planned to help Sara at the shop part time this summer, read chick lit at the beach every spare moment, and wait to hear back from the local school district about a teaching position this fall. With Aunt Sara's heart attack, subsequent surgery, and recovery…well, my grand plans just aren't feasible. In fact, everything is so topsy-turvy right now I haven't even gone back to pick up my things from Maggie. She's storing everything in her barn."

Matt just watched her and waited for the rest of the story.

"She and her husband own a horse farm just outside the town limits and were kind enough to pack up my apartment for me when I needed to stay for Aunt Sara. Most of the furniture is second hand, so I told Mags to keep what she wanted and donate the rest. I only have a handful of boxes with personal items and the remaining contents of my closet to bring back."

"What are you doing this Friday?"

Abby blinked in surprise at the quick change in subject. "Um, I'm not sure," she stalled.

"Well, since the shop is closed on Sundays and I have two days in a row off from the hospital, I think we should take a trip to Maggie's to get your stuff. It should fit perfectly in the bed of my pickup."

"That's a twelve-hour trip, Matt. We can't possibly make it back in time for you to go to work on Sunday."

"We can leave early Friday morning and arrive at Maggie's in time for supper. That way you get to spend most of the next day catching up with your best friend before we load up the truck and head out early in the evening."

"But that means driving all night, and I would have to figure out coverage for Friday and Saturday."

"I stay up all night quite often. You can sleep while I drive, and then we can switch halfway through. I'm sure your aunt can help you figure out the rest. What do you say? You up for a little adventure?"

She hesitated for mere seconds before recognizing his offer for the boon it was. After all, who else would volunteer to go with her in the immediate future? The answer was a big fat no one.

"Yes! Yes, I am most definitely in."

Definitely in over my head, she thought as she watched Matt walk out of the shop, the bell tinkling over his head.

Not only did they have plans to spend the weekend together on a road trip to visit her best friend, but Matt had asked for her phone number. Ostensibly in case he needed to get in touch with her about details for Friday. While it was a reasonable request, somehow in the last twenty-four hours they had gone from acquaintances who ran into each other randomly to friends who picnic, road trip, and call each other.

Abby felt giddy at the prospect of spending so much time with Matt, but she was also nervous. She was about to spend twenty-four hours in a car with a man who still barely knew her, although that wasn't his fault; she was the one playing her cards close to her chest. It didn't help that Matt knew nothing of her ex-fiancé, who also happened to call Midwell his hometown. How was it possible her life had become so complicated in the course of one conversation?

Abby moved behind the counter to prepare for the mid-morning tea drinkers, mostly other shop owners and tourists strolling through downtown before going to the beach. She picked up her phone to call Maggie back, but a wide smile overtook her face when she saw the text Matt had already sent.

> *Hey, just wanted to make sure you have my number too. Put it in your contacts, maybe under the heading Matt Is Irresistible or The Doctor Is In. Either is fine, both have a nice ring to them. ;-)*

Her thumbnail perched at her lips, she giggled over the way he managed to sneak in a wink at the end. She inhaled deeply and nodded decisively, reminding herself, *This road trip is no big deal. We're just going to pick up my belongings, one friend helping another friend move.*

She'd work out the schedule for the shop this weekend with Aunt Sara over dinner before calling Mags, who tended to make something out of everything especially, when it was nothing.

Fourteen

Dear Sunshine,

I'm glad to hear you've found a church where you feel a sense of belonging. I'm sending a few odds and ends for your new apartment. Now, don't argue with me, consider them a housewarming gift. You've worked so hard for this new step. I hope you're proud of yourself. I know I am. Perhaps now you can give Abby the chance to be proud of you too. Our door is always open for a visit if you should ever change your mind. Love you, to the stars and back.

Always, Sissy

Abby

Unfortunately for Abby, her aunt and Mags were ecstatic that she and Matt were about to spend hours upon hours in a tight space together. Dinner immediately went from a sedate discussion about each other's day, hers at the shop and Aunt Sara's in the garden, to a hallelujah and a declaration.

"This calls for dessert!"

"I'm never one to turn down dessert, but it's not as if this is a couple's weekend. More like an errand," Abby sought to convince her aunt, and maybe herself just a teensy-weensy bit.

"An errand that declares you're moving home, baby girl, and says a lot about the man helping you."

"Maybe, but it's a lot of time together without any distractions. What if we run out of topics to talk about, or we can't agree on what music to listen to, or we—"

"Whoa, slow your roll, sugar. I'm sure it'll be a pleasant trip. One in which you get to know each other better and check out his strong muscles in action."

"I am not going on this trip to check him out!" Abby exclaimed, bending over until her forehead was firmly planted on the dining table. "I'm going to get my boxes out of Maggie's barn. It's time for me to stop living with one foot in Midwell and the other in Homily. That's all there is to this," she mumbled.

"Whatever you say, baby girl, but I have no doubt Matt is going along to spend time with you. Don't get me wrong; men will do a lot for a friend if it's convenient, but they'll do anything for the woman who wins their heart. Obviously, that boy is interested in being more than friends."

Abby raised her head, confusion taking over her exasperation, and asked, "What exactly constitutes convenience?"

"Oh, you know, it doesn't interfere with work, food, or the game they plan to watch. Unless, of course, it involves the bribery of food, beer, or tickets to said game," Sara replied, ticking the items off on her fingers one by one.

"You sound a little jaded for someone who's never been married."

"Not jaded, just wise with experience. I certainly don't hold it against them. It's the way they're wired. Though there is always the exception to the rule."

"What about Papaw?"

"He wasn't the exception to the rule, but he was willing to do anything at any time for Nana. And in return she pampered him for his efforts."

"And for everyone else?"

"He'd nod his head agreeably and tell them he'd have to check his calendar."

"Which brings me back to the start of this inane conversation. We have a high tea scheduled for Saturday afternoon and Fridays are busy with weekenders. Who's going to fill in on such short notice?"

"You leave that to me, sugar. I can go in for a couple of hours in the afternoon, and one of the new high school gals keeps asking for more time. Not that you heard it from me, but I think she's helping her folks with the bills. Nothing in this town is ever your own business for long, but I suppose the upside is people knowing when to lend a helping hand."

Abby decided she'd be wasting precious breath if she tried to convince Aunt Sara the road trip was just such an example. She ate her triple scoop of rainbow sherbet in brooding silence, knowing the scoops would never be enough fortification for the upcoming call to Mags. Aunt Sara's reaction had been tame compared with the thrill sure to be her best friend's.

....

Twenty minutes later, she congratulated herself for anticipating the need for a third scoop. Yelling, lots of high-pitched yelling, forced Abby to pull the phone away from her ear.

"Oh my gosh! Abigail Hart, I can't believe you didn't call me back to give me details about your date last night, and yes it was definitely a date."

"It was not a date—"

"Yes, it was. Now stop arguing with me, because I plan to get all of the juicy tidbits from you even if I have to torture them out of you."

Rolling her eyes at her friend's harmless threat, she asked, "And exactly how are you going to torture me for information?"

"I'm going to make triple chocolate fudge brownies the next time I'm home and eat all of them in front of you. Besides, I'm your best friend. According to the universal best friend code, you have to tell me everything. Karma is real, and she's a—"

"Do not finish that sentence, Maggie Bradshaw!" Abby laughed hysterically.

"I was only going to say she's an ice queen on steroids," Mags said with such innocence anyone else might have believed her, but Abby knew better.

"Sure, you were. Your mother would be appalled."

"What she doesn't know doesn't hurt my backside. Anyway, I've toned it down since my sugar lump came along. Not that I don't tease Tuck mercilessly about our son's first real word being 'truck.' It's so cute, and sounds just like—"

"Mags!"

Maggie just cackled in the face of Abby's reprimand, though her own laughter entirely ruined the stern effect. Not that she meant it anyway. Being outrageous was one of the many traits Abby adored in her friend. She missed their talks over tea or meeting up for lunch on the weekend. Which reminded her why she'd called in the first place. "Actually, I was thinking about coming up this weekend to pick up my stuff—"

A new round of squealing commenced, forcing Abby to move the phone away from her ear once more. "Don't you have a baby sleeping?"

"Yes, he's sleeping like the angel he is and Tuck's bedding the horses down for the night in the barn. Stop finding reasons to extinguish my excitement, girlfriend."

"Fine, but it's going to be a quick trip because I can't leave until Friday morning—"

"That's okay, you can stay until Sunday and leave after breakfast."

"That's usually the case with the shop closed, but my ride has to be back at work on Sunday."

"Oh, someone's coming with you."

Abby could hear the disappointment in Maggie's voice. "Yeah, about that— "

"It's okay, I'm just jealous that I have to share my time with you. But I get it, and I'm glad you're not drivin' by yourself. Who's the friend? Someone from our school days? It's not Anna Mae Thorne, is it?" Maggie asked with utter disbelief. "Ugh, please tell me that viper is not your new best friend." She whined the last part, her Alabama drawl as present as the day she'd left.

Abby snorted. "Of course not, that would require her to have a personality transplant first. Besides, no one could ever replace you, Mags."

"You're right, I am pretty great now that I think about it. So, who is it?"

Maggie didn't lack confidence. She never had, and it was part of why Abby was drawn to her. They became instant friends on the first day of kindergarten, gaining a quick appreciation for each other's differences at a time when most children are more interested in those like themselves. Stuck like glue, people knew wherever one was, the other was close by. Their friendship made middle school bearable, and high school worth the roller coaster ride.

Maggie was outgoing where Abby was reserved. While Abby volunteered at the local library and tutored her best friend in almost every subject, Mags was on the pep squad, pulling Abby along in her wake to every sporting event and school dance. They'd looked out for one another at parties and bonfires on the beach, where Abby tried to blend in with the scenery. Her best friend always had some boy wrapped around her finger, while Abby usually had her nose stuck in a book.

Abby forced herself back into the present and focused on the question of who would be with her, and mentally congratulated herself for being so blasé when she answered, "Actually, it's Matt Dixon."

There was a slight delay as her best friend processed the unexpected information, quickly followed by another piercing decibel on the other end of the line. With her ear still ringing from the high pitch, Abby immediately tried to tone down her best friend's excitement. "He is simply a friend who offered to help when he realized I'd have to make the drive at some point, potentially by myself."

"Oh please, like Sara wouldn't come with you this fall when Homily turns back into a sleepy town after tourist season."

Abby could picture Mags rolling her eyes on the other end of the line.

"It's not like I'm in need of the space your handful of boxes are taking up in the corner of the barn. Nope. Nice try, girlfriend. You and I both know you presented the opportunity, albeit unintentionally, and the handsome doctor jumped at the chance to be both gallant and in close quarters with you. Looks like you have yourself a boyfriend or will soon."

Her best friend said the last part so smugly it rubbed Abby raw from a thousand miles away. "Not that I agree with you in the least, but promise me you and Tuck won't bring up Lon or the engagement while we're there. I'll probably tell Matt about it eventually, but there really isn't any reason for him to know yet."

The idea of sharing anything related to her past gave her a stomachache. Unless their friendship became something more, none of it mattered anyway.

"Abby, you don't have anything to be ashamed of. You made a mistake when you said yes to Lon, and broke things off before it could go any further. Broken engagements happen," Maggie said, concern lacing every word.

"I know, but the circumstances and my timing were unbelievably bad."

"Unfortunate for all involved, sweetie. You tried so hard to be who he wanted you to be that he didn't get the chance to know the real you, or your family. Whoever you wind up with should be someone you can share yourself with. I know you think your mother somehow rubbed off on you, but you are not her, and never will be."

"I know," Abby responded meekly, close to tears.

"No, sweet girl, you don't. But I love you like crazy, and I pray someday you realize just how amazing you are. My life is better for having you in it."

"Thanks, Mags."

"You're welcome. Now, tell me about this date with the good doctor you keep insisting wasn't a date."

Abby found herself profoundly thankful for her best friend once more. Being seen and accepted without judgment, despite her actions, became salve on her open wounds, the gift of friendship, a balm of grace.

Maggie

Maggie Bradshaw glared at the man she'd married, hands on her hips and steam coming from her nostrils for all intents and purposes. She liked to think of herself as a fierce, fire-breathing dragon in moments like this. Stomping her foot and narrowing her eyes to slits, she shook her finger at her nemesis of a husband even as he laughed at her performance.

"Tucker Bradshaw, promise me you won't—"

"Now, sweet thing," he tried to placate her in that deep gravelly voice of his, making her go a little weak in the knees. "I gave you my word I wouldn't say anything about Lon to whoever this guy is that Abby's bringing with her."

"Yes, you did, but that was while we were in the middle of more interesting things. And you and I both know promises made during sex don't count, because you'd promise me anything then."

"True."

Maggie raised an eyebrow and tapped her foot, waiting for the words she wanted to hear.

"Okay, fine," he said, resigned to his wife's need for reassurance of where his loyalty resided. Tuck pushed his weight up onto one arm and placed his right hand over his heart before saying, "Maggie Tallulah Bradshaw, love of my life and sweet as wild honey, I solemnly swear not to say a word about Abby's former engagement."

She tapped her foot and waited expectantly when he didn't continue. Patient woman that she was, she gave her husband a few seconds to respond but then her patience ran its course. With a deep breath in, she slowly exhaled and asked, "And the rest?"

Her husband let out a low chuckle, taking in her frazzled state and high temper. Maggie watched him admire the entirety of her, knowing he adored her more than his next heartbeat.

He finally conceded, "Or mention Abby's relationship with Lon Howard in any way."

"Thank you, baby," she said, her voice spun sugar.

"But the truth is bound to come out eventually. The four of us spent a lot of time together."

"Probably, but if we could keep some of those stories under wraps for this one visit it would ease some of Abby's worry."

"I can't even have a conversation with my best friend that doesn't involve his fists, or my guilty conscience, because I got to keep the woman I love as well as the one who wrecked his life," he grumbled.

"Lon's acting out isn't her fault," Maggie said softly, knowing she'd won enough battles on behalf of her best friend for one night. No need to poke the bear further.

He sighed. "I know, I just hurt for him. The choices he's making right now are going to haunt him later."

"Baby, we're all broken vessels. The only difference between us and Abby or Lon is that we know we can only be made whole by God. He's the one who heals our brokenness through grace. Nothing and no one else can."

"You're right."

"You can say that again."

"Ha, ha, very funny. Now, if you're finished with the theatrics we should get back to more important stuff, like sleep. You wore me out, woman."

Smiling at her bear of a husband, she took his outstretched hand and climbed into their queen bed, her back to Tuck's front with the weight of his arm a secure anchor around her waist. Maggie closed her eyes and sent up a worried plea and prayed over the coming weekend. Tuck squeezed her and breathed an amen in her ear.

Matt

The day before the road trip, Matt jogged down the long, sterile corridor and just managed to grab the closing elevator doors.

"John, you are just the man I've been looking for." Though he'd been heading to the cafeteria for a quick bite to eat, catching his colleague from the ER inside certainly made for serendipitous timing.

"Now if I could only get my wife to say those words," said Dr. John Radcliffe with a wry smile. He lifted amber eyes, a gift from his Cherokee grandfather, which were partially hidden behind a pair of thick-rimmed glasses, from the clipboard in front of him.

"What's up, Matt?"

"Any chance you could take my shift this Sunday?"

"Sure, I owe you one for taking Mother's Day anyway. Best surprise I've given Reese in years. We went to the tea place downtown, fancy hats and all."

"You mean The Christmas Tea Shoppe?"

"Yeah, that's the one. Turns out, Reese's little sister Maggie is best friends with the owner's daughter."

"Actually, she's Sara's niece."

"You say that like you have the inside track."

Matt smiled confidently. "That's because I do. Sara's niece, Abby, and your sister-in-law Maggie are the reason I need you to cover my shift."

"Oh?" John asked.

"When Abby moved back home suddenly to take care of her aunt, she asked Maggie to pack up her apartment. I offered to drive her north this weekend to get her stuff. We made plans to be back by Sunday morning, but I thought it might be a nice surprise for the girls to spend another day together."

"Oh man, you must like this girl if you're already trying to get on the good side of her best friend."

"I guess you could say I'm forward thinking, just in case I'm lucky enough to get the girl. She's not exactly jumping at the chance," Matt said with a healthy dose of self-deprecation.

"Trust me when I say persistence pays off. It took me months to convince Reese I was worth a second glance, let alone a date. Complete opposite of Maggie, by the way. My sister in-law was married within six months of meeting her husband. Thankfully, he's a good man so it all worked out. And my new nephew's so cute he has Reese thinking we need a third. I keep telling her sleep deprivation is nobody's friend."

Matt cocked his left eyebrow in confusion, "We do it all the time."

"Yes, but doing both at home and work is far from ideal, not to mention the pregnancy hormones," said John releasing a shiver.

Matt shook his headed and chuckled at his friend's response as the elevator dinged and Matt left John to get some charting done. Paperwork complete, he made the phone calls required to set his surprise for Abby in motion, excited for their time together.

Then he sent off a text to the girl who'd kept his thoughts captive for days.

> *Hey, looking forward to our trip. I'll pick you up at 5 a.m., breakfast in hand.*

....

Two minutes later…

> *Who gets up at such an ungodly hour? That's too early.*
> *I get up that early most mornings, and it's the only way to get there before everyone goes to bed. Come on, I know you can hardly wait to see Maggie. Besides, Gran says there are no ungodly hours. Turns out they all belong to him.*
> *Ha, ha. No promises I won't look like Medusa, but there is no way I'm getting up early to primp. You'll just have to live with the consequences of your actions.*
> *Pretty girl, I'm flattered you would even think to primp for me. Does this mean you're finally ready to admit you like me?*
> *Southern girls primp for everything and everyone. The only ones you dress down for are your best friend and your husband.*
> *What does that make me, then?*
> *The devil for making me get up so early.*
> *LOL.*
> *Seriously, we're road trip buddies.*

Matt frowned at his phone. He'd been enjoying their banter until Abby poked a hole in his hopes with her last statement. Like a bright-red balloon being pecked by a bird as it floats higher and higher into the sky, he watched the balloon deflate and fall to the ground in his mind's eye.

Hopes dashed, he dusted them off with a small measure of hubris and reminded himself persistence was often the winner of a fair maiden's heart. If everything went how he hoped it would, maybe he'd be more than Abby's road trip buddy by the end of the weekend.

Fifteen

Dear Sunshine,

I took Abby shopping for her first training bra last Saturday. She doesn't really need one yet, but since her best friend already wears one, I thought it couldn't hurt. We went for ice cream and talked about the birds and the bees. It went about as well as you'd expect it to, though I think I handled it much better than Nana did. Remember how she used to go on about Aunt Flo, and feminine hygiene products? At least I can say the words period and tampon without having to whisper like they're some disease. Love you, to the stars and back.

Always, Sissy

Abby

Abby watched Matt through the peephole of the front door. He'd arrived promptly at five and sat down on the porch steps in the morning air not yet ripe with the heat of day. The perfection that is summer in a coastal town lingered above him with promise in the minutes between night's retreat and dawn's appearance. She debated making him wait just to see what he would do, but he looked content with his lot, and she imagined there wouldn't be any point in dawdling. If anything, he'd probably tease her for taking the time to primp. The thought made her grin.

In a soft cotton t-shirt the color of sunshine, a navy knit skirt and flips, she was dressed for comfort more than style. Though she'd given her blonde lashes a swipe of mascara for color and coated her lips in her favorite strawberry flavored lip balm—to keep them from getting chapped, not to make them kissable—her curly hair was pulled back into an easy pony.

The screen door squawked with the sound of unoiled hinges and Abby grimaced, any hope her aunt would sleep through their departure evaporated. Sure enough, Abby looked back to see her aunt framed in the upstairs window wearing a silk dressing robe. Aunt Sara waved goodbye with a glint of mischief in her eye.

Definitely need to add WD-40 to the Hickam's list.

With a raise of her brow, Abby acknowledged her aunt with a small wave of her own, pivoting in time to walk through the gate behind her travel companion.

She gave Matt a thorough once over while he held the passenger door for her, taking in the worn-looking t-shirt he wore. Closer to rose than cherry, it complimented the faded blue jeans hugging his hips and rump in the best way. He wore a pair of running shoes that had seen better days and the whole ensemble was so Matt one side of her mouth rose in a half smile. No matter what he wore, he was at ease in it because he was comfortable in his own skin.

"I hope you like what you see, Miss Hart."

Busted. Though, by the twinkle in his eyes, he didn't appear to mind her perusal very much.

"Maybe," she said, forcing herself to meet his eyes, pink cheeks and all. "The verdict is still out."

Stopped at the last light in town, two blocks from where Homily completely disappeared in her side mirror, Matt handed Abby a bag of lemon chiffon cake doughnuts and an insulated travel mug with lavender Earl Grey written in sharpie on the side. "I have coffee, if you prefer," he said genially.

She eyed him with suspicion as she raised the cup to her nose to smell its contents.

"Why do I have the feeling you already know I don't? I mean, the doughnuts could be a coincidence. Everyone knows the best cake doughnuts for miles are found at Revolution Cake & Donuts, but not everyone knows that lavender Earl Grey tea is the perfect complement to them."

"Well, a little bird might have mentioned how much you like both of those."

"Your little bird would be right. Thank you."

"You're welcome," he said with a bright smile to match hers.

Abby's dimmed slightly. "Speaking of little birds, I have to admit I'm nervous about leaving Aunt Sara overnight."

He nodded in understanding. "I know what you mean. I arranged for Dot Hanson's granddaughter, a childhood friend of mine, to take Gran and Dot to lunch later today."

"Maybe Aunt Sara could visit your gran tomorrow? I could ask her to take Nancy some tea after her shift at the shop when I check in with her later tonight. That way they both have company during the day."

"Sounds perfect."

They made lively conversation through most of the morning, discussing the articles in a travel magazine Abby fished out of her handbag. She'd never been to Europe but had a whole list of places she'd like to go. London was her dream, and since her aunt had business connections there, she hoped to make a trip in the near future.

In return, he'd been to countless places abroad, having spent an entire summer backpacking through Europe and Asia before starting medical school. She listened with genuine interest to the stories he had about missed trains, his complete and utter debacle asking for directions in France, and how he'd stayed in a luxury hotel in Monte Carlo for free, thanks to his summers spent lifeguarding at a community pool.

"I can't believe you saved that woman's life *and* got to stay for free at her family's resort. I think I saw it on *Entertainment Tonight* once. That place is swanky. Not that you didn't deserve it, but come on, stuff like that just doesn't happen in real life."

"Scouts honor."

"Of course, you were a boy scout too." She said, entirely disgruntled. "Is there anything you don't do well, *Doctor* Dixon?"

He chuckled at her insinuation. "Don't go assigning me a complex. Besides, I only did what anyone in my situation would."

"Possibly. At least I can speak French better than you. Mags and I thought we were fluent in high school. We drove everyone nuts senior year when we spoke nothing but French spring semester."

"I bet you did. It's a shame you weren't with me on my trip; I could've used your help and delightful company."

"Oh please, I'm sure you had plenty of company along the way." Abby rolled her eyes, making him laugh again.

"True, but none as pretty as you." His wink and dimple prompted her to smile. Matt's congenial personality made it hard not to fall for him, but since he hadn't asked her out on a second date, she could only assume he'd decided friendship was all he was interested in. Abby on the other hand, was trying to keep herself from checking him out every chance she got.

Cheese and crackers, girl, it's not as if you can't ask him out if you want to. Then again, there's nothing wrong with flirting with a friend as long as you're both on the same page.

Was she on the same page?

"So, how do you feel about camping?" Matt asked, interrupting her thoughts of him.

That question resulted in a discussion on the pros and cons of backpacking. In the end, they decided car camping might be a good place for her to start. In spite of the long drive, the time passed rather quickly, and though Abby offered to drive after lunch, Matt was content to stay behind the wheel.

By the time she woke up from her late afternoon nap they were only an hour from Maggie's. She was so excited to see her best friend she literally bounced in her seat, her toes on the dash dancing to one of her favorite country songs on the radio. Since the farm was a little southwest of town, they wouldn't be driving through Midwell, which meant she could avoid Lon and his family altogether this weekend.

Pleased with her plan, she slipped into the hoodie Matt had kindly draped over her while she slept on the pretense that she was cold. His scent wrapped around her, a subtle citrus, reminding her of bergamot and tea. The feeling was akin to coming home— comfortable and warm.

Abby looked at his handsome profile and wondered if he felt it too, that little tug of recognition, like they knew each other much better than they did. When she'd woken up to the sound of Motown coming from the speakers, she'd almost laughed out loud over all of the foolish worries she'd rattled off to Mags. Turns out she had nothing to fret over.

Conversation rolled between them in an easy rhythm. They both enjoyed a variety of music genres, though his favorite was the oldies station while she preferred country. Taking turns was easy when they could appreciate each other's choice. If anything, the trip had gone so smoothly Abby began to worry about all the pitfalls she hadn't fully thought through until now. They were fifteen minutes away when Abby's anxious excitement turned into straight-up anxiety. With a frown firmly entrenched between her brows, she focused on the winding dirt road that led to the Bradshaws' farm, forcing down her sudden panic about all that could go wrong and shoving her prickly past into the back of her thoughts.

Matt

Watching Abby get in and out of the truck his granddad had left him and sit in the spot his gran used to occupy was a little surreal. When Matt drove away from Sara's curb, he experienced one of those rare moments in life when time seems to align, the past, present, and future overlapping for a quick glimpse.

The summer he'd turned twelve, he stayed with his grandparents while his mom and dad worked through the details of their divorce.

Matt remembered being on the precipice of adolescence and certain of all the possibilities the world could offer him even as he questioned everything. His gran had told him that while God works all things for the good of those who love him, some decisions a person makes hold more weight than others. She referred to them as crossroad moments. And, in those times, it was important to seek God's wisdom, because the path chosen can determine a whole future. Of course, he had argued that if God could do anything he wanted, and already had a plan anyway, why did it matter which path he chose.

"Pretty sure I'll get to where I'm supposed to be going soon enough, Gran."

She just smiled and said, "Yes, I imagine you will. And some of us need to go the long way around in order to appreciate the destination."

Her words had found their mark, and now he couldn't shake the feeling that the long way around would be just that, long, and he didn't know if he had the patience when everything he wanted was sitting next to him in all her glory.

With or without primping, Abby was beautiful. All her sweetness and attitude spilling over from the inside out, her strength and character were obvious in the choices she made. Very few people would change the direction of their whole life to take care of someone else. And smart too. She'd gone from teaching to managing a business in the blink of an eye. She was everything he never knew he wanted.

When he told Gran about the road trip, and his future hopes, she was thrilled he wanted to date someone, let alone a hometown girl like Abby. Of course, she also had all kinds of advice for him.

"Now, Matthew Lee Dixon, take it slow. I have no doubt you'll always treat her with respect, but you know what I mean. Sometimes the dimmer switch grows from a dull thrum to a mighty flame in the time it takes to snap your fingers."

He was gulping down a glass of water when she'd made that proclamation and fully choked on the last swallow, trying not to spew it across the kitchen floor mopped a few hours earlier. Heat traveled up his neck to infuse his face like a habanero pepper. Only his gran could make him feel like a boy of sixteen, foolish and guilty on every count.

Matt grinned as Abby bounced on the seat next to him. It wouldn't be long now. They'd arrive at the farm in another mile. Hopefully, he'd be more than a friend to the woman sitting next to him by the time they left.

He'd never been much of a ladies' man, despite Abby giving him a hard time that he was. Matt had always been so busy living the rest of his life that he made no time to worry about a serious romantic relationship. Sports and grades had kept him busy through high school, and though he'd attended parties with friends and had a date for every dance, he was mostly focused on his future. With a track scholarship and medical school on the horizon, college was more of the same. In retrospect, he could see how his teasing over the years might be misconstrued, but he sincerely hoped he had never hurt anyone. Besides, the joke was on him. For the first time in his life, he wanted a girl and she seemed immune to his charm. He could hear Gran's chiding now.

"Well, what did you expect? You've spent years flirting without intention. Guess you'll have to be more direct this time. Stealth is for spies and cowards."

Yep, just call him Doctor Direct. Before they went home, Matt planned to make Abby his girl. All he had to do was get her alone this weekend and define their relationship.

Sixteen

Dear Sunshine,

As requested, I bought Abby a quilt with the money you sent for her birthday. It was a thoughtful coming of age gift for our teenager. Maybe next year you'll let me tell her about the gifts you send each birthday and Christmas. The pictures of your garden are beautiful. I'm so glad you found a house to rent near work and church. I hope you're enjoying classes this semester. Love you, to the stars and back.

Always, Sissy

Matt

Matt couldn't imagine a couple more opposite than Maggie and Tucker Bradshaw, both in appearance and temperament. Matt found it fascinating to watch them interact. Maggie was bubbly and petite where Tucker was stoic and large. Her voice was high and girlish, while her husband sounded like he growled more than he spoke. But, you would have to be blind to miss the love in his eyes when he looked at his wife.

Tucker and Abby, on the other hand, acted like siblings. Ribbing each other from the first hello, he hauled her in for a bear hug and followed it up with a noogie to her head. Which in turn prompted a string of harmless threats from Abby.

Matt and Maggie looked at each other and in unison shook their heads as they moved toward the house, assuming the antics would stop without any interference from them.

From the outside, it looked exactly the way he imagined an old Virginia farmhouse would, a two-story white colonial with the addition of a front porch. Neither large nor small in size, it sat in the middle of rolling pastureland surrounded by trees, one barn within shouting distance of the house and what looked to be horse stables in the distance. The inside had been completely renovated, but maintained its charm with painted trim, wood floors, and a brick fireplace. Matt appreciated the practical lines of the open plan while trying to picture the original one with the eye of an amateur historian. He and Maggie made small talk with ease while Abby and Tucker finished their wrestling match outside.

"How old is the house?"

"It was built in 1772 by one of Tuck's ancestors on his daddy's side and remained pretty much unchanged, with the exception of an attached laundry and bathroom, until we got our hands on it. Renovating it was part of the deal when I agreed to marry him."

"That bad, huh?"

"I was happy to live out in the middle of nowhere, but only if I could make the house into our future instead of Tuck's past."

"The past is tricky like that. Sometimes it can hold onto a person so tightly it becomes a prison instead of an opportunity to learn from and move forward."

"Exactly. Tuck's mama died when he was little, and his daddy was a hard man. He expected a lot from Tuck when all his son really wanted was something else in life other than the family farm. Tuck got himself a football scholarship to some fancy school up north but injured his shoulder working with the horses the summer after graduation. Doc said there was nothing for it. So, instead of going to college, he enlisted in the army.

"Sadly, his daddy died while he was on his second deployment. Tuck didn't know about the cancer until it was too late, and they never reconciled their differences. Add that to all he'd seen overseas, and it doesn't leave a man whole."

Maggie gave him a half smile. "But God is good and faithful to bind our wounds and heal our broken hearts."

Her pointed look insinuated she meant more than the obvious reference to her husband. Whatever she intended, any further conversation between them was stifled by Abby and Tucker pushing through the door like a brood of unruly puppies tripping over one another to get inside first.

Not one to miss anything, Abby looked back and forth between the two of them standing on opposite sides of the kitchen counter and nervously asked, "What have you two been chatting about while I was wrestling the grizzly?"

Matt laughed at her description while Maggie said, "Oh, nothing too exciting. We were just talking about the history of the house and how the grizzly finally convinced me to marry him." She blew a kiss at her husband, who let loose a tiny smile as he drew her into his side for a quick squeeze and a kiss on the top of her red head, which barely reached his chest. Matt guessed he stood tall at six foot three, with tree trunks for arms and legs.

When the baby, who'd kept his own company in a pack 'n play, started to fuss, Abby rushed over to pick him up. Matt watched her pull him in close and nuzzle the folds beneath his chin, her face radiant with affection. After getting a giggle and coo from him, she placed him on her hip and reached for a toy to occupy him.

Abby with a baby in her arms made his heart jolt in surprise. Though he'd never considered fatherhood, the thought of a family with her made him pause to rethink. Matt was starting to see how he'd made his career his only plan. So much so, he'd forgotten to dream past it.

The girls interacting with each other was akin to watching children open gifts on Christmas morning. Abby was all lit up, completely animated and without a hint of the reserve she sometimes hid behind. Of course, he'd experienced glimpses of her carefree self in her tart retorts. Matt would take whatever she was willing to give him.

His offer to help with dinner preparations declined, he left the girls to catch up in the kitchen while he joined Tucker on the back patio. It wasn't a large space, most of it taken with furniture and a grill, but it was comfortable, and the cooler held ice-cold bottles of water, root beer, and peach tea. Matt grabbed a bottle of tea and sidled up to Tuck, who stood watching his son roll this way and that trying to get the ball just out of reach.

"How old is he?" asked Matt.

"Nine months."

"Any crawling yet?"

"More like a butt scoot," replied Tuck, a smile spreading across his broad face to soften the hard edges of his jaw.

"Yeah, I've seen that move a few times."

"Man, I laugh every single time. Reminds me of this yellow lab I had growing up. It was born with defective glands, and she'd scoot herself across any and every surface when things got bad." He laughed quietly in that gruff voice of his, then looked Matt directly in the eye. "Don't tell Mags. Makes her mad when I compare the two," he commanded.

"Course not."

"What are you two gentlemen goin' on about out here?" Maggie asked as she popped out of the house and set a platter of steaks on the glass-topped table.

Matt had never seen a guy with so much muscle mass jump so high in his life. He choked on a stifled laugh but rushed in to save his new wingman from impending disaster. "We were talking about the NFL draft."

Tuck blew out a deep breath and mouthed a thank you over his wife's head while she still had her back to him. Matt gave him an imperceptible nod to acknowledge the favor.

"I thought that was already over with this year."

"It is, babe. We were just talking about how we think it's going to go in the preseason with the new players," said Tuck, removing several ears of corn from the grill and replacing the empty space with steaks.

"Ugh, is football starting already?" Maggie asked.

"Next month, but I'll be recording most of it anyway. With the last of the foals coming in August and September, it's going to be even busier around here than it already is."

"Yeah, but busy means business is booming."

"All because of you, darlin'," said Tuck as he slung his arm over his wife's shoulder and led them back into the house.

Abby came outside and planted herself in a rocking chair at the edge of the patio, her eyes on baby Caleb, but she had a distant look on her face.

"Hey, pretty girl. Mind if I join you?"

To his great relief, she looked up with a smile, and whatever she'd been chewing on quickly vanished from her eyes. "Please."

He took a seat and looked at the scenery across from them. "The view is different than what I'm used to, but no less spectacular."

"Yeah, after living in Homily my whole life, the landscape took some getting used to."

"I know what you mean. I love the wild beauty of the coast."

"My favorite are the storms that roll in during early fall. It makes everything feel less predictable." She sounded almost surprised by the revelation.

He couldn't have expressed it better himself and yet added, "This is quieter. Peaceful compared to the ocean."

"When the fog descends in the early mornings with the sun making pinpoints of light through the leaves in the trees, it's almost ethereal," she said wistfully, reminding him that she'd called this town home not so long ago.

"I bet fall is amazing. Maybe we could make another trip to see Maggie and Tucker when the leaves change colors." The words were out of his mouth before he could snatch them back. And the wary look she bestowed on him made him want to do precisely that. So much for a direct conversation.

Fortunately, their hosts discreetly prepping dinner in the background announced dinner and the rest of the evening went without a hitch. Lively conversation, a bottle of red wine, and good food smoothed away any awkwardness between them.

Abby

Thanks to her late afternoon nap, Abby didn't sleep well that night, or really at all. She spent hour after hour tossing and turning over where she was and about who had come with her. Finally giving up around five-thirty, she stumbled down the stairs and into the kitchen to make coffee. As much as she preferred tea, some days called for the hard stuff.

Aunt Sara would reason that tea comprises every good part of the earth. It's why it smells heavenly, tastes sublime, and has multiple healing properties. Coffee, on the other hand, smells deceivingly good but tastes bitter, and only makes a person's heart race.

No matter how much Abby agreed with her, she also knew coffee sometimes made a sleepless night more bearable. Thankfully, Mags kept an obscene amount of vanilla creamer on hand.

"At least it makes the bitter taste better," she grumbled.

"What was that?"

Startled, Abby tossed the carton of creamer to the ground and promptly let loose an unladylike expletive. She rarely allowed such words to slip, but fudgesicle brownie was apparently more than her brain could contemplate this morning.

Nothing like a little adrenaline to get one's blood pumping.

With her hand to her racing heart, Abby turned to face Matt with an apology for her language on her lips. But absolutely nothing came out. Eyes wide, she was actually speechless. The man was busy pulling on a t-shirt to go with his pajama bottoms, but it didn't stop her from getting a glimpse of a well sculpted torso.

Stop staring! It's not like you've never seen a man's abs before.

She forced her eyes to his face, but it didn't really help matters.

Matt was handsome regardless of what he wore, but Matt first thing in the morning took the prize. The man's thick chestnut hair was tousled in every direction, the light coating of scruff along his jaw slightly redder than brown, and his sleepy eyes were drinking her in as much as she was him. Of course, she was also wearing his hoodie again, this time over her yoga pants and tank top. Positive the heat in her cheeks had left its mark, she turned toward the coffee pot tucked into the corner on the wood countertop and picked up the creamer, thankful it hadn't spilled.

"Coffee?" she asked, her voice an octave too high.

"Please," Matt replied, sleep coating his voice.

"How'd you sleep?"

"Pretty good. I can sleep anywhere at any time."

"Must be a nice ability to have," she said, cranky about her own sleepless night.

"More like a learned skill, but an important one to have in my field. And you?"

"No such skills on my part. I always sleep best in my own bed, and the afternoon nap yesterday didn't help my endeavors." She scrunched her nose up with the last part.

The smell of coffee permeated the air while she watched the trees in the distance from the sink window. She'd spent so much time at the Howards' farm with Lon, she found herself thinking of all the morning sunrises she had watched with him. Her past wrapped around her until she turned around to find Matt on a stool at the kitchen island, his head propped in his hand, silently surveying her.

"It looks good on you."

Confused, she asked, "What does?"

"Morning."

"I'm not sure I get your meaning."

Laughter rumbled out of his chest. "Morning looks good on you. Bedhead, sleepy eyes, the whole package wrapped up in my favorite hoodie."

A smidge embarrassed, she said, "Sorry, I forgot to pack a warm layer for the cool mornings here."

Lame excuse officially lobbed. Put an L on my forehead.

"No problem. Keep it."

"You just said it's your favorite."

"It is."

"I can't keep your favorite hoodie. You probably wear it all the time."

He just smiled until his dimple made an appearance and said, "It looks better on you."

She promptly rolled her eyes but followed it with a cheesy grin and handed him a cup of black coffee, to which he added nothing, while she filled half her cup with vanilla creamer.

Because, hello, it only tastes good if you add something to it.

Coffee in hand, they headed for the back patio in silent but mutual agreement and the outdoor couch instead of the rocking chairs. This morning called for comfortable cushions to sink into. Matt had thoughtfully grabbed the blanket he'd slept with from the living room and sat close enough to Abby to share it and the warmth he emanated. He made sure to tuck the blanket around her feet.

"Thank you."

"For what?" he asked looking baffled.

"For being you."

"Well, that was easy."

"What was easy?"

"Finally convincing you I'm a great guy."

"Now, wait a minute; I didn't say that exactly."

His ridiculous dimple came out to play again. "It was implied, but that's okay because I think you're great too."

Abby tried to scowl at him, but found the effect entirely lost on Matt when he gently tucked a wayward curl behind her ear and slowly leaned in to kiss her cheek.

Abby was nothing but a melted puddle. Matt stared directly into her eyes and took her coffee cup gently from her hands. Placing the mug on a short side table next to his own, he wrapped his arm around her shoulders and drew her in closer.

She automatically snuggled in until her head was on his shoulder, practically comatose until he spoke, breaking the spell.

"So, what plans do you and Maggie have for the day?"

"I'm sure we'll probably catch up while we get things done around here. Running a farm is a full-time job, and I thought I could help out with Caleb today to lighten the load for Mags."

"No interest in horses?"

"Actually, I used to be a decent rider, and I've spent my fair share of time in the horse barn. I'd just rather spend my time with Atilla the Hun today."

"Yeah, I've got to admit he is pretty awesome, rolls and all."

"What about you? Last night it sounded like you and Tuck were making plans."

"I figured while I was here, I could lend a hand with the horses and learn a thing or two."

"Do you know how to ride?"

"Passably, though no one would ever mistake me for a cowboy."

"I'm intrigued, please continue," she said, trying to shake the image of Matt in a cowboy hat, boots, and tight jeans. His shirt was nowhere to be found. How unfortunate.

"My mom went through this phase of thinking horse lessons

were good therapy for divorce. I went with her, and while I can't say it fixed everything, it gave me an appreciation for horses and those who work with them. Maybe somewhere along the way I also forgave my folks for the heartache they caused all of us," he said, raw with exposure.

Abby took his hand in hers, squeezing gently. "A parent's betrayal, even unintended, is never easy to cope with," she consoled in perfect understanding.

Matt watched her, a question in his eyes, when a banshee wailed from inside the house. Alarmed and desperate to make it stop, he covered his ears while Abby belly laughed so hard tears streamed down her cheeks.

"What is that?" Matt yelled over the sound.

Abby snorted and tried to grasp some self-control. "That is the sound of a hungry Caleb. My guess is that it's Tuck's turn to feed him, which means he's about a half hour behind his son's schedule. Mags is probably kicking him out of bed right now."

Sure enough, as they stepped back inside, they could hear Tuck shuffling down the stairs and telling Caleb to hold his horses.

"Hey y'all, didn't expect anyone else to be up this early. Hope the Hulk didn't wake you," said Tuck when he noticed them at the kitchen island, his son cradled in one burly arm as though he were nothing more than a football.

"Nah, man; we've been up for a while now," Matt replied, amusement lacing his words.

Tuck scrubbed a hand over his face. "Please tell me that's coffee I smell."

"Mm-hmm. I'll fix you a cup," offered Abby, her arm brushing against Matt's as she got up from the island, sending a shiver of awareness through her.

"Thanks, Abs. It's Maggie's day to sleep in, which means I'm on sumo-feeding duty."

"I can feed Caleb if you'd like so you guys can get ready to head to the stables. I'm not sure what time we're leaving this afternoon, so I figure the sooner you get started on the day's chores the less we'll interfere with your time."

"Which means Matt hasn't told you his plan yet." Tuck looked at Matt conspicuously, his dark brows raised in question.

"Just hadn't gotten around to it."

"Well don't let my being here stop you." He smirked, and Abby couldn't tell if he was challenging Matt or simply knew too much for his own good. Probably both. He tended to be a little protective of her. Most of the time she felt blessed that her best friend had married a man who treated her like a sister, but sometimes she wanted to kick him in the shins.

Matt turned to her and casually said, "I got a colleague to cover for me tomorrow and since the shop is closed on Sundays, I thought we could stay another night and leave after breakfast tomorrow morning instead. That is, if you'd like to have extra time with your best friend."

Abby stood in stunned silence for all of two seconds before throwing her arms around Matt in excitement. It wasn't until he looked down at her, eyes lit up in reflection of her own, that she noticed how close their lips were to one another. The world seemed to stop, and her breathing grew shallow as she waited, for what she wasn't sure, but it felt as though she'd been waiting her whole life for it.

"Morning y'all, what'd I miss?" Mags asked with a loud yawn, effectively breaking the spell. Abby stepped away from Matt to find her best friend grinning like a fool and Tuck staring pointedly, his jaw tighter than a cinch, as though she'd committed some grave *faux pas.*

Okay, maybe she had. After all, she'd almost kissed someone who wasn't his best friend in the middle of his kitchen. With an internal groan, she wondered how she could possibly move on when her actions continued to cause others so much pain. Abby excused herself to get ready for the day, chewing on the side of her cheek as much as the problem at hand.

Seventeen

Dear Sunshine,

Abby went on her first date last night. Per our agreement, it was a group date which included Maggie, another gal from school, and three local boys. Knowing the families made it easier to send her out the door, and the girls and I talked about watching out for each other. The boys all agreed there would be no drinking or parking at the beach. Honestly, making them squirm over the last part was the highlight of my night, because I spent the rest of the evening worried about our girl. Love you, to the stars and back.

Always, Sissy

Abby

Thirty seconds after they entered the bar, Abby considered tucking tail and running for the exit. Technically it was a honky-tonk, offering nightly music, and—from what she could tell—a popular spot Saturday night. Even so, the option to leave the farm had never occurred to her when Matt sprung the surprise of staying an extra night. Another nice quiet dinner or smores over the fire pit was more of what she'd envisioned. However, everyone else seemed to think a loud bar in the middle of nowhere was the perfect way to spend the evening.

In fact, Tuck was so eager to have a night out with his wife that by the time he and Matt came in from the stables for lunch, he'd arranged for the neighbor's teenage daughter to babysit. When Abby tried to get out of it with an excuse about not coming prepared for a night out, Mags gave her the stink eye and started pulling shoes and clothes out of the closet, some of which were Abby's.

"What are my clothes doing in your closet?" Abby asked, not because she cared if her best friend borrowed anything, but their cup size and height difference made it nearly impossible to share.

"Because I didn't want the moths to get to them in the barn, silly."

Unfortunately, that made way too much sense. Abby shook her head. It wasn't as if Maggie was trying to sabotage her efforts to steer clear of her ex-fiancé. Where they were going was in the middle of nowhere. There was absolutely no good reason to avoid the place.

"Please," wheedled Mags. "I can't remember the last time I had an excuse to get gussied up for a night out." She batted her lashes and when that didn't garner Abby's agreement, she resorted to good, old-fashioned guilt.

"You wouldn't deny your best friend a date with her husband." And the real kicker, "I know you don't want to see a grown man cry. Tuck never puts this much effort into a date unless he's desperate."

"Oh please, I know for a fact you two still behave like newlyweds despite the sugar lump's arrival.

"Just because I go easy on the man doesn't mean we couldn't use a little romance."

"Fine. But you're in charge of making me presentable."

What Abby didn't tell her best friend, who did a little victory dance while she plugged in a large barrel curling iron, was that it was the least she could do for Tuck after her stunt in the kitchen. Chiding herself again for nearly kissing Matt in front of everyone, Abby still couldn't believe she'd gotten so caught up in the moment that their audience fell off the radar.

On top of that, Maggie's obvious excitement over a night out was hard to ignore, not if Abby wanted to be a friend worth her salt. She gave Mags a smile that didn't quite reach her eyes as she tried to pull her grinchy, selfish, and terrified heart out of the vicinity of her stomach.

Which is why an hour later she found herself in full makeup, hair tamed to within an inch of her life, wearing black skinny jeans paired with a royal blue blouse and heels.

When they arrived at the bar, Abby's guess was proved right, that her friends planned to spend the night wrapped up in each other on the dance floor. And, though Matt tried to convince Abby to join him there too, she'd pulled the 'I'm famished' card.

Ever the gentleman, Matt pulled out her chair, and let her order before him.

"I'll have the loaded baked potato, extra butter, with bacon on the side." Abby firmly believed a girl needed to indulge in carbohydrates every now and then. Tonight's escapade might also require the chocolate brownie alamode she'd spotted halfway down the menu.

"And I'll take the house burger with extra fries, please. Oh, and an iced tea," ordered Matt.

The place was packed out by the time they were done with dinner, and the crowd at the bar had become more boisterous since the band went on break.

"Thanks to this crowd, I'm pretty sure the waitress won't be back to refill our drinks anytime soon. Can I get you something from the bar…a glass of wine or another coke?"

"Just a glass of ice water would be great," Abby said, fanning herself with her hand. "The air condition must be working overtime and failing miserably. So many people must have raised the temperature."

"I've been trying to tell you all night how hot you are," said Matt with a wink before disappearing into the crowd.

Abby brushed him off but reconsidered a turn on the dance floor upon his return. Heaven help her if he two-stepped as well as he winked.

Matt had been gone for at least five minutes. She looked over her shoulder toward the crowded bar, glancing down at her watch, and fanned herself with her hand.

"He's a grown man and can take care of himself. Just relax," she chided under her breath. She knew she had become a worry wort in recent weeks. If it wasn't Aunt Sara's health, it was the continued secrets between them, and now the one she had kept from Matt about her engagement to Lon.

Another five minutes had passed when the noise at the bar registered as something more than the lively din it had been only moments before. She scanned the crowd, slightly concerned about the mob gathering closer to the far side of the bar. In fact, she was almost sure she heard Tucker's growl in the center of it. Abby stood up, almost knocking her chair to the ground in her hurry, and anxiously searched the throng of people for Maggie. She spotted her best friend pushing through the crowd, no doubt swearing as she went, until it parted like the Red Sea for Moses. Through the gap of people, in the middle of all the commotion, stood her ex-fiancé with his hand fisted in Matt's shirt, and a snarl ripping from his throat. Tuck reached for Lon's arm to pull him back from Matt, but he simply shrugged him off, becoming more belligerent by the second.

Oh, sweet Jesus, Abby prayed desperately as her palms began to sweat and her stomach churned in earnest. *Just stay put, you'll only make it worse!* she pleaded with herself.

No good would come from her interference, and yet, Abby wasn't able to walk away any more than Pharaoh had been from the Israelites. "You'd think the seven plagues would've been enough to warn him," she moaned, watching the scene unfold as she marched on shaky legs toward the impending brawl, trepidation in her every step. There was only one way for this to end, badly. Abby's stomach cramped painfully again as though it agreed with her thoughts.

The men stood eye to eye, but Matt looked calm and steady even as he asked the other man to remove his hand. Tuck placed a hand on Lon's chest in an effort to force him back to reason. Abby had never really seen her ex angry, at least not like this, and never towards her. But that changed the moment she made her way through the crowd and next to Matt.

"Should've known," he slurred. "Course you're here. As if my night weren't shi—"

"Whoa, buddy, there's no reason to take it out on the lady," Matt told him firmly. "I'm the one who knocked over your drink. I apologized and offered to buy you another, although water might be in order."

With a cynical laugh, Lon released Matt, who immediately placed his hand on Abby's lower back. She could see the exact second Lon realized they were there together, if not actually as a couple. Instead of letting Matt guide her back to the table, like any sane woman in this situation would, she stepped forward.

"Lon, I didn't mean—"

"Don't bother, Abs," Lon said, interrupting her. "You got nothin' to say I wanna hear."

She stumbled back a couple of steps as though he'd slapped her and watched him pull a brunette in daisy dukes and half shirt into his side, kissing her in a way that left little to the imagination about his intentions.

Lon looked Abby over from head to toe, a hard edge to his jaw and a nasty leer on his face as he slurred, "Careful with that one. She's kinda like a natural disaster. Only leaves destruction in her wake."

Matt ignored the warning and simply took her by the hand, gently tugging her in the direction of the exit.

Despite Aunt Sara's health, leaving her job, and the secret letters, the emotional lacerations on her heart had begun to heal subtly over the past few weeks. Being home in Homily, her new friendship with Matt, and The Christmas Tea Shoppe had all wrought a tender hope that she could leave her past behind. But with a few cruel words, Lon had ripped those wounds wide enough to make her bleed out.

Matt

Moonlight spilled through the gauzy curtains in the living room where Matt lay on the sofa, arms tucked beneath his head while he watched the shadows play on the walls and creep into his heart.

He could still hear Abby's sobs coming from the back of Tuck's crew cab where she'd fled into the arms of her best friend. Tuck concisely explained on the drive home that Abby had been engaged to the man at the bar—the same one Matt wished he'd hit, even if it wouldn't have solved anything.

Abby had kept her eyes averted when they entered the house, stopping only long enough to say how sorry she was for ruining everyone's evening. After which, the ladies disappeared upstairs while Tuck paid the sitter and followed them shortly thereafter. Nobody came back down, and nothing else was said.

Jealousy was a new emotion for Matt, since he'd never cared about a woman the way he did Abby. She'd been engaged and never alluded to it in any of the time they spent together. Not that he blamed her after meeting the man. Matt could not for the life of him figure out how the callous drunk who went around picking fights had snagged such a sweetheart.

Snagged my *sweetheart,* he amended.

Sighing into the dark, he reminded himself she'd been under no obligation to tell him anything. If he'd played the fool, he could only blame himself for not making his intentions clear sooner.

Rest eluded him, though he felt exhausted, his body blatantly denying him the oblivion sleep brought. Eventually giving up, Matt grabbed his shirt from where he'd carelessly tossed it on the back of the sofa earlier and pulled the old cotton tee over his head. His bare feet padded silently to the backdoor. The cool air washed over his fevered skin, sparking goose flesh down his arms to his hands, which were clenched into fists.

A few moments later Tuck joined him.

"Heard the door open from upstairs and thought maybe you could use some company."

Tuck held the shot glass in his hand out to Matt. "Personally, I'm not a proponent of the strong stuff when life is hard, but sometimes a single can fortify a man for the battle ahead."

Eyeing the caramel liquid, Matt released a pained laugh but declined the offer. "Fairly certain the only thing able fortify me now is a word from the distraught woman upstairs."

"I figured, but I wouldn't be a very good wingman if I didn't at least offer." The guilty expression that accompanied his words said more than enough.

"Well, then, as my wingman, tell me what I need to know about Lon Howard. The guy tried to pick a fight with me, but worse, he disrespected one of the kindest people I know."

"You're right on both counts. But Abby's also complicated, man."

"What woman isn't?" Matt asked with levity.

A small laugh reluctantly rumbled in Tuck's chest. "True. But she's more complicated than most. Honestly, it isn't my story to tell. But since you almost got yourself hammered by my best friend, it's only fair to give you the parts of it I can. The rest is up to Abby."

"Fine, let's start with how a man like Lon Howard is your best friend."

"First off, the man you met tonight isn't the man I've known my whole life. That man would've done anything for anyone, including a stranger. Loyal, generous to a fault—the man I knew would have gone to the ends of the earth to keep his word."

Matt's eyebrows rose in disbelief.

"The man you met tonight is a broken shell trying to fill all of his hurt places with liquor, fighting, and women. God knows I've tried to intervene, only to find myself black and blue for my efforts. The last time it happened, I swore I was done. I won't continue to watch him treat others, or himself, like trash. People matter, and Lon used to understand that."

Matt tried to have compassion for the man Tuck described, but when he thought of how the man had tread all over Abby's feelings, he found himself curling his fists at his side all over again.

"Anyway, I hoped my words would mean something, but after tonight's escapade it's obvious Lon is too busy wallowing to acknowledge how he's hurt himself and others. From my own experience, I know staying angry about the past won't change the future. The only thing any of us can do is try to make tomorrow different. Lon isn't ready to hear that God is bigger than his circumstances."

Watching Matt with a sympathetic eye, Tuck continued, "There was a time I would've said your anger's justified. But I've long since realized if not for God's grace, I might be just like the man you met tonight…broken and lost."

Matt waited for further explanation, sensing it might be hard to swallow anything Tuck had to say about Abby with another man.

"Abby met Lon at her school's auction shortly after the girls moved to Midwell. A lot of the town's education fundraising is supported by wealthy families in the area and the Howards are one of those families, not that you'd ever know it. Not long after their initial meeting, Abby introduced me to Maggie."

A reminiscent smile tugged at the corners of his mouth and a faraway look entered Tuck's eyes. "We were like oil and water at first, but it was obvious to me I'd met my match. She agreed to marry me a week after the house renovations began. At the time, I was stoked with what seemed to be an ideal situation; I was going to marry the love of my life and our best friends were in love. But my wife told me those two would never make the long haul. Mags said they probably just felt like they were being left behind. Frankly, I didn't know what she was talking about until Abby broke it off a year ago. Timing was bad, but that's a whole other story."

The two men were quiet for a while, taking in the night sky and the sounds of insects in the field.

Finally, Tucker continued, "But I believe God can work through and overcome any situation to achieve *his* plan. I think how I treat the people around me is more important to the Almighty than who I vote for or which church I attend. How well do I love my neighbor, who blows his leaves onto my driveway every freakin' fall? Do I treat people with respect and common decency even when we disagree? Am I kind to the checkout person moving at a sloth's pace?"

Matt pondered the big man's words. He still felt the awkwardness between them, knowing Tucker had a loyalty to Lon he could never understand.

"Definitely easier to be selfless when it's convenient, and I rarely ask myself what my personal freedom costs those around me. Heck, if I'm really being honest," Tuck confessed to a starless sky, "I fail at most of what I just said. And, as much as it pains me to watch my best friend send his life up in flames, Lon is responsible for how he treats others."

Tuck's words left a bitter taste in Matt's mouth, and he searched his own soul, trying to quell the worry consuming him. Abby and Lon's relationship must have been something special to tear a man up to the point of self-destruction.

"Still, your friend seemed pretty devastated to me. Maggie could have it all wrong."

"Believe me when I say my wife is rarely wrong, as much as it pains me to admit it. Besides, I don't know about you, but I find life is generally better when I trust God with the outcome. Maybe not easier, but better," finished Tuck with a nod of his head.

....

Dawn emerged as a watery gray blanket over the hills. The snippets of sleep Matt managed to get between restless thoughts and troubled dreams was not nearly enough for the day that lay ahead. Breakfast was a solemn affair; Abby had opted out, claiming she needed to do some packing.

The men loaded Abby's boxes and two large suitcases into the back of his truck, a tarp bungeed over the top to protect them from the moisture. Abby took the final five minutes to hold Caleb, his gurgles almost bringing a smile to her face, but it quickly disappeared as she said goodbye to her best friend.

Matt closed Abby into the passenger seat and said his goodbyes quickly with a hug from Mags, who whispered in his ear, "Be patient; have faith. She'll come around." The handshake from her husband might have broken a lesser man's hand, except Matt gave as good as he got, earning him a nod of respect.

"Don't be a stranger. Take good care of our girl," said Tuck solemnly.

Matt's head bobbed in return, grateful for their encouragement.

Abby slept most of the morning away, wrapped in a long cardigan this time instead of his hoodie. When she'd informed him the rest of her wardrobe had been found in Maggie's closet, he'd told her to keep his hoodie anyway, desperate to comfort her with or without his arms. The silent drive persistently reinforced what he knew deep in his gut. Their tentative relationship wouldn't withstand the onslaught of running into Abby's ex. What he found baffling was why it was such a big deal.

Five miles outside of Homily, the night sky full of stars and foreboding, Matt finally gave in to the thought that had tumbled through his head most of the day.

"Do you still love him?" he asked, afraid to disturb the facade of peace covering them like the fog over the hills they'd come from. Tuck had said she didn't, but he still wanted to hear the words from her. His question coaxed her from her silent vigil while dread prowled closer, poised to strike.

"No. In fact if I'm completely honest, I don't think I ever loved Lon," she said, continuing to gaze out the window. "I wanted to," her voice pleaded. "But in retrospect, I think I loved the idea of someone like Lon more than I actually felt anything for him."

Shame saturated the admission, and though he wanted to assuage her guilt, he longed for the truth more. "Then why did it wreck you to see him?"

She hesitated briefly searching for the right words. "Because I hurt him, and at a time when he really needed me to be there for him. I just…"

She stopped, forcing him to ask, "You just what, sweetheart?" The endearment came out unbidden, but honest all the same. If Abby noticed the slip, she didn't acknowledge it.

"I couldn't lie to myself anymore." She swallowed hard once and then again, trying to get the words past the lump in her throat. "Not when I understood the extent to which he would go to make me happy. Look at all the pain I've caused him, simply because I couldn't be honest with myself."

"Hold on a minute. You're taking far too much of the blame on yourself. I understand you feel guilty for hurting him but he's still responsible for his own actions."

"The man we saw last night is nothing like the man I knew, but the words he spoke were true. I only leave destruction in my wake. I'm just like her."

With the car idling at the curb in front of Sara's house, Matt leaned across the cab and took Abby's upper arms gently in his hands, willing her to look at him. Tears cascaded over the contours of her face and for a brief moment she bent to his desire, allowing him to draw her close. All too quickly, she yanked herself from his embrace, leaving him cold and her shuddering with pent-up emotion as she stumbled up the walkway.

He numbly began taking the tarp off the back of the truck. When the boxes and suitcases were stored in Sara's garage, Matt watched helplessly as his future walked away from him, her last words desolate and thundering in his ears.

"Just like who?" he asked into the empty cab of his truck.

Eighteen

Dear Sunshine,

Our girl left for college today. Where has the time gone? She promises to come home on the weekends and holidays, but I know it will never feel like enough. I guess I'm going to have to get myself a hobby, at least until I get used to having an empty nest. I'm glad your counseling job with the church is going well. Love you, to the stars and back.

Always, Sissy

Matt

The next seven days were brutal. Matt lost count of how many shifts he'd taken at the hospital and the miles racked up running. His only goal became pushing his body hard enough to fall into a dreamless sleep each night. He rubbed his chest right over the place his heart stuttered every time Abby crossed his mind, as if he could rid the soreness her absence from his life caused. She haunted his days, hounding his thoughts with what ifs and picking away at the plans he'd foolishly made.

Forget defining the relationship, he just wanted her to call him back. Text, voicemail, anything would be better than this stonewall. Matt mocked his image in the mirror for being such a lovesick fool. He was angry with Abby for ignoring his attempts to reach her even if he knew his charm would never be enough to convince her their relationship deserved the chance to grow.

The heavens were dark outside, awaiting the dawn's celebration of light, when Gran walked into the front entryway and caught him sitting on the stairs, mid shoe tie. Normally, Matt mused, this would be no cause for alarm. However, he'd been avoiding her as much as possible since his return. Aside from the occasional few words from her about overworking and proper meals, to which he always gave a grumbled assent—acting more like a surly middle school boy than a grown man—he'd managed to go without a proper debriefing of his recent trip and subsequent turmoil.

"Good morning, young man. You're up awfully early again."

She said it as a statement, but he gruffly returned the sentiment and answered as though it were a question. "Yes, ma'am."

"Sweet boy, I didn't get to be my age without some serious powers of observation."

Curiosity caught a fly in the web every time, but he gave in anyway. "Okay, I'll bite. What, exactly, have you observed?"

"You. Now, I'll admit it took me a mite too long to put all the pieces together, what with you carrying on the way you have been," she said with a frown between her brows and a dip of her cupid lips.

"I have no idea what you could possibly be alluding to. My routine is the same as it's always been."

"Maybe when you first moved in, but then you began to make time for the more important things in life. Now it's even worse. You work all hours of the day and night and you're running holes into the soles of your shoes, literally. And don't even get me started on your eating habits. A granola bar doesn't count as a snack, let alone a meal."

Raising his eyebrows at her tirade, he finished tying his laces, another mumbled comment rolling off his tongue without thought. "Then maybe it's time I moved out."

Gran tapped her foot, and when that didn't garner his attention, she swatted him with the tea towel in her left hand, shaking a finger within an inch of his nose. "Don't play dumb with me. Callous comments only leave you feeling regret and a mite foolish in hindsight, Matthew Lee Dixon."

She'd garnered his attention with the use of his full name, making him cringe and feel appropriately chastised. Any man raised in church knows he should never hurt the women God has so generously placed in his life. Not with words, or otherwise. Being a doctor only underlined the point. "Do no harm" sat at the forefront of his mind every day, but this morning he'd lashed out like a wounded dog. Head hung in defeat, he took a deep breath and looked up to meet his gran's stern gaze.

"I'm sorry, Gran. Both for my words and actions lately," he said, the words soft and remorseful.

Gran grabbed the handrail and slowly, with what seemed like all her bones cracking, took a seat next to him. She wrapped her short arms around as much of him as she could. He pulled her in close, resting his head on top of hers, the comfort he'd been pining for in Abby's absence almost in reach.

Gran leaned back to find his eyes, the same shade as her boy's. "Have I ever told you about the day you were born?"

"No, ma'am."

"Your father was waiting on a flight out of Germany, so we drove to be with your mother. They hadn't been stationed at Fort Benning long, and your mother's parents had passed shortly before your folks met. You were overdue by almost two weeks, behavin' like you were in no hurry to be anywhere. Your poor mother, on the other hand, was wilting in the sultry summer weather. I could only do so much to ease her discomfort, as any pregnant woman will attest to. No one bears the burden a mother does when waiting for her child to come."

Matt smiled and leaned back into the bench, realizing he should settle in for a while. Once Gran started a story, the telling took a while.

"It was another three days before you finally made your appearance in this world and then you had the audacity to come out breech. Bottom first. Make of that what you will, but in my experience that all amounts to a heap of stubbornness."

He acknowledged the truth with a nod of his head and a low chuckle.

"The whole experience was the complete opposite of your father's birth. We were thrilled to finally be parents, but when he came three weeks early after a short labor, we almost felt unprepared for the shooting star who'd entered our lives. And when I held him to my bosom for the first time, I knew…"

Gran had that far off look in her eye. The one which reminded him she might be with him physically but wasn't entirely present. He waited another moment before asking, "What did you know, Gran?"

A look of sadness crept into her expression. "I knew he would only really be ours for a brief time. Even then, I recognized the restlessness within him. Life in a small town would never be enough to hold his interest." She looked directly at Matt, and the corners of her lips perked up. "But not you, sweet boy. No, the first time I pulled you close I knew you would lay down deep roots somewhere, someday. You were in no hurry to go anywhere, and if you wanted to take the long way around, you would."

"Gran, I think I know where you're going with this story."

"Good, because Sara and I have become good friends, thanks to the little visit you and Abby arranged while y'all were out of town."

His mouth gaped wide enough to catch flies. Aware of the mischievous gleam in her eye, she confirmed with just one look he'd been caught. Hook. Line. And sinker. After spouting off the juicy morsel about her new friendship, Gran said "We spoke on the phone yesterday and decided it's high time for y'all to get over whatever this tiff is and make up."

Which is why he found himself driving downtown toward The Christmas Tea Shoppe the following afternoon. Never let it be said Nancy Dixon wasn't wily. He had no doubt she'd planned for this precise outcome when she'd ventured onto the stairwell with him bright and early the previous morning.

As far as schemes went, this one was rather simple. Matt would stop in at the quaint little shop nestled on the corner of Main Street and Second Avenue to pick up some tea Sara had ordered last week for his gran. Right about now, he was hoping the name of the latter street was a sign of things to come—a second chance, of sorts, to get things right with Abby. At a stop sign a block from his destination, he looked up at the blue sky, his hands gripping the leather steering wheel, and made a quick request for courage and faith.

Faith was easy to have when everything stayed laid out in front of a man, but Matt wanted to have the kind of unfettered belief that shone a light on any situation, especially when life tipped on its axis. His grandad had always said, "Son, it isn't the absence of difficulty, but the presence of God, which leads to genuine hope and joy."

His priorities straight and eager to find a parking spot, Matt rounded the corner and put his truck in park directly across from the large picture window anchoring the front of the shop's brick façade and green-and-white-striped awning. Purpose blazing anew in his every movement, he jogged across the street and pushed on the brass latch of the door handle without hesitation.

Abby

Aunt Sara's advice was usually helpful. After all, if a woman didn't want to look like her heart had been blown to smithereens, then the first step was to stop carrying on as though it had. Sadly, her advice only went so far after days spent sobbing into her pillow, running through every minute of her weekend with Matt. Her face had become a portrait of solemn despair. Or as Aunt Sara pointed out, not unkindly but nonetheless with brutal truth, she looked like she could use an avocado mask and several dozen cucumbers.

Fortunately, The Christmas Tea Shoppe was in Aunt Sara's capable hands once more. They'd gone over the books together at the end of the week, and though the regular patrons had asked after her in concern and curiosity, her aunt assured her no one knew the real reason for her niece's absence. Which meant it was time to get a grip, fix her puffy, splotched face, and pull on her big-girl knickers.

On the bright side, her wardrobe had grown by astronomical proportions. If only she'd been able to avoid Lon, the trip might have been worth the acquisition.

To make matters worse, she'd ignored Matt's numerous phone calls and concerned text messages, but tortured herself by playing them back daily.

"Abby, it's Matt. Call me back. Please," he implored. "I'm sure we can work through this."

"Sweetheart, it's me. Again. I miss talking to you."

› *Why won't you call me? I'm certain this is just a big misunderstanding.*

› *I know if we talk, we can figure things out.*

› *Abby, who is it you think you're like?*

It was the last one that kept her from responding. She was far too much like her mama for anyone else's good. Matt was better off if she walked away before their relationship went any further. If she called him back, he would try to talk her out of it, charming her into being friends again until one day she let him hold her hand. Again. Eventually he would put his arms around her because a friend gives hugs. Often. Until one day, she would find herself looking at his lips, forgetting the world around her and wishing for something that could never be.

No siree. It would only end in ruins, and I care about Matt too much to lead him on.

Look what happened to poor Lon Howard, all because she'd said yes when she should have said no. This was better. Abby knew she'd already done enough damage. Staying away from Matt would be much safer for both of them.

Decision made, Abby forced herself to get ready for work and caught Aunt Sara in the kitchen with a breakfast burrito, Paige Reyes style, filled with eggs, seasoned papas, spinach, tomatoes, and avocado inside a corn tortilla with salsa verde on the side. Abby's mouth watered in anticipation.

"Well, look who found the shower and some pep in her step this morning," said her aunt by way of greeting.

"I don't think it's pep, but resignation is a powerful motivator."

"And what exactly are you resigned to, sugar?"

"Not having Matt in my life," said Abby, refusing to release one more tear in vain.

"Unh-unh." Aunt Sarah shook her head and clicked her tongue in disapproval. "I don't know what this nonsense is about, but if you've decided to martyr yourself because of what the Howard boy said, it might be time we talked about your mama."

"I told you, there's nothin' to talk about. Mama left and never looked back, right?" Abby taunted.

Aunt Sara stared back but didn't speak. How could she?

Anything she said would either be a lie, or a confession. Abby wasn't sure which was worse. The secret between them continued to grow the longer they kept it, but Abby didn't know what she really wanted, let alone how to ask for it.

....

Abby was adding up the receipts from afternoon tea when the bell above the door rang. The last customer had left ten minutes prior, but she kept the door unlocked in case the delivery kid came by in the half hour after closing. Aunt Sara had spent years developing global partnerships for The Christmas Tea Shoppe in order to purchase a wider variety of tea for her customers. But everything else was purchased at Dandelion Grocers a few blocks away, giving her the opportunity to support another local business.

Abby assumed one of the Yang children, who ran deliveries for their parents, would set everything inside the door without a peep. Her aunt thought it was rude not to engage in conversation, whereas Abby recognized the hurry they were in. It wasn't that they were ill-mannered; they were simply teenagers with other exploits on their mind. Anticipation of adventures that could only be sought once they finished their rounds was the real impetus for their silence.

It was quite the conundrum when they were both present at delivery time, and almost comical to watch the kids be polite yet deter her aunt from any long enquiries. Abby was fairly certain her aunt kept them longer than necessary to teach them a lesson in politeness she thought they were sorely in need of.

When Abby saw Matt at the front counter instead, she tried to get her legs to move—where, she didn't know, but anywhere else would have been preferable. Unfortunately, there was no avoiding the face of the man she'd ignored for the past week. She wished the floor would open up and swallow her whole.

In her efforts to keep him at arm's length, she'd been unkind. Why hadn't she called him back to explain the situation? Oh yeah, because she was a sucker for his green eyes, constant teasing, and the way he called her sweetheart.

To her aunt's credit, she had tried to change Abby's mind, repeatedly. But Abby had stubbornly refused. They lived in a small town, so it wasn't as if she didn't know she would see him at some point, though she had definitely lied to herself about how it could unfold without any embarrassment on her part or hard feelings on his.

Liar, liar, pants on fire. Turns out denial is a cloying temptation that can only end with one outcome…humility.

"I'm so sorry, Matt," she blurted out without an ounce of eloquence. She winced over the inept delivery and waited for what was sure to be a well-deserved set down.

"I forgive you," he said, without hesitation. "I've missed you, pretty girl."

After a week apart, Matt stood there, drinking in her presence like a thirsty man on a hot day, and once again she wanted to be the water to quench his thirst. His right hand clutched at his heart like he was trying to hold it inside of his body, but his eyes said so many other things she wanted to hear, all of it stealing the air from her lungs.

Matt

Matt's forgiveness hung in the air between them. Time ticked away without a care for the organ in his hollow chest as Abby stayed frozen and silent behind the counter. Matt took a deep breath and jumped in for the plunge.

"Just give me a chance. Give *us* a chance," he begged. Yep, he definitely heard begging in his tone. His pride tucked tail and ran, nowhere to be seen, but Matt knew his pride would be worth nothing if he walked away without putting all of his cards on the table.

Abby stood there, wide-eyed, but finally gave a jerky nod of assent. Whatever leash tethered Matt to his spot came unraveled. His long legs ate up the space between them as he rounded the corner of the counter, took her face in hand, and leaned in slowly, giving her time to adjust to his nearness.

Chastely, he kissed her once, twice, and again, waiting for her to catch up while the world dropped away around them. When Abby rose on her toes and reached her arms around his neck to draw him in closer, his hands slid to her waist. His attentions were tender, giving more than taking, but his heart felt like it might beat right out of his chest beneath her hand. Each pulse a demand: *here, take me, I'm all yours.*

When the world finally intruded upon them with a bell chime, Matt pulled back, entwined her hand in his and asked, "Can I drive you home, sweetheart?"

Breathless, Abby nodded yes, wearing an utterly foolish grin to match the one on his face. Entirely wrapped up in each other, neither of them noticed the box of groceries against the wall to the left of the door.

Nineteen

Dear Sunshine,

Our girl is off to Virginia to teach. Though I can't figure out what that small town has that Homily doesn't, unless it's the cloak of anonymity. It's a fresh start, and I'm doing my best to be supportive. At least Maggie is going with her. I suppose they'll find their way, much like we have. Let's get together for lunch soon. I'll come to you as usual. Love you, to the stars and back.

Always, Sissy

Sara

Sara peaked through her living room curtains for the umpteenth time to see if Abby and Matt were still cuddled up and talking in hushed tones on the porch swing. They sat so close, she almost couldn't tell where one ended and the other began except for their heads, one light and the other dark. Abby was tucked under the wing of Matt's arm, her head on his shoulder while he spoke.

Thank goodness for old, single-paned windows, thought Sara, listening to their sweet declarations between stolen kisses. When pecks turned to locked lips and tight embraces once more, she left the lovebirds to make up.

Hallelujah, she declared to herself. Though she had no intention of being nosy, what started out as a casual glance outside upon their arrival had quickly morphed into a phone call to Nancy Dixon, with repeated check-ins.

Their plan had gone off without a hitch, not that Sara had ever doubted it wouldn't. She and Nancy had a direct line to Heaven for a reason. God was bigger than any problem, and he already knew the solution to every single one. Now, if only she could figure out why her mile-high meringue kept falling short. Maybe the man upstairs had more important things to do than enlighten her on proper whisking technique, but he had managed to feed five thousand with two fish and five loaves of bread. With visions of blue ribbons won at the county fair the following month, Sara left the lovebirds to entertain themselves with affection.

An hour later, she was still agonizing over her recipe when Abby came floating into the kitchen, looking dreamy eyed and well kissed.

"By the look on your face, I'd say that was one doozy of a goodnight kiss, baby girl."

Abby blushed to the roots of her blonde curls that looked like they'd been recently tousled. "Aunt Sara, how could you possibly know that?" Eyes wide with exasperation she said, "Please tell me you weren't spying on us."

"Of course not, sugar. Well, at least not for that part." Sara raised her brows in implication. "The two of you looked cozy on the porch swing, though, and it's not hard to recognize a thoroughly kissed woman."

With another dreamy look falling over her countenance, Abby slid onto a stool near the counter where Sara had her ingredients laid out like warriors ready to sacrifice themselves in her quest for perfection.

"So, I take it that everything broken has been mended?"

"I guess so. I haven't really thought about it, or anything else for that matter, since Matt kissed me," said Abby with a wary glance.

"Papaw used to say the easiest way to tell a story was to start at the beginning."

Abby filled her in on the details, starting with her failure to mention Lon to Matt before the disastrous night out in Midwell. After that, the story was simply a case of honesty and forgiveness.

"The words 'I'm sorry' and 'I forgive you' are powerful ones, especially if they're given freely with truth and action behind them. But you might have to do a little more than kiss and make up."

Sara watched Abby squirm in her seat, knowing she could be a bit of a prickly pear when it came to matters of the heart. It was a natural defense mechanism and Sara couldn't blame her after all she had gone through, both in childhood and more recently with the Howard boy.

"Sugar, I know the words Lon said were hurtful. However, they aren't true."

"But what if they are?" Abby's sorrow over the possibility was evident in her tone and countenance.

"They're not. You aren't destructive, and you aren't your mama." Though Sara said it emphatically, it wasn't enough to change the doubtful look on Abby's face.

"Baby girl, no two people are ever exactly alike. You have some of your mama's physical traits, and people are drawn to you the way they were to her, but your temperaments are entirely different. Grace was popular and loved being in the center of everything. You have an inner light people want to warm themselves with even if you'd rather blend in with the scenery.

"You make me sound like a wallflower," Abby said, obviously disgruntled.

"You are definitely not a wallflower, but sometimes I think you live your life worried about what others are going to say. Sugar, you can't continue to live your life in the shadow of everyone else's expectations or disappointments. You can only live the life God intends for you to have."

"I'm trying to, but what if my careless actions caused—"

Sara quickly interrupted what was sure to be another tirade about how Lon's actions were her niece's fault. "Marriage is meant to be until death do you part, and while it doesn't work out that way for everyone, divorce is a particular breed of grief I wouldn't wish on my worst enemy. I promise no matter what that boy said, in the long run you've saved yourself and him from heartache further down the road."

In the quiet that followed, her niece made spaghetti at the stove, perhaps finding comfort in the rhythmic motions and routine of an easy meal, while Sara resumed baking and conversed with God.

Abby had become the beautiful, independent person Sara had known she would. But now, it was time. Time to share the little girl she'd been blessed to raise with the woman who had given her life. Her niece needed to move toward the future God had for her, and the only way for her to do so would be to face her past. The time had come to write Grace a different kind of letter.

Matt

The heavy front door closed with a loud thud as Matt came through the door calling, "Gran, where are you?"

"Stop all your fussin'. I'm in the kitchen prepping dinner, and I know I taught you better than to yell in the house."

He removed his shoes and placed his bag on the entry bench before he made his way to the kitchen, where Gran was elbow deep in a large bowl of buttermilk.

"And I told you I'd cook tonight so you could spend some extra time in the yard. It won't be long before we get our first hurricane. Frankly, I'm surprised we haven't had one yet."

"Thank the good Lord," she interjected.

"I also know how much you like to get your beds prepped for fall planting. Besides, it was my attempt to apologize for my boorish behavior of late."

"Hush now, can't an old lady make dinner just because she feels like it?"

"I didn't mean to sound ungrateful. You know how much I love your cooking, especially your fried chicken. No one, and I mean no one, makes it better than you." He leaned in to kiss her cheek, smoothing any waves he'd made.

Matt slid onto the footstool Gran used to reach the upper cabinets.

"Not so fast, young man." Her left eyebrow lifted all the way to her white hairline as if he'd lost his mind.

"You're in charge of making the apple slaw."

Matt rose to do her bidding, not daring to chuckle, even under his breath.

"Yes, ma'am," was all he said on his way to the fridge, grabbing a Granny Smith from the fruit bowl on the counter as he went.

"Don't forget to wash the apple and mind the container of potato salad on the second shelf. It's a little precarious."

He muttered under his breath, something about being a doctor and certain he could make a simple apple slaw without anyone's help.

Gran's sight might have been going, but her hearing was clearly just fine. After swatting him with a towel, she watched and waited until he was wrist deep in shredded apples and carrots before she said, "I had an interesting conversation with Sara Hart today."

It was a trick she'd used time and again when she wanted to get him to talk about something he wouldn't bring up on his own. Come to think of it, she'd used it on his dad and granddad too. Busy hands led to chatter, like idle hands led to trouble.

"Oh, and what did the two of you lovely ladies talk about?"

When she didn't respond immediately, he turned around to look at her, catching the smirk on her face. His face flamed all the way down his neck, and Gran couldn't seem to help herself as she chortled with glee, which at her age might have been a feat, but laughter was good medicine for the soul at any age.

"Well, should I assume the two of you made up, then?"

"As a matter of fact, we did. The whole thing couldn't have gone better. She apologized. I forgave. And your smirk suggests you know the rest."

"So does this mean you're officially courting the lovely Miss Hart?"

"Abby and I are dating. Which sounds funny to say at my age but courting sounds too old fashioned."

"Courting is dating with intention. Do you have intentions, Matthew?"

"Actually yes, Gran, I think I do. No pun intended," he grinned and stared at Gran, his heart full of revelation.

When he'd left for the shop, his hope had been to reconcile with Abby enough to be friends, or at the very least find closure. Instead, he'd kissed her, and then he'd kissed her some more. Combustive, electric, dizzying, whatever words he used to describe the meeting of their lips, sparks had flown. He had to remind himself more than once to keep it rated PG on Sara's front porch.

Matt thought back to Abby curled into his side on the swing, her puzzle piece fitting itself perfectly into his own. She'd rested her head upon his shoulder while they caught up on what had happened in their time apart, all while stealing kisses from one another in between words.

Whether it was telling Abby about his day, making plans to see each other, or sharing each other's burdens—even making her laugh had somehow become vital to him in a short time. Though meeting Abby had been a complete surprise, being drawn to her, seeking out her friendship—it all felt so natural, it was as easy as breathing. Which was part of the reason why being apart had been so difficult.

Today only reaffirmed what he'd felt on their trip. Abigail Jane Hart was the girl for him. He may have taken the long way around to find someone he never knew he needed, and in the only place he'd ever called home, but now that he was headed in the right direction, he could hardly wait to arrive at the destination.

Gran smiled and patted his cheek with her soft hand, the scent of vanilla lingering with its departure. She returned to dinner preparations and hummed an old tune, swaying with each dunk of chicken breast into the batter, while Matt smiled what was no doubt a dopey grin and tossed the coleslaw with honey-poppy-seed dressing.

When Gran was done, she continued to hum one of her favorite tunes while Matt took her in his arms, slowly moving them around the kitchen the way his granddad used to. She patted his cheek, a suspicious wetness in her eyes. He knew how much she missed his granddad, and he was beginning to understand the reason for it.

Matt poured dish soap into the water on one side of the sink as he leaned into the Formica countertop, scrubbing pots and pans, and listened to the sounds of Gran getting ready for bed echo through the old wood floors of the house. He slid his phone from his back pocket and pulled up the contact he'd put in weeks ago. Matt considered listing Abby's info under Gorgeous and discarded it, not because it wasn't true, but because he wanted her to know she meant more to him than just the way she looked. Granted, holding all of her beautiful curves close that day had been pretty outstanding. Forcing himself to focus, he sent off a text.

> *Thanks for a great afternoon on the front porch swing ;) I have an early shift at the hospital, so I'm headed to bed. I'll call when I'm done to see if we can catch up at the shop. Dinner this Friday?*

A few minutes later his phone pinged with an incoming text while he was brushing his teeth.

> *Are you telling me you go to sleep at the same time as your gran?*
> *Always giveng me guff, Miss Hart. And yes, I thought it might be wise to get some sleep for the sake of my patients. Old folks know if you have to get up with the sun, then you go to bed with it too.*
> *Does your gran know you call her that?*
> *Of course not. Nobody but a fool ever refers to a woman's age unless she's under twenty. Even then it's questionable. Why?*
> *Hmm, I think I'm going to save that little tidbit for a rainy day…*
> *You wouldn't dare.*
> *Guess we'll find out the next time you make me spitting mad. Friday sounds fun. Talk to ya later. Sweet dreams, Doctor Dixon.*

He was sure to have sweet dreams after spending the day with her, no doubt about it.

> *Goodnight, sweetheart.*

Though he'd used the endearment with her before, somehow

writing it down made it official. Abby was his sweetheart in every way, and he wanted her to know it.

Securing a reservation at Portia's downtown for a Friday night took weeks if not months, according to his colleagues. If not for Shelby, he'd be up a creek without a paddle, snakes and all. Unbeknownst to him, the owner was her son, Franklin. After working the food scene in New York for the last decade, he'd moved back home to be closer to his parents following his father's health scare the previous year. With his years of experience, Franklin had decided to start his own restaurant, a favorite with locals and as far away as Montgomery.

"Heard everyone talkin' about your date. Franklin would be more than happy to find a spot for you."

"Thank you, Shelby. Once again, I owe you. Just let me know what I can do for you and George. Gran's pie, a little carpentry, my firstborn…all of it is yours."

"Keep your firstborn; I can barely handle you, let alone a mini-Dixon. Must be someone special if you're going to such lengths."

Said casually, Matt knew she was actually asking *whom* he'd be going to dinner with.

"As a matter of fact, she is. Her name is Abby Hart, and her aunt owns The Christmas Tea Shoppe in Homily."

"Oh, I know Sara. She's on the town's business advisory board. In fact, she's part of the reason why they approved Franklin's application. I believe her exact words were, 'His concept is the wave of the future, and innovation is the key to a thriving downtown.'"

Matt said, "Sara is certainly a force to be reckoned with when she makes up her mind about something. Kind of like her niece. Those two don't do anything halfway."

"Then I wish you the best of luck winning her hand. A good woman is worth more than rubies, and a wise man knows how to appreciate the treasure she is."

Without a word goodbye, Shelby turned on her heel and headed for the phone at the registration desk, where Matt assumed she would make the reservation for his date in her usual brisk fashion.

It was simply one more example of the generosity displayed by folk in Homily, rooting for one of their own and providing what they had to offer. On the flip side, everyone within a five-mile radius, including so and so's third cousin, would know he and Abby were dining together at Portia's. After which, phones across the county would ring again with the details of what she wore, and whether or not he'd been able to make her laugh before dessert was served.

Twenty

Dear Sunshine,

My knitting hobby finally perished just like all the others. I wonder if all women search to fill their empty nest with new activities only to realize what they're really hoping to find is themselves. And though I've sorted myself out once more, I miss the gift you gave me so long ago. Love you, to the stars and back.

Always, Sissy

Abby

Abby flopped onto her bed. She'd been through her closet and dresser twice. The same clothes took up residence in the crammed space, her wishful thinking doing little to change the available options for her date. She let out a defeated sigh, picked her phone up from the nightstand, and tapped out Maggie's number.

"Girlfriend," drawled her best friend on the other end of the line before Abby could say hello. "You've been holding out on me. For weeks you've left these sad messages on my phone and played phone tag like it's an actual game. Then just this morning I told Tuck you were going to call me for dating advice. Now I can totally forgive you for acting like a mop of a friend if you confirm your date is with Matt Dixon."

Mags referred to her uncanny ability to know things before they happened as her extra superpower, but Abby called it friendly intuition. Still, Aunt Sara said folk might consider it a gift of the Holy Spirit.

"Gifts are either embraced, tempered, or ignored all together, depending on the church. Personally, I like to think God is capable of anything. He created the universe, so why not superpowers for his people," she'd said with dainty shrug.

Abby reeled herself back into the present conversation and said, "Of course it's with Matt. You don't think I'd be going out with anyone else when I've been so miserable without him."

"Sweetie pie, while I expect you to spill every last detail I missed, especially the making up part, right now all you need to know is LBD."

"LBD?" Abby asked, thoroughly confused.

"What am I going to do with you?!" Abby could picture the flustered gestures her best friend was making, even with a thousand miles between them. "Repeat after me: Little. Black. Dress."

"Um…" By Abby's calculation, Friday night had taken its sweet time arriving, but it appeared she was no better prepared now than when she'd agreed to the date.

"Wait. Don't even tell me. Cheese and crackers! You don't own one. That's why you don't know what those three very precious letters stand for. How can you claim to be a woman, let alone a southern one, and not own that one article of clothing?"

Abby didn't know whether to be ashamed for her lack of fashion sense or bust a seam over Maggie's obvious horror.

"It's okay, Abs. I've got this. I'll call my sister. She lives in town—"

"I know, Reese comes into the shop at least once a week these days. We carry her favorite ginger tea. Oh, and I saw Liv last week when she was in town visiting your folks. She said to tell you you're on her list for not calling her back. Looks like I'm not the only one in trouble."

"Ah, that's sweet honey. Now stop distracting me. We can fix this little blunder and still have you ready in time for your date with Doctor Hotstuff. You and sissy are roughly the same size and build. Lucky for you she didn't get my large—"

"I get the point, Mags. Just tell her to hurry."

"Done. Love ya!"

"Love you too." Leave it to Mags to put her in her place and solve her problem all in the course of one conversation. Thank God for best friends—and their sisters, it would seem.

The doorbell rang twenty minutes later, just as Abby finished the smokey look she'd applied to her eyelids after watching several YouTube tutorials. The eyeliner was a bit dicey but, overall, she thought she would pass muster. That is, until she opened the door to see Maggie's very elegant and put-together sister standing on the other side, the beginnings of a small baby bump visible under her stylish clothes and in her glowing cheeks. On second thought, she probably looked more like she had two black eyes.

"Come on in, Reese. Thank you for coming over on such short notice. I don't know what I'd be wearing tonight if Mags hadn't called for reinforcements. Probably a burlap sack." She laughed with self-deprecation, but the look on Reese's face assured her it was warranted. Desperation coated her tongue.

"If you can make me look half as good as you do right now, I'll give you free tea for life."

Abby said it with so much sincerity Reese laughed out loud. The sound was light, airy, and matched the Chanel No. 5 she wore. "Maggie always did say you were dramatic, but without a penchant for center stage. I think I finally understand what she meant. Now, let's see what we can do to help you feel more like the beautiful woman you already are."

Her raccoon eyes wide with disbelief, Abby countered the other woman's confident smile with a look of utter doubt.

Reese ignored her, took Abby's arm, and tugged her in the direction of the stairs. "Don't worry, honey; it's nothing a little Pond's cold cream, a light touch, and bronzer can't fix."

Matt

When Abby answered the door, he seriously considered staying in instead of going out.

He finally stammered out a compliment shortly before they arrived, no doubt looking as dumbfounded as he felt. Matt hoped his ability to speak and be charming would reassert itself over dinner. Seeing Abby dressed to the nines was worth any amount spent on flowers for Shelby the following week.

Matt placed his left hand on Abby's lower back while reaching to open the screen door for her. The critics cited the restaurant as "a beautiful fusion of old and new in both its design and menu." The article went on to mention a farm-to-table concept, with most of the food being locally sourced. He let his eyes wander over the space and plates in front of diners and found the description from this month's *New Around Town* publication to be an accurate one.

Most of the walls were exposed brick with a high ceiling of dark wood beams that formed a crisscross pattern overhead. Taking up the far back wall was an open concept kitchen; crates and baskets took up rows of wood shelving which held loaves of bread, fresh fruit, and vegetables. A metal spiral staircase led down to what could only be a cellar, sporting a sign on the wall beside it with the word "Restrooms" on it, followed by an arrow. The wooden stairs above it led to another seating area overlooking the main dining room.

After giving his name to the hostess, they were escorted upstairs, much to Matt's surprise. Filled with plush leather couches and chairs, the space could be rented for private parties. Abby's hips swayed in front of him as they climbed the stairs, and he tried not to pay attention to how the little black number she wore hugged her curves in all the right places. Franklin stood at the top of the stairs and introduced himself to Matt with a handshake.

"Mama took the liberty of ordering hors d'oeuvres and drinks for y'all, thinking you might enjoy the quiet here. Heads up, though; the cocktails are the real deal. We share a basement hallway with Desk Set Cocktail Club and provide small eats for their menu while they create fancy drinks for ours. It allows each of us to do what we do best but reach more customers."

"Sounds great. And thanks again for the reservation on such short notice."

"No thanks needed. Always happy to help out one of Mama's colleagues," Franklin said and gave Abby a quick dip of his head.

"I'm honored to be one. Shelby keeps me in line and out of trouble, for the most part."

Franklin chuckled lightly. "Mama can be a handful sometimes. Thank goodness for books. They've saved me from her wrath once or twice."

"Books, not flowers?" Matt asked, to clarify.

"Oh no, she likes flowers too. Irises are her favorite. I only give her books when I need to pull out all the stops. Forgotten dates and the like."

"Which authors?" Matt asked on the chance he screwed up majorly in the near future.

"Her current library favorites are Edward P. Jones and Diane McKinney-Whetstone, but she reads the complete works of Jane Austen at least once every few years." With a shake of his head he said, "Mama says it's best to come at life from all sides. According to her, the world through your own window offers a narrow view, and books provide a wider lens."

"Sounds like your mama is a very smart woman," said Abby.

"Smartest woman I know, and she never lets me forget it," Franklin smiled tightly.

Sensing his tension around the subject, Matt lightly added, "No doubt about it; she makes the rest of us at the hospital look like slackers."

"I think I need to meet your mama, Franklin, if only to meet the woman who keeps so many men on their toes. Aunt Sara asked me to say hello and tell you she'll see you at next week's business advisory board meeting."

Franklin latched on to Abby's words, visibly grateful. "Tell her I'll be there, and I've got those spreadsheets she requested."

"Will do. Between you and me, I think she's relieved to hand over her responsibilities as board treasurer."

"I'll endeavor to be worthy of her confidence. Let me know when you're ready for dinner. Then y'all can decide if you'd like to stay here or move to a table downstairs." A genuine smile lit up Franklin's face as he bounced down the rough-cut stairs stained in the same dark patina as the wide boards throughout the restaurant.

Abby seated herself on a couch, taking in the sight of diners below with food-laden plates and various drinks. It would seem they both enjoyed people watching, though his favorite person to watch was her. She invited him to sit next to her, the smile on her face demure and engaging all at once.

"I've never been here before," she said.

"Neither have I, though my colleagues have been talking about it since it opened."

"Well, it would seem you have friends in high places then, because I've heard it can take months to get a reservation here."

"Shelby is one of the charge nurses on the pediatric floor, and her husband George helps out around Gran's place on occasion. In fact, he jumped in to help with her plumbing a little while back and refused to take payment after spending an entire weekend working on it. They're generous people, and I count myself lucky to have them in my life."

"Sometimes it's easy to forget how fortunate we are to live in a place where people help each other without the expectation of anything in return."

Matt released an internal sigh and the thought he'd been wrestling with since he and Abby reconciled. "All of my happiest memories in life are associated with Homily. Don't get me wrong, no place is perfect, but leaving a place for a while can give a person perspective and help them appreciate what they left behind."

"Maybe," she conceded. "For a long time, I only ever wanted to leave, and I probably wouldn't have come back if things had worked out—" Abby stopped the rest of the words from slipping off her tongue and withdrew her hand from his.

Matt reached for the bourbon cocktail on the side table to his left. It was warm in his throat but light on his tongue with a tangy citrus after taste. He forced himself to slow down even though the topic of conversation encouraged the opposite.

Abby tried to delay the inevitable by reaching for a mushroom stuffed with bacon and gruyère cheese, and practically whimpered over the taste.

Matt ignored the jealous twinge in his heart, reminding himself that Abby was here with him. He smiled at her reaction to the food while reaching for a slice of brie with chutney and prosciutto. Agreeing with her sentiment, he added a spiced almond to the mix when he caught her smirk. So maybe he was humming out loud.

"I won't apologize for singing over the food. It deserves the accolade."

Abby giggled and said, "You're right; it does. Besides, you have a nice voice."

"Thank you, sweetheart, but don't expect a serenade any time soon."

"Oh really, and why is that? Am I not deserving of a song or two?"

"I'd lasso the moon for you if I could, gorgeous. Nope. The sad fact of the matter is I sound better in a group. I wouldn't want to scare you off." Matt winked and added, "But I have rhythm like Fred Astaire. We can go dancing anytime you want to, Ginger Rogers."

"Slow dancing doesn't count. Anyone can sway."

"True, but I'm talking about real dancing. I can ballroom, swing, two step, and line dance."

"Are you trying to impress me, Doctor Dixon?"

He chuckled, swallowed the bite in his mouth, and replied, "Not really. My salsa is atrocious, but I was one of two escorts to the daughter of a family friend at her debutante ball. The experience was more fascinating than I was impressive."

"From a historical perspective or as a gentleman?"

Abby already knew him well, making him smile as he answered, "Both, but personally, I think it's an antiquated tradition built on a patriarchal system."

"I agree," she said, seeming pleased with his answer. "The fact that they're exclusive to wealth and social status just rubs me the wrong way. And maybe the idea of being introduced to potential suitors for those reasons feels a little like a woman's value is in who her family is," she added somberly, as though it had touched a nerve.

"I much prefer a quinceañera or bar mitzvah," he replied lightly.

"So, you like birthday parties?

"Yes, though I'm more interested in what we were talking about before you so aptly sidetracked me."

"What were we talking about before?" she asked, feigning ignorance.

"How you only ever wanted to leave Homily." Matt's heart stuttered a bit at the thought, and the implication she would have stayed gone if she had married her ex.

"Oh, that. Nothing really. Homily is like most small towns... quaint, charming, nosey. You know what I mean."

"Yes, but I also know everyone in town respects your aunt and The Christmas Tea Shoppe is a successful business. One the people in town speak highly of."

"I know. It's just, well, Aunt Sara's not my mama, and this town never lets me forget that."

Matt wasn't sure how Abby's mama fit into the equation, but at least they were talking about her. Slowly treading into uncharted waters, he asked, "Sweetheart, what exactly happened to your mama?"

Abby wrung her hands together and looked at her lap. "I don't know. She gave me to Aunt Sara when I was four. I think she signed away her rights."

"Is she still living?" he asked, not daring to bring up her father in the same question. The man obviously wasn't around now, and if what she'd said about her mother was true, he probably never was. It was a situation Matt couldn't fathom; the idea of a man not taking care of his child or the woman who'd given him such an incredible gift.

When she didn't answer, he circled back. "You mentioned the town gossip mill. Have people ever said anything unkind to you about your mama?"

He almost vibrated with adrenaline, prepared to fight her battles if it meant she'd stay in Homily. Abby was more than capable of defending herself, but sometimes it was important to know who stood in your corner.

"No," she shrugged. "It's more like a feeling I get sometimes. I think she disappointed them, and they're waiting for me to do the same. Most of my memories from back then are…unclear. But as far as I know, Aunt Sara never told anyone why I came to live with her. I don't even know the full story, but I don't know if she's protecting me or her sister."

"If your mama disappointed folks, it's up to her to right that wrong Abby, not you. You aren't responsible for her choices."

"I know, but I can't help wondering what if they're right and I'm just like her? What if I disappear when things get hard? What if my mama left because she knew I wasn't worth stickin' around for?" She whispered the last question while tears pooled in her eyes.

Matt drew her into his arms and handed her the handkerchief tucked into the breast pocket of his blazer, only able to offer small comfort for hurts that ran so deep and long they might be impossible to overcome.

"Those are a lot of what ifs, sweetheart."

She left his embrace still dabbing at her cheeks and excused herself to the restroom to powder her nose. Matt stared after her soberly. There was nothing like making the woman you cared about cry, in public no less, to make a man feel helpless. He only hoped they had come far enough in their relationship for her to stick around this time.

Twenty One

Dear Sunshine,

Our girl is dating some boy whose family has a horse farm in Virginia. She says he's a good man and comes from a nice family. I miss her, but I understand she needs to spread her wings and fly. Meanwhile, the shop could use a face lift, but I'm not sure what direction to take it, or who I'll upset if I do. I wonder when being comfortable became more acceptable than being brave. Love you, to the stars and back.

Always, Sissy

Abby

Abby pulled out her cell phone as soon as the bathroom door shut behind her.

"Mags, it's me. Call me when you get this. I just made the biggest fool of myself, and only you can make it better."

Abby grabbed a few tissues from her borrowed clutch, along with a tube of lipstick Aunt Sara had forced on her for the evening. While wiping the mascara beneath her eyes, her phone began to vibrate with a call.

"Thank goodness—"

"I'm pretty sure only chocolate makes everything better, but I'll do my best to stand in the gap. First off, where is Doctor Hotstuff?"

"Upstairs in the restaurant."

"Where are you?"

"Downstairs in the ladies room."

"Okay, we'll make this the quick 'n dirty version of kiss and tell."

"Mags! I did not call for quick 'n dirty anything." Abby did her best to sound shocked, only to chortle with a snort thrown in for good measure.

"No, but you *are* laughing. I think my job here is done."

"Wait, no it's not," Abby said and rushed headlong into the details. "I cried in front of Matt after spilling my guts about my mama." Just the thought of it had humiliation filling her veins again.

"Honey, it can't be that bad. You don't actually know very much about your mama. Mostly, you have a lot of worries, none of which are concrete. The biggest question is how did he handle your tears?"

"He held me and let me blubber all over him."

"And after?"

"He pretty much said the same thing you did."

"I knew I liked that man. Now, how's your face?"

"A little worse for wear," Abby hedged.

"I can't help you if you're not honest. Are we talking a little touch up?"

"Worse." Abby's shoulders slumped as she assessed her reflection once more. "I look like the crazy guy from that one movie. You know, the one with green hair and clown paint. Unattractive is an understatement."

"I am so going to lay into Reese. She knows better even if you don't. Only waterproof mascara is acceptable for all situations."

"In all fairness to your sister, she probably didn't expect me to cry on my date tonight."

"True, but I think it's the pregnancy hormones. They poke holes in a woman's brain like Swiss cheese. The brain cells fall right through."

Abby started to laugh again.

"It's official, I can quit my day job and become a standup comedian. Now, once you have yourself under control, remove as much of the damage as feasible with a light hand. You don't want to look like a tomato afterward. Blend whatever is left—again, lightly—then slather on a fresh coat of lipstick."

Abby looked back at the mirror, cringed over the pitiful portrait she made, and started removing the mask around her eyes.

"Okay, I can do this."

"Of course, you can. We are B-A-B-S-W."

"Do I even want to know what that stands for?

"You're hopeless. Born and bred southern women. We kick A-S—"

"I get the point, Mags!" Abby shouted with more humor than exasperation.

"Good, now go have some fun with the sexy doctor. Love you, sweetie."

"Love you too, Mags."

....

In spite of her earlier breakdown, the rest of the evening was rather enjoyable. After Abby returned, they finished a lovely meal in the main dining room. The creole crab cakes were a perfect blend of spicy seafood spread over a bed of greens topped with a poached egg and a side of grits, but the venison medallions in cherry compote with Yukon gold mashed potatoes and petite green beans stole the show.

Contentment brought on by good food and even better company saturated the air as they walked hand in hand toward a bench near the playground in the square. "That meal was Facebook worthy. I can't believe I ate so much," Abby said, tempted to run her hand over her stomach.

"I don't post much on social media, but the food was amazing. Shelby told me half the menu comes from her great, great Grandmother Portia's recipes, updated and passed from one generation to the next since emancipation."

"Now the name of the restaurant makes sense," Abby said thoughtfully. "What a beautiful way for Franklin to commemorate his kin and celebrate resiliency."

"Shelby mentioned the transition from New York back home has been a difficult one for Franklin."

"Then I'm especially glad for his success."

"Me too. Anyway, I planned to take you out for ice cream after dinner, but I have to admit I'm too full. Any chance I can get a rain check for tomorrow afternoon?" asked Matt with a hopeful expression.

"I'd like that. You're not at the hospital tomorrow?"

"I am, but it's an early shift."

"Oh, I see how it is," said Abby and poked him in the ribs. "You don't want to stay out late because you have to be up early. What was it you said the other night? Oh yes, just like the old folks."

Hanging his head in mock defeat he returned her playful banter, "You are never going to let me forget that are you?"

"Probably not, but if you buy me as many scoops as I want tomorrow, I might not tell your gran."

"Deal," Matt said, but instead of reaching for her extended hand he leaned into her space and said, "Let's kiss on it."

She didn't think twice and let him pull her in for a kiss which quickly became a few more, the feel of his lips on hers at once smooth and hard.

Abby assumed they were just getting started when Matt gently pulled away, entwined his fingers with hers, and led them to the swings. She toed off her heels and took a seat on the swing next to his, allowing the gentle breeze created by the up and down motion to cool the fever left on her skin from their somewhat public make out session. Her eyes traveled over her handsome date, who wore a suit the same way he did everything: with complete ease.

"Let's see who jumps first," Abby suggested feeling carefree and brave. "Winner gets another kiss."

Matt smiled until his dimple came out and a full grin spread across his face. She beamed in return as they both pumped their legs until soaring through the air in a giant leap toward the ground. Anyone watching would have called it a draw, not that it mattered. As far as kisses went, Abby knew she'd won.

....

With blue skies and sunshine as far as the eye could see, the last week of August arrived in typical fashion, as the end of summer and a slight pause before fall. Abby practically skipped to the shop, looking forward to her time with Matt on the porch after his shift. On second thought, it was going to be a long eight hours until she saw him. Business was steady but winding down as school began, families returned to routines, and vacationers went back to work.

Around noon, a delivery of flowers wrapped in brown paper and twine came in from Flora 'n Fauna, located on the corner of Oak and Second Street, across from the donut shop and a bridal boutique. A combined flower and pet shop, it was rumored the owner, a great nephew of the Michaelson twins, had named the store in honor of his aunts. Or rather, maybe to annoy them.

Oohs and titters from patrons filled the shop with a great deal of speculation over the arrangement and who it could possibly be from. As if everyone within fifty miles of town didn't know. Abby rolled her eyes and bit her bottom lip as she read the attached notecard written in Matt's atrocious script.

Happy one and a half months, sweetheart. Let's play a little game. Start with, "He likes me…"

A cheeky grin spreading across her face, Abby knew how the game would end but played it all the same. She pulled the string attached to a single petal and hummed to herself, lighting up the entire shop with her happiness. They had fallen into an easy pattern of stolen moments at Bean, late afternoons at the beach, and a night out whenever Matt wasn't on a late shift. They spent as much of their free time together as possible. She'd even started running with him on occasion. He kept up a steady stream of chatter while she sucked wind and tried to keep up, but she treasured every moment regardless of sore muscles and a pesky side cramp.

Abby feared she was falling in love for real, the kind where she held her breath between dates and her stomach dropped whenever she saw him. The rollercoaster was thrilling and terrifying, simultaneously making her want to yell in exhilaration and puke.

Whoo-hoo! Blech.

With Matt at her side, she became more involved in the goings on in town, even if her aunt said it had more to do with her choice to be an active participant than anything else. Though she agreed, Abby wasn't silly enough to ignore the positive way he contributed to her confidence. He sought her opinion on matters with colleagues and family, and encouraged her decisions rather than telling her what he would do. She felt fearless next to him, like Joan of Arc, wielding a spatula and tea bags, fiercely caring for the shop and those who entered its peaceful confines.

With a secret smile, she stashed her feelings close to her heart and placed the bundle of white daisies in a vase to display prominently on the front counter, along with the small changes she'd made in the shop for the start of the school year.

Tiny pencils, apples, and books hung from the tree with a garland made from brightly colored construction paper rings. Backpacks were placed under the tree in lieu of gifts, where folks donated school supplies for children whose families might not be able to afford them. When one was full, an empty one took its place, only to be filled before Abby could blink. Delivering the supplies to the district office for distribution had become a weekly occurrence, and Homily's generosity only continued to grow, shoes of varying sizes and basic toiletries finding their way beneath the tree anonymously.

As Dot Hanson had pointed out on her weekly visit, children grow so fast they're always in need of something.

"When we give to them, we take care of our future."

Being part of something so meaningful gave Abby a deep satisfaction.

Maybe it's good to be home, no matter what the future holds.

....

The middle of September strolled in with cooler temperatures and a meeting Abby had deliberately tiptoed around for months. But the Michaelsons were persistent, if not impatient. She sat with them on either side of her, a polished silver tea set the demarcation line between them.

"Miss Florence, can I get you another sandwich or more shortbread?" Abby asked, politely. She'd pulled out her most traditional offerings for their teatime.

"No, thank you, Abby. I see you share your aunt's relish for new additions," said Florence.

Similar to the awning, they were not fans of the changes within the shop. Apparently not everyone thought twigs tied with burlap and layered with apples, pears, and nuts made for appropriate trappings in early fall.

"Yes ma'am, but I'm not sure I understand why the new awning is so…unpopular with Homily's Historical Preservation Society. The building's structure remains the same and there was an awning before this one," Abby explained, trying to hold her frustration in check.

"But the old awning was burgundy with gold lettering," said Faunella sternly.

"It was tasteful and didn't stand out. The one Sara replaced it with is green and white striped," jumped in Florence.

"In short, it stands out like a sore thumb."

"With all due respect, Miss Faunella, standing out was Aunt Sara's point. She moved the gold lettering to the center of the window to better showcase the shop's name and replaced the awning with one that would stand out more, hoping to draw attention and therefore business."

"Still, the burgundy blended better with the brick," said the twins in synchronous harmony.

Abby tucked the annoying curl within her line of sight behind her ear, folded her hands demurely, and channeled her aunt's pragmatism.

"I understand your disappointment, and perhaps Aunt Sara should have run her idea by the society first, but I assure you she never intended any disrespect. She knows how hard HHPS works to make sure the history of Homily is remembered," she implored, pulling in another calming breath. "However, I think the awning actually makes the architecture stand tall. The last swallowed the classic elegance of the building, whereas this one allows it to shine."

"Different but better?" asked Florence, uncertainly.

Abby ran for the finish line. "Absolutely. Similar to you and Miss Faunella. Clearly two individuals, but one in purpose, championing history in all its tarnished glory." Oops. She may have gone too far with the last bit.

"Well, isn't that what we've been saying all this time?"

"So, it's settled then: the association will approve the new awning's addition to the building?" asked Abby to clarify the outcome.

"Of course, dear. Every grand dame needs a makeover every now and then. Come Florence, our work here is done."

Phew. Abby swiped anxiously at her hairline and the sweat that had gathered there. Aunt Sara's advice from the night before came back to her. "A butterfly spends most of its life becoming something new. People are the same, except we fear change. Listen and be gracious. You'll always catch more flies with honey than vinegar."

....

Abby threw her hands in the air. Of course, Matt thought the entire conversation was hysterical until his gran turned to him and gave him the same lecture. He took Abby's hand in his under the table and replied, "We're all on the same page, Gran, but it's important that we spend time with y'all too."

Matt and Abby were having afternoon tea together with his gran and Aunt Sara at Nancy's house after church. Apparently, Aunt Sara and Nancy felt the need for an intervention. According to the two women, the couple was still far too occupied in keeping their elderly relatives' company instead of using all of their free time, which was hard to come by, to hang out with each other.

"Perfect. Then you won't mind if Sara and I arrange to have another dinner in a couple of weeks, after you've spent more time with each other than you do us."

While Matt and Nancy worked out the date around his hospital schedule, Abby whispered in her aunt's ear. "His gran is pretty great, isn't she? It's not surprising y'all have become fast friends."

"Can you blame us? It's the only way we stay in the loop. Besides, she's got spunk."

"According to Matt, she's got it in spades. She informed him yesterday that if he didn't quit spending time at home fussin' over her then he would need to find a new place to live. She's not getting any younger and she'd like great-grandbabies soon. I almost died when Matt relayed their conversation," said Abby, fanning her beet-red face at the memory. Matt and babies in the same sentence made her ovaries tingle.

"See? Spunk, just like I said."

"You like her because she reminds you of yourself," Abby responded with an astute look.

"Maybe, sassy britches."

"Matt said he'll probably work Halloween, but he's already asked for Thanksgiving off. His mama is coming here this year. Her husband has a business trip that weekend and Matt doesn't want to leave Nancy alone. Since his daddy goes hunting for the holiday, it works out for everyone."

"And explains why we received an invitation already," said Aunt Sara.

"Matt mentioned Nancy was going to extend one. What do you think?"

"I think we'll bring twice-baked sweet potatoes and Nana's streusel apple pie. And that boy is more than smitten if he's ready to introduce you to his mama."

"You really think so?"

"Yes, sugar, I do. What about you? Are you as crazy about him?"

"I am, though it scares me. I feel like I'm teetering on a tightrope, waiting for someone to cut the rope out from under me."

Aunt Sara gave her knee a gentle squeeze. "If this is about your mama again, we can talk about her whenever you're ready."

And there it was, the manatee in the room. Why would Aunt Sara bring it up now, of all moments. Abby hated those letters she'd found. They'd made her mama a real entity, filled with breath and a soul so that she could no longer ignore her or the memories from before Aunt Sara.

Abby blanched and promptly turned back to the conversation at the table. She watched from the corner of her eye, until Matt slid his arm around her with a dimpled smile and kissed the top of her head. Yep, she was definitely more than smitten.

Every action and word spoke volumes, but Matt hadn't brought up her mama since their dinner at Portia's, and she had decided it was better to leave the topic alone. If her mama didn't want her, then there was no reason to involve her in Abby's other relationships.

Matt

Halloween in Homily was more treat than trick, but the emergency room became busier as the night wore on. Food allergies, alcohol, and costume-related injuries were just a few of the accidents to come through the hospital's doors. Glancing at his watch, Matt jogged to his truck in the parking garage. If he hurried, he could make the end of Safe Sweets on the Square and steal a kiss from his girl, before the inevitable late-night gore fest of drunken crashes, alcohol poisoning, and weapons gone wrong.

The line of families wound in and out of business doorways downtown where bats, spiders, and cotton cobwebs hung from lamp posts or awnings. A small hay maze set up on one side of the square corralled a group of small superheroes, zombies, and various

Harry Potter characters while exhausted parents counted down to bedtime. Folks blew on hot cider steaming from paper cups, and volunteers dashed to grab children bobbing for apples before they toppled headlong into the fountain.

"Dr. Dixon, it's good to see you out for the festivities," waved the mayor as he sprinted from one station to the next to offer a hand.

"Yoo-hoo, Dr. Dixon," tootled the Michaelson twins from a bench by the playground. Dressed in identical costumes, they vividly resembled a scene from a horror movie. He flashed an amused smile and replied, "Good evening, ladies."

"Hi, Dr. Dixon," said a tiny voice as she hopscotched by him in a tiara and layers of tulle, her memaw shuffling up behind her.

"Well, if it isn't two of my favorite people," he said, offering his arm to Dot. "How's the candy hunt going?"

"Pretty good, so far. My pillowcase is half full. We're goin' to the tea shop. Wanna come?"

"Course he does, child. He's Miss Abby's sweetheart," Dot said in a superior tone, causing Bella to giggle.

"Yes, ma'am. I'm signed, sealed, delivered, and hers," he quoted from the old song.

Abby stood in the doorway of The Christmas Tea Shoppe wearing a Goldilocks costume, with a teddy bear attached to her white, frilly apron, and tossing caramels into the bags thrust before her every three seconds. She smiled for each child, wishing them a spooky Hallows' Eve, and Matt waited for her to greet the new arrivals as he stepped up next to her.

"Mrs. Hanson, Bella, I'm so glad to see y'all out tonight. Hmm, let me see, are you a princess?" she asked the little girl, a sparkle in her eyes.

"Mm-hmm. But I bet you can't guess who," taunted Bella.

"Well, let's see if your costume gives me any clues. A tiara, a gold dress, and…is that book in your other hand?"

"Yes, ma'am."

"Hmm. Think, think, think. Are you a pirate princess?"

"No silly, then I'd have a funny hat, and say things like, 'Awgh, me hotties!'"

"I think you mean, 'Argh, me *hearties*!'" said Matt in a rather decent impression of a pirate.

Bella giggled. "Come on Miss Abby, you can do it!"

"I don't know," she said, pretending to think hard again. "Are you Belle from *Beauty and the Beast?*"

"Yep! 'Cause she's a worrier princess," the little girl stated emphatically.

"You mean a warrior princess?" asked Abby.

"Thass what I says. Belle's real smart cause she reads all the time, and Memaw says a sharp mind is the best kinda weapon to have."

With those parting words of wisdom, she skipped away before Matt could blink, Dot's hips swaying in a wide berth behind her.

"And what, pray tell, are you?" asked Abby, straight faced.

"Impressive?" he teased, looking down at the white coat he'd forgotten to leave in his truck.

Her laugh was low and sensuous. "Nope, but you're all mine."

"Say it again."

"You are all mine," she complied and placed her hand on his chest, moving in closer.

A growl rumbled from his throat as he pulled her in, hungry for the taste of her lips. He'd never get enough of her sassy mouth.

Someone coughed discreetly at a short distance, and like a bucket of ice water thrown on them, the spell was broken. Abby blushed profusely for the kids giggling at them with open sacks while Matt preened beside her like a puffed-up rooster.

"I think caramel is my new favorite flavor," he commented and watched the pink creep back into her cheeks. He chuckled when she swatted his chest as though he was a pesky no-see-um.

"Good, because your lips are my new favorite, no matter the flavor."

"Lord have mercy, woman; if you keep saying things like that, I'm going to embarrass us both. My self-control is hanging by a thread, gorgeous."

"Good, now you know how I feel 24/7," she flirted, a hand fanning her warm face.

If he didn't change the subject soon, the gentleman he was would be lost to the inner caveman begging to stake a claim.

Me, caveman. Girl, mine.

He shook his head to clear it and hooked a thumb over his shoulder, saying, "The shop looks great."

"Thanks, I was going for old school Halloween."

Candy corn garlands encircled the tree with Frankensteins and vampires hung from its evergreen limbs. Cobwebs covered the front of the fireplace alongside spiders, and a stuffed black cat kept watch over the room next to jack-o'-lanterns in every shape and size. Pumpkin lanterns hugged the windows and bathed the doorway in a soft glow, casting the room in eerie shadows for the evening.

"On second thought, we should step inside to further investigate your decorating prow—"

His beeper went off, effectively cutting their time short.

"The ER calls. Probably only a few peanut allergies this early, but it won't be long before it really picks up."

Abby leaned in close, chastely pecking his cheek and then his lips. "Stay safe, handsome."

"Always. I'll text after I get home," he said lifting her hand to kiss the inside of her wrist, watching a shiver glide over her skin. "Hold onto that thought, sweetheart," he said with a wink.

Twenty
Two

Dear Sunshine,

Maggie is getting married. Though Abby is happy for her, I think she feels like an unmoored boat now that her best friend has roots in the Virginia soil. Our girl is still dating the stable boy, and an engagement feels imminent. I want her happiness more than I want my next breath, and yet I fear she's more in love with the idea than the man. No one likes being left behind. Love you, to the stars and back.

Always, Sissy

Matt

With Halloween a distant memory and Thanksgiving around the corner, the morning's forecast had caught everyone on the Gulf by surprise, including the weatherman, it would seem. Matt drove toward downtown Homily, the windshield wipers on his truck working double time to combat the rain.

The weather had turned from blue skies to a raging tropical storm overnight. Thankfully, he'd remembered to throw sandbags in the back of his truck before leaving for the hospital in the early hours of this morning. Certain a quick prayer and those bags were the only thing keeping him from fishtailing, he tried to focus on the road in front of him instead of worrying about Abby.

Two text messages and a voicemail had all gone unanswered, so instead of heading home after his shift he'd called Gran to let her know where he was headed. She tried to reassure him the Hart women were probably taking care of things at the shop. A dry summer and an even drier fall had lulled everyone into believing they'd come away from hurricane season unscathed.

Gran's house sat far enough inland and high enough off the ground that he knew she would weather the storm fine. Unless the weather made a turn for the worse and everyone evacuated, he planned for her to sit tight.

Matt pulled into a spot a block from The Christmas Tea Shoppe just as his phone rang. He quickly answered, thinking it might be Abby, only to hear his gran's voice on the other end.

"Matthew, I got a hold—Sara and she's on—way here."

Gran's voice cut in and out, but he got the gist of what she'd said. "I'm at the shop now. I'll help Abby finish up and then we'll head your way." Static crackled in his ear and the line went dead. Hoping she'd heard him, he stepped inside the shop and found Abby in the back, delving through a desk drawer.

"Hey, sweetheart!" he called. "I see the Homily Fire Department delivered sandbags to all the businesses. Fingers crossed; they'll help keep out some of the water."

Abby jumped at the sound of his voice and said, "Matthew Lee Dixon, you should know better than to sneak up on a woman like that."

He grinned and apologized, "Sorry, but I really wasn't all that quiet. What has you so engrossed in that drawer?"

"I'm looking for a hammer and nails. Hickam's is already closed, but I thought I should be prepared to board up the windows in case this storm turns."

"Sweetheart, I didn't see any of the other businesses boarded up. The last news report I heard on the radio said this nasty weather would head back out to sea by tomorrow morning. They expect heavy rains and wind, maybe flooding in some places, but not of the hurricane variety."

"I know, but it's my job to make sure the shop can weather anything," she replied while worrying at her bottom lip. Over the last few months, he had come to understand her little tells and the hidden emotions that came with them. His girl took her responsibilities seriously and he admired her all the more for it. He also knew how much the shop itself meant to Abby.

"Something tells me The Christmas Tea Shoppe can weather the worst of storms, thanks to its solid foundation. This building has endured worse things than this before. However, if we're going to make it out of here before the streets flood, we need to leave soon."

She let him take her hand and relinquished her fears in place of common sense.

"Aunt Sara called a half hour ago to say we should meet her at your place."

"Great minds think alike. We'll be further from the coast and far enough off the ground to avoid the flooding."

"Don't forget your gran's home cooking and cuddling up on the couch together in front of an old movie."

"Your wish is my command, and your chariot awaits." With a dramatic bow, Matt followed her to the front of the shop, where he almost plowed her over when she stopped abruptly in her tracks. The big picture window televised the torrential rain falling sideways in sheets, lashing everything in sight as the wind picked up speed over the Gulf. Water flowed over sidewalks and the streets resembled shallow rivers intent on returning to the sea. What had been hazardous had become impassable in the short time he'd been inside.

"Any chance your truck turns into a boat, because that is the only way we are going to make it anywhere other than here," said Abby with wry humor.

"Sadly, my truck is not a transformer and is probably going to flood if the waters keep rising."

"I'm sorry, babe."

"Me too, but I'm not sorry to be here with you." Ever the optimist he added, "At least we have tea and cake."

She deflated in disappointment.

With a nudge in the direction of the kitchen, Matt countered, "Let's bake first and then while the cake is in the oven we can curl up in front of the fireplace." *Because every situation is made better with creativity and making out, so long as you're with the right person.*

Abby's smile was pure sunshine on a cloudy day. "Deal," she pronounced, as she rose up onto her toes and wove her hands through his hair. "Let's kiss on it."

Abby

Abby wasn't sure how they went from making out in the kitchen to her crying and yelling. She could still hear the echo of it in her ears as she made her way home to Aunt Sara.

"Leave, Matt. Just leave. Please, I'm begging you."

"Sweetheart, I don't understand. What is the big deal? They're letters from your mama to her sister. How does that have anything to do with us?" He shook the equivalent of Pandora's box in his hand, straining to keep his voice calm as her own rose frantically.

Sobbing, she tried to catch her breath and hiccupped. "Everything. They have everything to do with us. Don't you get it? She gave me away because she didn't want me. Why didn't she want me?" she wailed the last words and Matt reached for her.

When she twisted away from him once more, he tried a different approach. "Baby, have you read the letters?" he asked softly as though she was a wounded animal. "It might not be as bad as you assume. Maybe she just couldn't be the mom you deserved."

He said the words reasonably and with such tender concern, Abby hated him as much as she loved him in that moment. The fine line between the two emotions ran like a drippy watercolor painting and all she wanted to do was lash out, to hurt him and make him feel the pain she was feeling as it clawed its way through her. She had been too much of a coward to read the letters or even ask her aunt about them. It was far easier to be ashamed of what she thought she knew than seek the truth. Better to believe a potential lie than to have her frail hope trampled upon.

"Please leave," Abby sighed, beginning to cry again.

"Abby, sweetheart, let's take a deep breath and step back from this for a minute. I'm sure we can work this—" he paused, shoving his hands through his hair in obvious frustration and searched for the right words to change her mind.

"There is no working through this! I don't want you here," she screamed before he could finish his thought.

The next time Abby told him to leave, he did.

She watched him walk away from her and crumpled to the floor. He'd done what she'd asked, just like she knew he would, because Matt would always do whatever she needed. Why had she expected for him to act any differently now? Why would he stay when she told him to go? She pulled her legs in tight, burying her face against her jeans as her whole body shook, painful sobs wracking her body.

The storm moved back out to sea sometime after midnight, leaving the shop eerily silent without the rain and wind pounding against the building. The place that had always been a refuge had become a tomb, absent of life.

Where Matt sat out the rest of the storm, Abby could only guess, but he was gone from the shop by the time she stumbled into the office the next morning, exhausted and emotionally wrung out. Sara had left multiple messages on her phone and the shop's voicemail, but the only one of any significance had been left by Matt the previous day.

She held the phone to her ear and bent over as her legs began to give out beneath her, anguish tearing through her body at the sound of his voice.

"Hey sweetheart, I'm on my way to the shop to pick you up. I love—"

The message from the previous day, before she had ruined everything, cut out, and she felt pain puncture her heart once more.

Her mama had broken the little girl she'd left behind, and now Abby had broken her relationship with Matt with her own callous words. Lon was right; she only left destruction in her wake.

Twenty Three

Dear Sunshine,

I've been feeling a little tired the last few weeks. I'm sure it's probably nothing, but I'll check in with my doctor soon. Our girl is finally coming home. She sounds heartsore, even if she thinks she can hide it. I wish she'd stop beating herself up over her broken engagement. Brunch Sunday after church? I'll come to you as usual. Love you, to the stars and back.

Always, Sissy

Sara

Sara waited on the porch stairs with a thick quilt beside her, surveying the damage to her yard and house. She'd caught a lift home with Officer Tooey, who was going door to door to check on folks, leaving her car stuck in two inches of mud at Nancy's until Matt had a chance to tow it out. Yesterday's storm had stripped the trees on her street and the flowers in her garden of any remaining foliage, depositing leaves and branches in soggy yards. Her porch swing hung askew, battered from high winds and debris, but perhaps the most distressing damage was the sight of Abby trudging up the walkway.

Though the waters had receded enough for Abby to walk home, it was obvious her girl had been through the wringer. Soaked from crown to pinky toe with tears, dirt, and rainwater, a look of utter devastation on her face, she more closely resembled the abused little girl from so long ago than the empowered woman she'd become. Sara stood up and opened her arms, waiting for her niece to step into them.

"Hush now, baby girl, it's going to be all right. Nothing a little tea can't fix right up, I'm sure," Sara whispered gruffly, pulling Abby into her safe embrace. She led her niece into the sunroom where she placed another heavy blanket on Abby's sodden lap.

"I don't think tea can fix it this time," she said, her teeth chattering with every word. "I told Matt to leave me alone and he actually listened. I think we broke up."

Abby began to cry in earnest again while Sara rubbed comforting circles on her back.

"I know, sugar. I was still at Nancy's when he got home early this morning. He looked like a dead man walking when he came in. Apparently, he spent the night in one of the dining room chairs at the shop. I guess he didn't want to go very far in case you changed your mind."

"Or he didn't want to wade out into the street," Abby muttered unkindly, a bitter aftertaste on her tongue.

With a hard look, Sara tried to temper her own words and failed. "I'm fairly certain he could have made it to the firehouse if he wanted to," she said with fierce determination. "Trust me when I say he stayed for you."

She left Abby to wallow in her blanket cocoon and went to put the kettle on. A cup of tea remedied most difficult situations in life, especially those of the relationship variety.

"Now, are you going to tell me what happened?" Sara called back into the room. But Abby stood in the doorway, holding a wooden box similar to the ones she kept her recipes in.

"I found this, that's what happened," she stated flatly, extending the item to Sara.

Sara took the box out of Abby's hand, wondering how she hadn't noticed it before, and lifted the lid. "How on earth could a recipe box cause so much—" she trailed off. Eyes wide over its contents she said, "I wondered if you'd find these."

"I discovered them a few months ago while I was searching for your hummingbird cake recipe."

Sara looked at Abby hopefully when she asked, "Did you read them?"

"They're not addressed to me."

"No, but most of them are about you in some fashion or another. I never intended to hide my relationship with your mama from you forever."

"Why didn't you tell me the two of you keep in touch? That my mother was alive? That you knew where she was and were talking to her?" she asked and accused all at once.

"It's a pathetic excuse, but at first, I didn't know how long Grace would write back. Our relationship was fragile and required... distance. The letters were initially brief, and she sent them to the shop instead of the house. Though she never asked me to hide them from you, I think she was afraid of what you might learn through them at the time."

"Obviously she didn't want me, or she wouldn't have given me away. If she loved me at all, she wouldn't have kept herself from me."

"That's not true, baby girl."

"Then why did she do it? I'm all grown up, so why hasn't she tried to see me?" Abby folded her arms across her chest in a protective manner.

"I'm afraid it's your mama's story to tell. Besides it's not like you went looking for her either, baby girl."

"Like that's ever going to happen." Angry and hurt, Abby's words came out sharp. "Are there other letters?" she asked pointedly.

Sara waded into the waters of truth cautiously. "Yes. We write to one another on a very regular basis. Though we also talk on the phone and meet up. She came to see me after my surgery. I hoped your paths would cross then, but when they didn't, I trusted the timing wasn't right."

Abby looked crestfallen, shocked, and bitter, all at the same time, but Sara needed her niece to understand the position she was in.

"Grace is my sister. I did what I thought was best at the time. Sugar, you were only four when you came to live with me. The more I brought her up, the more withdrawn you became. Regardless of how this all looks, I am sorry I hurt you. Being the chord that binds the two of you together hasn't exactly been easy for me either."

When Abby stayed silent, she pressed on, "I still don't see what the letters have to do with you and Matt breaking up."

"Those letters, it's everything about my past. Everything wrong. Everything hidden from me. Every single letter in the box is a time my mama could have reached out but didn't. Every single letter reminds me I wasn't wanted, and that I might be just like Mama. I don't have to read the letters; I know every single one is a reminder I'm not wanted by that woman. And look at my life; I've destroyed everything, like she did. I only hurt the people who love me," Abby sobbed. "Or worse, what if I hurt the people I love?"

"That's a bunch of nonsense if I ever heard it. You are not your mama, baby girl. And your mama isn't the same person she was back then. However, you are as stubborn, independent, and strong as the rest of the women in this family. Not to mention, smart as a whip and delightful to be around, most of the time."

Abby's lips wobbled at the last part, but she had stopped crying. Sara decided to take what she could get. "In case I wasn't direct enough the first time, what happened between you and Matt last night?"

"The streets were flooded so we decided to hunker down inside the shop for the night. Matt suggested we have tea and cake, only he wanted to bake one together. I went into the office to print the file I keep all of the recipes in and when I came back out Matt had that stupid box in his hands."

She glanced over to where it rested next to Aunt Sara on the counter and continued, "Matt said he found it in the back of the pantry, which is where I'd shoved it months ago. Then I accused him of being nosey and told him that he had no business snooping around the shop. He apologized but I wouldn't let it go. When I started to cry, he asked why the contents upset me so much. At first, he assumed they were hidden keepsakes from Lon, as if I could possibly have any feelings for him when I'm so clearly head over heels in love with Matt," she expelled with a heap of annoyance.

The kettle whistled in the pause, and while Sara prepared tea, Abby shuffled into the sunroom, blankets twisting further around her body.

A few minutes later, Sara pressed a warm teacup into Abby's cold hands and coaxed her niece on. "I'm almost positive you didn't declare your undying love and affection, otherwise we wouldn't be having this little tête-à-tête."

"No, but I did tell him about the contents of the box. After which I had a complete meltdown and told him we couldn't be together because he didn't know the real me. I tried to explain to him that I might be just like my mama and only capable of hurting people I'm supposed to care about. Then I told him to leave."

"And when he did, he was doing exactly what you expect of yourself, only you forced him to do it instead," said Sara, disappointed. "Sugar, that is unfair to him, and your mama. I can promise you Grace did what she thought would give you the best chance at a good life. Your mama paid the price for her actions twenty-five years ago. Now it's time for you to own up to yours," she said and kissed Abby's head.

Abby

Tremors shook Abby awake as they filled her limbs. Her pillow was soaked with sweat and tears, her heart in a hard gallop for an imaginary finish line. This was the third night in a row she'd had the dream. In every version of it, her mama tried to hide her from the man who yelled obscenities and stomped through a dirty house. Under the bed, in a closet, or the small space between the garbage cans by the back door, all while her mama picked a fight to distract him.

The words Aunt Sara used to comfort her with in the middle of the night when she was a child played on repeat in her head.

It's not real. You're safe. You're safe now.

She'd forgotten about the violence and uncertainty of her world before Aunt Sara came into her life.

"Mama, my tummy hurts. I'm hungwy."

"Shh. Be silent as a bunny, baby girl," her mama had slurred, curling her body around Abby's.

"Mama, wake up. Please, wake up," she'd pleaded, afraid.

Tonight's dream was different though. Matt had been waiting on the other side of the front door this time instead of the nice man in blue. He was calling for her, his hand outstretched and ready to whisk her away, but she'd turned from him to look for Mama.

Abby curled into a tight ball and let the empty ache in her heart swallow her body whole. She wanted to make things right with Matt, but she didn't know how to move forward while mired in her past. She avoided every opportunity to talk with Aunt Sara and still lacked the courage to read the letters double daring her from their place on the dresser. A coward, she let them hold her life hostage, in limbo. Unable to ignore the dream that had started with or without reading them, she lied to herself anyway.

Reading them will only make it worse. Better to let your demons lurk in the edges than fight them head on.

But with every day she ignored them, they came like thieves in the night to steal away her peace.

....

Morning arrived with bruises beneath her eyes, her face a mirror of how she felt. She dragged herself from bed anyway. Abby knew better than to hope she could mope her day away at home. She'd missed a week after her doomed road trip with Matt, but this was different. In the few days since they'd broken up, she'd made no attempt to right her wrong. Her soul hurt with missing him as much as her battered body did from rotten sleep. Incapable of giving him what he deserved, she punished herself for it mentally, and pushed herself physically.

Flipping the light switch on, she took in the shop properly outfitted for a Thanksgiving feast. Leaves twisted over and around every surface in a cornucopia of colors, the tree's branches weighed with food ornaments from turkey to green beans and pie, while boxes of canned goods waited to be picked up by the county shelter at lunchtime.

Business slowed to a crawl after the mid-morning caffeine break with preparations for family, friends, and a large meal on the forefront of everyone's thoughts. Abby closed the shop an hour early and headed home with the intention to crawl into bed. Aunt Sara had other plans.

"Oh good, you're home! We still have a lot to do tonight if we want to get the turkey in the oven by five a.m. tomorrow."

Abby dumped her coat over the stair rail and left her canvas shoes on the steps with her purse, her keys forgotten in the front door.

"Yippee," she replied without enthusiasm. "I'm really tired, Aunt Sara. I think I'm just going to go to bed."

Her aunt ignored her and started in with directions. "The deviled eggs need more of everything. Dust the top of them with a dash of paprika when you're done filling them."

"Yes, ma'am."

"How did it go at the shop today?"

"Fine."

"Are you ready to talk about your mama?"

"Nope."

"Fine, you can make the streusel apple pie and twice-baked sweet potatoes. I already made the cranberry sauce."

Abby sighed, weary. They were supposed to be having Thanksgiving dinner with Matt, his mom, and Nancy. Now it was just the two of them, which until recently had always been enough, but Matt had left a six-foot-tall hole in her life. Added to the Mama-shaped one she'd had most of her life, she didn't comprehend how her heart kept beating. A silent tear dropped into the yellow blob of mashed egg yolk with mayonnaise, mustard, and sweet relish.

"I invited a few people to join us tomorrow," said Aunt Sara, quietly.

Hope flared within her; a jolt of adrenaline rushing through heavy muscles to revive them.

"Abe and his son in-law are coming with the baby. Jazmyn has to work."

The air whooshed right out of her lungs.

"Great. It'll be good to catch up with them," Abby offered past the lump in her throat.

They worked, dancing around each other in their separate tasks until the turkey was laid to rest in brine and the smell of butter and sugar permeated their pores.

Matt

Matt helped his mom into her coat and kissed her cheek as he opened the door.

"I'm sorry Abby couldn't make it. I hope she's feeling better soon. Maybe we could meet over Christmas?" his mother asked, oblivious to the white lie he'd told all weekend. The one Gran overlooked once more as she purposely left them to say their goodbye.

Initially, he'd done it to protect Abby from poor opinion, but if he was honest with himself, he'd also done it to protect the organ failing in his chest. False hope was still hope.

"Maybe. I don't have my schedule yet, but thanks for coming this way, Mom. It was good to see you."

She placed her hand on his cheek. "You too, sweet boy. I'm glad you're here for your gran, even if I wish you'd settled closer to me."

Matt watched her walk to her car before he shut the door and leaned against its sturdy wood. Every day spent apart from Abby made him question the point of the last few months. He tried to rest in the knowledge that God knew best, but seriously doubted the outcome. They'd been meant for more than friendship, he was sure, and yet he'd stumbled through the past week waiting for her to come to her senses.

His head hung in defeat and worry as he thought of what he'd said on her voicemail that fateful day. Three little words, solid in their truth, had burst from his lips without a second thought.

Had she heard them before he stopped at the shop the night of the storm? Did that have something to do with how wrong the night went? Those words now haunted him, a brand upon his heart. Had she gotten his message? Did it matter if she had? She wasn't here in his arms, so she obviously didn't feel the same way. With a loud *thunk*, his head smacked the door he had shut behind his mother, those perfect words hounding every thought.

Twenty Four

Dear Sunshine,

It's time to come home, little sister. Be brave for Abby if not yourself.
Our girl can't move into her future without working through her past.
The weight of our choices is too heavy for her. It's time for her to know
the truth. We can't fail her now, not when our girl needs us both. Love
you, to the stars and back.

Always, Sissy

Grace

Grace entered The Christmas Tea Shoppe slowly, the tinkling chime of bells over the door unable to cover the blood pounding in her ears. Sara had sent pictures of Abby regularly through the years, but even without them she would recognize the young woman behind the counter. She looked around her sister's shop, the very one which had inadvertently helped change her own life and took a moment to slow down her rapid heartbeat and compose her thoughts.

It occurred to her, albeit a little late, that perhaps she should have spoken with her daughter on the phone first instead of this ambush. *No, this kind of conversation was meant to be had in person,* Grace reminded herself. Sara had said as much in her letter, again in a phone call, and reiterated at the house where they'd met for lunch an hour ago. The sad truth was, she feared running into someone from her past almost as much as meeting Abby. Though her sister came to see her on a regular basis, Grace had not stepped foot inside Homily's town limits in almost thirty years. And she couldn't begin to fathom what her daughter's reaction would be.

Abby glanced up from the cash register where she was removing the day's till. "I'm sorry we're closed for the day," slipped from her mouth. Delicate features shaped her face, and her slight frame lent her a willowy grace, with curly blonde hair pulled back into an elastic and eyes the exact match to her own.

"Mama?" The word came out as a question, but Grace saw the recognition in her daughter's eyes.

"Hello, Abby." Grace paused, took a breath, then spoke again. "Sara said I would find you here. I'm sure you're surprised to see me, but since you know about the letters, I hope it's not a complete surprise."

"I'm still not sure I've forgiven Aunt Sara for keeping them a secret." The words came out with a quiver, which Grace ignored.

"Please don't blame Sara. Though I never asked her to keep our correspondence from you, I sent my letters to the shop with the hope you'd never see them."

Her words only lit a blaze of anger in her daughter that tore through Grace.

"But why?" Abby demanded. "What were you hiding, other than yourself, from me?"

Grace gathered her strength and said, "Not a day has gone by that I haven't thought about you. I made the only choice I felt I could under the circumstances. I was so lost, and I didn't want you to have to be lost with me any longer. It wasn't fair to you, and I knew Sara would be a better parent."

"Well, you don't look very lost now. You could have come back for me, so why didn't you?" Abby asked and dashed furiously at the tears gathered in her eyes.

"Because it wasn't fair to y'all for me to sweep back into your lives. Selfishly, I wanted to, but I knew it would be another disruption for you. Sara always said I was welcome to be a part of your life as long as I was clean and sober, but I didn't want to create any more confusion or instability in your life than I already had. By the time I was healthy and whole enough to try and be a good mother, you were in middle school and thriving under Sara's care. But my sister seems to think you need me now. Point of fact, she was quite adamant about it," she said, disgruntled.

With a low laugh Abby conceded, "I know exactly what you mean."

"Sara always was a bit bossy. Unfortunately, she's usually right," Grace said with a half-smile.

Abby agreed with a nod of her head, and remembering the manners so ingrained in her, offered her mama a seat at one of the tables. She then excused herself to the kitchen to prepare tea, and, no doubt, have a moment to process.

Hands giving her away with a slight tremble, Abby set her burden on the white, linen-covered table and tried not to look at her mama as she poured two cups of tea, placing a plate with cookies in between them.

"I see you've adapted the southern adage that all awkward situations can be overcome with tea and sugar," Grace commented lightly to cover her own nerves.

"Some would say a little bit of hard alcohol never hurts either, but Aunt Sara only keeps peppermint schnapps in the pantry for baking. I checked."

Probably a smart decision, thought Grace.

"Based on my personal experience, I'd say sugar might leave behind a few extra pounds, but the hard stuff only leaves you with a headache and additional problems come the morning. I'll take the extra pounds, thank you very much."

Squirming in her chair, Abby shuffled back and forth.

The silence was becoming oppressive, sitting heavily on Grace's shoulders, and wrapping her in discomfort like an itchy wool sweater instead of the knit she preferred.

"Mama, would you like some milk or sugar for your tea? I hope you like Assam. It's a malty and robust blend Aunt Sara prefers. Here, have another gingersnap," said her daughter, but Grace heard the questions she didn't ask.

Why did you abandon me? Don't you understand how messed up I am because of you?

She waited patiently for her daughter speak.

Once Abby started, there was no forcing the wave of words back inside. She almost choked on them as they bubbled up and over, rushing out of her.

"Why didn't you want me? Did I make your life so awful? Do I remind you of my father; is that why you sent me away?"

The words were said with such terrible anguish, and Grace wanted nothing more than to cradle her daughter and brush back her curls, to explain she was never to blame. Doubting her comfort would be welcome, she gave her daughter the only thing she could.

She latched onto Abby's last question and started with what made the most sense.

"Unfortunately, I don't know who your father is," she spoke plainly. "After what happened to me in high school, I couldn't stomach being with a man unless I was drunk or high. Usually both, and more often than not I was with someone who would pay for my next high, or who I was paying for the current one I was on." Years later and the words still tasted acrid in Grace's mouth, but she knew better than to be dishonest with herself, though she wished for her daughter's sake she could skip over her ugly past.

Abby shied away from her words, but one sentence caught her attention. The one Grace didn't want to tell.

"After *what* happened in high school, Mama?"

Trepidation wound tightly through her already aching heart. Not even Sara knew all of the details. Grace exhaled, letting detachment envelop her as she often did to cope with reliving that night and reminded herself the girl in the story may be her, but not the woman she became.

"Sara was away at college by the time I started high school. Contrary to the perception most folks in town had of me, I wasn't doing anything their own kids weren't. Rumors are funny that way. They hit some people square in the chest while never touching others. In fact, most of my rebellion was an act. I enjoyed being the center of attention, but I was only willing to go so far for it.

"My best friend was the quarterback of our football team.

We'd known each other our entire lives and it was only natural to keep each other's secrets. But by the time we'd finished middle school, our secrets had grown in magnitude as much as we had in inches. I wanted to be a part of the popular crowd without the usual channels to get there, and in return he got to look like every other boy with a pretty girl on his arm. Even though I wasn't his type. No girl was."

Abby's mouth dropped open with an *Oh* of silent understanding.

"Bonfires and partying were a regular occurrence at the beach on Friday nights, especially after a local game. Even law enforcement looked the other way as long as nobody got hurt. At the start of each bonfire, I would pour out my beer into the reeds when no one was watching and replace it with water from a bottle I hid under the front seat when I left to find my lip gloss. If my performance wasn't flawless, it didn't matter because most of the other kids were too busy flirting or getting drunk to notice anyway. I never wanted to be out of control, just fit in with the cool kids."

Eyebrows to her hairline, Abby waited anxiously for the story's end.

"That night was different from beginning to end. It was junior year, and we were making plans for prom. A group of college kids I didn't recognize were also at the beach, probably for spring break. No one else knew them and the boys were older, more sophisticated, compared with my classmates. I remember walking down the beach to talk with some of them. A boy with dark blonde hair asked if he could get me a refill. I said no thanks and lifted my solo cup, a beacon for all to see," said Grace with a shudder.

"Eventually we wandered over to sit behind a pile of driftwood on the high bank. The feeling was intimate, and I'd convinced myself he thought I was interesting and worth his attention even if I was only some girl from a small town.

"We didn't exchange names or other personal details, and when he leaned in to kiss me, I panicked. Talking was one thing, but my best friend was home sick, and I didn't want the kids from school to think I'd cheated on him. It would have ruined our entire ruse. My limbs were heavy as I tried to push him away, and "No" slurred from my lips. Darkness swallowed me after that."

As she went on to relate to Abby, Grace had woken up with her face pressed into the sand, the cadence in her head growing intensely as she sat up. Her shorts and underwear were discarded next to her like a calling card. And, Grace continued, nothing was the same after that. Any real friendships she'd had went to the wayside, and any new relationships had been based solely on her need for oblivion.

"I have so many regrets about where my life went from there. I did everything and anything to forget that night. I know that's not an excuse for the choices I made and can't change. The only thing I wouldn't change is you. You were never a mistake. God remains faithful even when our circumstances are less than ideal. He has a plan for you, just like he has one for me."

"How can you say that?" whispered Abby before her voice rose an octave, "You were raped, Mama. Tell me, why didn't God step in if he's so faithful?"

Abby said the word Grace hardly ever let herself concede. But not saying it hadn't made it disappear all those years ago either. She had been drugged and sexually assaulted. The proof had been in every sore muscle, bruise dotting her skin, and blood smeared on her inner thighs. Rape was an ugly word only amounting to one syllable in the English language, yet its power over her life and that of her daughter's resonated to this day. Grace looked Abby directly in the eye and answered her question honestly.

"I don't know why God didn't intervene then. But I'm not sure I would be the woman I am today if he had. I know that sounds like cold comfort instead of the pretty package tied up in a bow you're looking for. A stranger made me a victim, but it was up to me to become a survivor. In retrospect, I should've told someone, anyone, what happened. But when that kind of trauma happens, it's hard not to let fear take over. And more than that, shame. I was so sure someone would blame me that I began blaming myself."

"That man assaulted you. It wasn't your fault, and his behavior can never be justified," Abby urged with righteous indignation on her mama's behalf.

Abby watched her mother with fierce blue eyes.

Grace took a deep breath and continued, "With hindsight and a lot of counseling I know what happened to me was someone else's wrongdoing. Of course, it wasn't my fault. But as a young woman, I convinced myself I must have led him on, or I should have been more responsible with my cup. The longer I kept my secret, the longer my list of reasons became until I was drowning in them."

The tea sat cold between them. The only movement in the room the reverberating sound of Grace's words.

"My shame grew into self-loathing. I turned to drugs and alcohol to numb myself from the pain, all of which soon led to stealing from those I loved, and later prostitution. Anything for a hit.... until you, that is."

Tears streamed down Abby's cheeks, and she asked, "Really? Then how did I wind up with Aunt Sara?"

"When I realized I was pregnant, I knew it was time to get my life back under control. I found a women's shelter that helped me get into a sobriety program. For the first time in three years, I was clean; working the steps of the program until you were born had been easier than I thought it would be. A healthy baby was an incentive, of course, but more than that, I loved you from the moment those two pink lines appeared on the little plastic stick. I was, however, unprepared for the hard realities of being a single parent without a job and very little support. Instead of asking for help, I spiraled. Once shame had its claws in me again, I couldn't see any way out. It was easier to get high and forget the pain."

She watched her daughter struggle with the feelings her admission caused. Grace no longer saw her life as a tragedy, but rather one of triumph and redemption, and she hoped Abby would one day as well.

"None of what happened is your fault. I made my choices, poor as they were. The day I was arrested became your salvation and mine. Sadly, I wasn't afraid of serving time. I was so jaded by then; my heart could have been stone for the cold beat it pumped in my chest. It wasn't until I spoke with the social worker that I understood the meaning of rock bottom. Instead of protecting my precious little girl, I'd neglected you, and allowed you to be hurt by others. I failed you, baby girl, not the other way around."

Abby's body shook as she wept. Grace didn't know what to do, and if her daughter wept for her mother's innocence and the years of painful regret that followed or for the little girl she once was, a child who longed to be wanted. Grace could tell not much had changed between then and now.

"My shame was never yours to bear. In fact, it was never mine to bear either. God's grace says come as you are, but I let shame deceive me into thinking I was unworthy. When presented with the choice to sign away my rights to Sara or put you in the foster system, there was no doubt in my mind she'd give you a better life. I knew my sister would love you the way you deserved to be loved."

They sat in silence as Abby wept. Grace knew those sobs. The ones that wracked your body so hard your chest hurt. The ones that that have been buried for too many years. Finally, Abby's jagged sobs silenced; she sat still as a corpse.

"I am so very sorry, baby girl. I hope you'll forgive me. I don't expect you to want me in your life, but I also don't want to be your excuse for not moving on with it either."

Grace rose from her chair after a few minutes of silence, knowing she had said what she had come to say, and her daughter would have to make the next steps. She was almost to the door when Abby snapped out of her reverie.

"Wait," her daughter croaked through an emotion-laden voice. "Maybe we could see each other again in the future?" she asked with hopeful sentiment.

"I'd like that very much, but I'll leave the ball in your court. Obviously, Sara knows how to get in touch with me," said Grace, the corner of her mouth rising self-consciously. With the truth laid bare there would be no more hiding, but today didn't have to be the end of a sad story, rather a new chapter in a life still unfolding.

Sara

Sara watched her niece lean into the doorframe of the sunroom for support. Abby resembled a wrung-out dish sponge, the conversation with her mama draining the last of her reserves. When Sara patted the cushion beside her, Abby pushed off the wall and sat down next to her.

After giving her a good squeeze, Sara rose from the couch to do what any southern lady who loves her kinfolk does—make tea and prepare a plate of red velvet brownies. Returning with a tray filled with comfort, she set it down and spoke her peace.

"Baby girl, I can see it was an emotional intervention. You can't keep living your life like this, one foot out the door, afraid Matt will find you lacking and leave first. Now, I'm not going to force you to rehash everything. Instead, we'll put on a movie and have some tea. You'll see, everything looks brighter in the morning light."

"Only because the sun is shining," she said under her breath with a slight roll of her eyes.

Sara decided to let it pass. If Abby was feeling feisty then it meant there was some fight in her yet. The Hart women never could concede a battle graciously. It was one of her favorite traits most of the time, though it rankled a bit under current circumstances. She may have ambushed Abby with her mama's visit, but it was exactly what her niece needed. Kind of like a swift kick in the patootie.

By the end of the movie, the only thing left on Sara's plate were a few crumbs she valiantly tried to pick up with her fork while Abby licked hers clean and dabbed at the corner of her mouth with a napkin.

"I just love Tom Hanks and Meg Ryan," Sara crooned. "Their chemistry on screen reminds me of Bogie and Bacall or Hepburn and Tracy. Though my personal favorite has always been the dynamic duo of Bing Crosby and Danny Kaye."

"Danny Kaye and Bing Crosby have never played a romantic couple, unless I missed something," Abby's eyebrow rose in question.

"Let's not start any rumors!" Sara exclaimed. "All I meant was their comedic timing was perfect. Did you know I saw them on the big screen for the first time with Nana and Papaw at the theatre that used to be off Third Avenue?

"How old were you?" asked Abby

Lost in her memories Sara replied, "Probably not much older than you were when you came to live with me. Maybe five or six years old? My hair was more orange than brown then, but Danny Kaye made ginger hair look glamorous." She winked and continued, "Back then the theatre alternated between two classic holiday films every week from Thanksgiving through Christmas, until the oversized Cineplex went in at the mall in Mobile. It's one of a few reasons The Christmas Tea Shoppe exists."

"What do you mean?" Abby asked with some confusion.

"Every time I watched George Bailey help his neighbors in *It's a Wonderful Life*, I wanted to have a similar sense of purpose. I may not be lucky enough to get a second chance to see the effect my life has on others, so I wanted to get it right the first time around. The shop is my way of sharing the gift of God's grace, sent in the birth of his son. Christmas is a miracle meant to be experienced all year long." Sara stood up and kissed her niece on the head. "Night, sugar. Sweet dreams."

And for the first time in weeks, Abby did. The dream started the same, but the ending changed. When Matt reached for her, she stepped away from her past and into his embrace.

Twenty
Five

Dear Mama,

I thought I'd try writing to you myself. I feel like you know so much about me from Aunt Sara, but I still have so many questions for you. Maybe we can start simple, like what's your favorite color and which kind of music can't you live without? I love every shade of red, and country is my music soulmate. No matter how I'm feeling, country music always has the words to describe it.

Anyway, I hope you'll write me back.
Abby

Abby

Christmas Eve arrived in the form of one of the coldest days on record. Abby's room in the old house carried a nip that wasn't usually present, while the hiss and pop of the old radiator confirmed the temperature. If she didn't know any better, she just might believe the weather forecast coming from the clock radio next to her bed, but she couldn't remember the last time it snowed on Alabama's coastline, let alone for Christmas.

Some adults might hate living in their childhood room, but Abby didn't mind so much. This morning, the memories of Christmases past kept her company and would have filled her with excitement if she thought there was any chance of making new memories with Matt.

"Bah humbug," indeed, she thought.

Rising to a cloudy day and cold floorboards she debated staying in bed.

I'm going to hide beneath this mound of cozy blankets. Who cares what day it is? Not me.

The idea had merit, but she quickly discarded the plan. As sure as cotton bloomed in July, Aunt Sara would come in search of her if she chose not to make an appearance for breakfast. The shop was closed until the 27th of December, but that didn't mean her calendar was clear.

Abby stared at the ceiling counting off the hours, days, and weeks since she'd last seen Matt. Four weeks and five days. Or roughly thirty-three days, ten hours, and fifteen minutes since those awful moments in the shop. Time had slowed to a snail's pace, and forever had passed yesterday.

She'd read her mama's letters to Aunt Sara during that time, creating a whole new reality, and berated herself for waiting so long to start. It had been such a waste of time. Instead of embracing her relationship with Matt, she'd spent months being afraid he'd find her unworthy and leave, or worse, that she'd hurt him. And, like a self-fulfilling prophecy, she had.

They say you can't really know someone until you walk a mile in their shoes, and it had turned out to be true about her mama. It was easy to make assumptions from rumors. As it turned out, her mama was a typical teenager who wanted to fit in and be liked. Being sexually assaulted had changed the course of her life.

Hurt and scared, she'd started down a dark road, but what could have ended in tragedy had become triumph all because of a child, a tea shop, and a sister who'd held on tight when letting go would have been easier. Though Abby couldn't change the past or even forget it, she held the power to forgive her mama and forge a new future with both of them in it.

Slowly descending the stairs ten minutes later, Abby heard her aunt call from the direction of the kitchen.

"I hope you haven't forgotten we have deliveries to make today. It'll be fun to make the rounds with you. Just like the good ole days."

What she wanted to say was, "Yippee skippy!" punctuated with large amounts of sarcasm, but it would have been largely misplaced. Leave it to Aunt Sara to find a way to prevent her from drowning in self-pity. With an immense amount of effort, she tried to infuse her voice with sincere excitement as she replied, "Looking forward to it."

Okay, so it came out a little flat. It was a valiant effort. Go team.

Grumbling under her breath, she started up the stairs again to get dressed.

Abby pulled on a pair of leggings with an oversized Fair Isle sweater, then dug into the recesses of her sock drawer for the only pair of thick and wooly ones she owned, doing a little dance when she successfully pulled out a match. She would find her fun where she could, pathetic as it was. Prepared for the cold, if not for her aunt's itinerary, she gave herself a quick glance in the mirror and tried to trade her grimace for a smile.

By the time she entered the kitchen, Aunt Sara was pulling brioche French toast out of the oven and giving it a light dusting of confectioner's sugar with a sifter. She then added a large scoop of strawberries to the mounds of buttery bread in front of them at the table and bowed her head to bless the food. Abby only managed to get one eye closed before the prayer was complete, which was just as well because she had every intention of giving her aunt the stink eye.

"This doesn't look like a heart-healthy breakfast," she said flatly.

"Hush now, sugar. I'm not even adding Bailey's whipped cream, which is what the recipe called for. A little brioche won't kill me, and besides, it's Christmas Eve today. All bets are off until after New Year's Day."

"All right," Abby deadpanned.

"Don't all right me in that tone, young lady, and stop squinting like that or your face will get stuck. Trust me when I say it's not a pretty look."

"Yes, ma'am." Abby said, disgruntled, while Aunt Sara jumped in, eager and upbeat.

"I thought we'd start our deliveries right after breakfast so we can have enough time to rest before Christmas Eve Service at church.

Keeping her sigh to herself this time, Abby allowed herself an internal *Ugh* as she searched for some Christmas cheer to hoard within her bankrupt heart, at least enough to spread with the people of Homily.

Dressed in an evergreen satin blouse with an open red cashmere sweater, a pair of black slacks, and pearls in her ears, Aunt Sara resembled the classy woman she usually was, but all wrapped up in Christmas trimmings. With a look down to survey herself, Abby pondered her own choice of dress.

Perhaps it could use a little tweaking. Maybe merry is as merry looks?

In her unladylike quest to be done first, Abby inhaled her breakfast in record time and dashed upstairs to throw on a pair of dark jeans. Her blonde curls pulled into a relatively neat chignon, she added an amethyst pendant and earrings to match the purple in her sweater. Swiping on a little mascara, she hurried to meet Aunt Sara at the door, where they both pulled on a pair of suede ankle boots and their warmest dress coats in burgundy and camel.

"Well, don't you look like a picture of glad tidings. That combination of blue and purple makes your eyes pop." Aunt Sara was no dummy and knew exactly how much goodwill a sincere compliment produced.

"Thank you," said Abby and stood a little straighter, cheeks colored with pleasure.

"You're welcome, baby girl. Here, put this on your lips. It's just the right shade for today." Her aunt also believed lipstick could transform any woman into a beauty queen.

"Sugar Plum. Nice, and may I say extremely fitting," said Abby as she smeared the deep shade onto her pale lips and admired herself in the entry mirror.

Not the fairest in the land, but not bad if I do say so myself.

External armor in place, she rallied her heart to join the festivities.

The backseat of her aunt's car was filled with baskets of bagged goodies and tins filled with tea. Uncertain of her choices, Abby said, "I think the Darjeeling loose leaf pairs well with the fudge, and the chai was a big hit paired with the divinity when the customers sampled it last week. Unless you decided to go with the pecan shortbread, which —"

Aunt Sara jumped in before she could finish her anxious tirade. "I did all three, and don't worry; everyone who receives a gift will appreciate the thought regardless of the combination. 'Tis the season for tea and goodwill to all."

"I know, but I still want our gifts to be a perfect reflection of the shop."

"We provide a place for friends and family to slow down and catch up over a freshly brewed pot of tea and cake served with a side of grace no matter the season. Reese Radcliffe was saying just the other day how our new peppermint ginger tea has made her morning sickness bearable. Your presence makes a tangible difference in people's lives every day."

"Did you know Reese's husband works at the hospital with Matt?" asked Abby softly, her heart doing a back flip over the thought of him.

"You don't say."

"She mentioned him the other day. Apparently, he had dinner with them last week."

"That's nice."

"Aunt Sara, is that all you have to say about it?"

"Baby girl, what do you want me to say? You're the one who let him go. Not once, but twice. Apparently, you don't want him. I had hoped you would come to your senses once you calmed down about those letters and spoke to your mama, but it would seem your past is too much to overcome."

Following her no-nonsense statement, both occupants in the car went silent. Aunt Sara because she was right. There wasn't anything else for her to say on the subject, without her calling her niece a fool outright.

And Abby, because her aunt's words were burning a hole through her digestive tract like coffee on an empty stomach. It didn't help that Mags had said something similar on the phone the night before.

Abby watched as the colors of familiar places blurred together into a diminished impression outside the car window. Until recently, her life had looked that way, undefined yet finished.

Do I have the courage to create a new future for myself?

It was the question she'd been asking herself for the better part of a week.

....

Aunt Sara had stopped sending Christmas cards years ago in lieu of a more personal gift from the shop. She said it felt more like the meaning behind the season to give away a little something she'd made, but Abby thought it was good business plain and simple, not that her aunt would ever admit it.

After making deliveries to nearby neighbors, they dropped off a token for every business downtown, before stopping at Homily's House for the Elderly. The complex consisted of three large Victorian homes sporting gingerbread trim and bright colors. The interior of the painted ladies had been updated to serve the needs of those who lived there, and while the inside smelled of disinfectant, the residents appeared content as they visited with friends and family in the large community spaces on the first floor. Happiness filling every nook and cranny didn't leave much room for wallowing. It was Christmas, and time for Abby to get over herself. Only later did it occur to her that Aunt Sara must have had the same thought.

"Aunt Sara, I think you missed the turn," said Abby, pointing and looking over her shoulder as they drove by.

"No, I didn't, sugar."

"I thought this was our last stop."

"I never said that."

Confused by her aunt's vague response she asked, "Well, where to next then?"

"You'll see. We're almost there."

"Okay," Abby acquiesced, trying to hold onto a little bit of Christmas spirit, but she had a growing suspicion in the pit of her stomach.

Don't panic yet; Mrs. Hanson lives out in the sticks.

For a woman who usually had a fair number of words to use, Aunt Sara had suddenly clammed up. Abby liked a surprise as much as the next person, but she calculated just how far she could run if she was desperate enough anyway. When they pulled into Nancy Dixon's driveway a few minutes later, she wanted to kick herself for not heeding her worry two turns back.

Time to panic.

"Why are we here, Aunt Sara?"

"Because Nancy and I are friends. I thought it might be nice to stop by and wish her a Merry Christmas. Grab the last two bags in the back please."

Right. Aunt Sara and Matt's gran were friends. Except she'd brought two gifts and had ambushed Abby yet again.

"But Aunt Sara—"

"No buts, young lady. Get the bags and join me on the porch. Thank you." It wasn't a request so much as a command.

Grousing under her breath about a bossy busybody, and perhaps saying a few things she would have to take back later when she finished freaking out, Abby did as she was told. She stopped at the bottom of the stairs, gifts in hand, to see Aunt Sara standing by the front door.

"Maybe they aren't home. I don't see two cars in the driveway." Translation—she hoped Matt wasn't home. Everything suddenly felt topsy turvy.

"That's because Matt sold Nancy's car a few weeks ago. When I spoke with her on the phone this morning, she said they'd be here until service tonight."

"Oh." So much for hope. Abby trudged up to the porch to stand by her aunt but refused to face her.

Aunt Sara took a hold of her hand, exerting just enough pressure to force Abby to turn and look her in the eye. "Baby girl, I know this is hard. However, y'all have to live in the same small town. So far, you've managed to avoid Matt, but that won't last forever. Take tonight for example."

"What about tonight?" she asked, worrying at her bottom lip.

"I thought you might have forgotten. Homily Baptist and First Pres combine services for Christmas Eve."

Abby's eyes grew wide as the implication sank in.

"Exactly. At least this way y'all can make your peace beforehand, and in relative privacy. The good Lord knows you won't find it in church tonight."

Abby nodded as her stomach churned. Now might be a good time for some ginger tea.

Her aunt squeezed her hand once more, this time to imbue Abby with strength, and gave a determined rap on the door.

Twenty
Six

Dear Sunshine,

Our girl is a little worse for wear, but she's beginning to accept the dents in her armor for the beautiful story they tell. Shame is a sham and only grace takes us as we are. God's love is faithful, where everyone else's fails. Love you, to the stars and back.

Always, Sissy

Matt

Matt sat on the living room floor, paper and ribbon strewn about his legs, tape and scissors at the ready, when a perfunctory knock sounded through the house.

"I'll get it," he called toward the kitchen where Gran fussed over a chess pie. His family had always celebrated Christmas Eve with a full dinner and gift exchange after church service, saving stockings and leftovers for the next day.

He'd spent the past two days preparing and had lost count of the number of grocery trips, gift deliveries and visits to Main Street he'd made hither and yon for last-minute trinkets and ingredients on Gran's behalf. Fortunately, Reese Radcliffe had taken mercy on him and removed The Christmas Tea Shoppe from his list, going in his stead. Though he longed to see the shop decorated for the actual season, and more so the woman whose vision had helped create it, he'd been fairly certain his heart would never forgive such a betrayal on his part.

Gran's drawl carried gently back to him. "A friend said she'd be stopping by with a little something."

He pulled the door open with a flourish, expecting to see Dot or one of her friends from church. What he didn't expect was Abigail Hart, beautiful as ever, tearing the wound on his heart wide open again, one which refused to heal no matter how much he tried to stitch it closed with work and running.

There she was, the woman he loved, standing on his front porch, looking for all the world like she was going to vomit on his feet any second now.

Wait, vomit?

"Sweetheart are you okay?" he asked, the endearment instinctive. "You look like you're going to be sick."

"Um, no?"

"You're not okay, or you're not going to vomit?"

She chortled under her breath, and Matt wondered if she was on the verge of hysterics or genuinely amused by the absurdity of their conversation. He couldn't help but notice the similarity to their first meeting.

"I'm definitely not okay, but I'm also not going to puke," she replied before uttering, "Because this situation is mortifying enough without the contents of my breakfast."

He gave her another once over to reassure himself that she was well enough and reeled his traitorous heart back into his body long enough to speak to Sara.

She waved him off and almost sang, "I'm off to the kitchen to give this to your gran." She waved an overstuffed wicker basket in his face. "Y'all carry on."

Matt let Abby pass in front of him into the living room, watching as she looked around the space filled with family heirlooms and antiques collected by his grandparents through the years. Abby admired the Swiss cylinder music box on top of the mantle he'd recently found at an auction, and he followed after her like a moth drawn to a flame. A pregnant silence filled the room instead of her usual litany of questions and insatiable curiosity, making him hesitate a moment as she sat in front of the fireplace. He knelt down to add another log to the pile before he joined her on the settee covered in a mauve floral brocade.

"The tree is beautiful. I like where you placed it in front of the window. Did it come from the lot on First and Oak, like we talked about?"

With a sad smile Matt said, "Of course. How could I not after our debate?"

"The entire house smells like pine and sugar. Nancy must be baking for an army."

"No doubt Sara is too."

"Uh-huh."

"Abby—" he paused, shaking his head before saying, "Not that I'm not enjoying our small talk, but why are you here?"

Abby let out a frustrated groan. "Because Aunt Sara ambushed me. Again."

"I have a feeling she's not the only one in on it," he replied with a dismayed chuckle.

Matt's lips inched up at the corner, but not quite enough to bring his dimple out of hiding. "It's fine, Abby. I understand why you don't want to see me," he said a touch coolly, and the complete opposite of his typical demeanor with her.

Abby blinked, caught off guard.

"I've wanted to see you every day since I told you to leave," she said so silently Matt had to lean in. "You're my first thought upon waking and my last memory before I drift off into a restless sleep. I feel like I've made the worst mistake of my life all because I was afraid that I might mess things up. And I behaved badly, not once but twice. I'm certain you'll never forgive me, and yet I desperately want you too, even if..."

"Even if?" Matt asked with bated breath.

He watched as shame flared across her cheekbones before she continued, "I know you can't possibly want me anymore, but I'm sorry for the way I treated you. I am sorrier than this pathetic excuse for an apology can say."

The fire sizzled and popped as it consumed the last piece of wood in the grate. After an awkward silence, Abby stood. She'd made it as far as the hallway when Matt asked with quiet determination, "What's changed? How do I know you aren't going to walk away again the next time things are difficult?"

He stood a short distance away, eyes on the ground and hands shoved into the pockets of his jeans. He wore the green sweater she'd bought him in early November, the one she had said matched his eyes. Matt wanted to be brave, which meant having faith, believing God could do the impossible, and was in fact, bigger than their circumstances.

"My mama came to see me. And I'm reading her letters to Aunt Sara. You see, someone hurt my mama, and in turn she hurt a lot of other people, including me. But her life is different now, and it would seem God really is in the business of second chances. In my case, I'm hoping it's more like thirds or fourths, but I'll take what I can get," Abby said with a wry smile.

She watched him with such hope in her eyes, hope he desired to fulfill as longing for her rushed in, filling the empty space she'd left in his life.

"I need some time to process all of this," Matt said, even if all he wanted to do was hold her close and try to forget about the last month.

Abby clutched at her stomach and started to breathe rapidly. "I understand. I'm the one who broke us. Maybe we could work towards being friends again, or grab a coffee once in a—"

Matt set his hands on her shoulders gently and pulled her in to kiss the top of her head, effectively cutting off her ramblings.

"Breathe in one, two, three. Breathe out one, two, three. Nice and easy, baby." He tugged her fully into his arms, resting his head on top of her soft hair, and breathed in her subtle scent of soap and wildflowers. "I only said I needed some time to think, not that we should start all over again. Let's talk after service tonight. I'm willing to bet those two colluders planned for a family dinner tonight anyway," he said with a small chuckle.

Reassurance settled deep within him as she brought her own arms up to hold him around the waist, bringing with it a deep-seated contentment.

Of course, Sara's timing was as perfect as her shade of lipstick. She walked down the hall, a feline grin in place and Gran radiating pleasure a few steps behind her. Everyone said goodbye with promises for later before Matt walked the Hart women to their car. After seeing Abby into the passenger seat, he kissed her cheek, lingering long enough to make her aunt laugh. With a wave and smile big enough to showcase his dimple, he watched them pull out of the gravel drive.

A bounce in his step, Matt took the stairs two at a time and bounded back inside the house. He could hear Gran singing carols in the kitchen mimicking those in his head, his heart full of Christmas cheer and Abby. Repositioning the present he'd wrapped only moments before her visit, he brought it closer to the front. The gift was a testament to God's faithfulness, and he could hardly wait to see the look on her face when she opened it. With his head bowed in humility, he asked for grace to cover their steps in the days ahead.

Abby

They had just found their seats when Abby felt her phone vibrate in the pocket of her burgundy wool dress coat. She fished her hand into the satin lining, almost certain it was Matt texting her, late to church as usual.

> *Dropping Gran out front now. Save us seats?*

> *Does a bird have wings?*

> *Always giving me guff, Miss Hart.*

No doubt grinning like a fool, she looked around for Nancy Dixon. Spotting her as she entered the sanctuary, Abby waved her over to their saved seats at the end of a pew located halfway down the aisle and to the left of the choir. Aunt Sara preferred to be front and center of the pastor's podium, but they would take what they could get with such a full sanctuary. It would be a tight fit, though Abby didn't mind so much knowing Matt would be the one sitting next to her.

The pews overflowed with Christmas blessings for those near and hollered hellos for those a little hard of hearing or farther afield. The din rose to a crescendo before dying to a hum as the choir began to file in. Matt slid into the seat beside her just as Pastor Kirk welcomed family and friends to celebrate the birth of Jesus Christ with an opening hymn.

"Nice of you to join us, Doctor Dixon," Abby said quietly for his benefit. "It's a good thing the service is here tonight. The Presbyterians would've made you sit up front."

He turned toward her and laid his arm on top of the pew, letting his lips brush the shell of her ear as he whispered back, "All that attitude wrapped up in one little Baptist. Now I know why God had to rest on the seventh day."

She shivered from the contact, and it took her a second to find a response. "And why is that exactly?"

"Because you broke the mold, sweetheart," he answered with a dimpled grin.

Abby swatted his knee when he just laughed low and winked at her while reaching across to take her hand in his. With a little sigh of content, she told herself she'd scold him for his corny joke later. Her time was much better spent soaking in his presence.

Best gift ever.

In one of her early letters to her sister, Grace asked why The Christmas Tea Shoppe was named after the holiday, the same question Abby had asked recently. Aunt Sara's familiar words rang through Abby's head as Christmas carols filled the room.

"The name was born out of the need we all have for a constant season of miracles. God gave humanity the gift of grace in the form of a tiny baby. After all, Easter morning only became possible because of a birthday. Divine yet human, God's son came to seek and save the lost, which is all of us."

In the letters that followed, Abby watched those words unfold in her mama's life as she realized there was nothing that could ever separate either of them from the love of God. His grace is always enough; to break the chains of shame, to cover every wrong, to heal the broken hearted, to bring the lost home.

Matt shared the light of his candle with her, and she watched as the golden hue passed from person to person, filling the dark room with its warmth. Abby listened to the choir sing and soaked in the truth of Christmas; grace had always been God's plan to conquer shame. Whether real or perceived, shame cannot stand in the light of God's love. Her family was proof that his love has the power to reach into prison cells and tea shops alike.

When the congregation joined in with the choir, her soprano mingled with Matt's tenor to sing, "Till he appeared, and the soul felt its worth. A thrill of hope the weary world rejoices, for yonder breaks a new and glorious morn; Fall on your knees, oh, hear the angel voices! O night divine! O night when Christ was born."

God's love had rescued her mama. Knowing the truth meant Abby could no longer continue to live as though her mama's past decided her future. It was time for her to step into the light of a life filled with grace. She was loved, forgiven, and worthy regardless of her past, her present, or her future.

With the song's end and a new beginning burrowing into her soul, Abby blew out her candle and placed it on the bench.

....

When the service ended, Matt appeared to be as eager as her to leave behind the sounds of holiday cheer calling across the sanctuary once more. With a quick glance at each other, they left by way of a side door and rushed into the cold night air.

"I told Gran we'd meet her and Sara at home. Parking was awful. I'm on the other side of the square," said Matt, leaving behind tiny clouds as he rubbed his hands briskly together.

"I don't mind a brisk walk."

"Atta girl."

Matt entwined her fingers with his and led them across the grass field past the fountain toward the far northwest corner where he'd parked next to a wrought iron streetlamp. Like glitter shaken from the sky, the first snowflakes fell from weighted clouds as they reached the band stand, landing on their hair and tongues as tiny presents from Heaven.

"Mind if we take a detour?" he asked.

"Is it with you?"

"Always."

"Then I can't imagine anything more ideal," replied Abby.

With a stop to take it all in, Matt held Abby close for a moment in the falling snow before drawing her inside the small pavilion doused in twinkling white lights. Wreaths hung from every shop and streetlamp on Main Street, their red bows smiling wide. The men and women on duty at the firehouse called out season's greetings to an occasional passerby while loading toys to be delivered tomorrow morning by Santa and his elves at Grant Hospital. Everywhere they looked was a little bit of Christmas magic created by the goodwill of folks in town.

"Tonight, is a night for miracles, Abby. The least of which is the snow, but I couldn't have asked for a better backdrop."

"I can't remember the last time it snowed in Alabama for Christmas."

"So, tell me all about your mama, sweetheart."

"I'm not sure where to start."

"I find the beginning is usually a good place."

"Smart—"

With a finger to her mouth he said, "Entirely, but let's not digress." Too late. His eyes followed his finger, drawn to the lips he touched. A fire igniting along her skin, she waited as he leaned in to meet hers with his own. Once. Twice. Three more times. The kiss becoming a little deeper with each pass.

A pitchy whistle caught their attention, and they laughed self-consciously while looking around for its source.

"Nice night for a visit to the square folks, but maybe it's time to move the show, it being a public place and all."

"Sorry sir. We'll do just that," said Matt, trying his best to keep a straight face.

"I tell them every year not to hang the mistletoe in the gazebo, but they never listen to me," said the man wearing a thick navy coat and gloves.

Matt smiled unabashedly and Abby giggled.

With a tip of his uniform hat in their direction, the officer called out, "Night, Dr. Dixon. Ms. Hart, always a pleasure. Merry Christmas, y'all."

"Goodnight, Officer Tooey," they returned in unison.

"I can't believe we got caught making out in the bandstand," Matt said with a smirk.

"I blame it entirely on you."

"Happy to take the blame, sweetheart." Matt gave Abby one more peck on the lips before heading to his truck. The wipers swished back and forth with steady purpose as they made their way in the snow, their anticipation for the evening to come and the days ahead a joyful noise whispered into Heaven's ear.

Twenty Seven

Dear Sunshine,

Happy Christmas, little sister. Praise God for a baby born in a stable! Talk about humble beginnings; the King of kings and Lord of lords, our eternal gift of God's grace wrapped in swaddling clothes and laid in a manger. And isn't that exactly how we come to him? Lowly in spirit if not poverty, and in need of a savior, one who loves us no matter what. Love you, to the stars and back.

Always, Sissy

Abby

Aunt Sara placed her cloth napkin on the table. "Thank you for the wonderful meal, Nancy. It was the perfect accompaniment to tonight's service."

"You're welcome, but I can't take all of the credit. Matt was the sous-chef. Besides, it's nice to have more people around this long table again. The two of us make a poor showing when it can seat eight."

"I agree with Gran, and no thanks are necessary. Really, it's me who should be thanking you, Sara. If you and Gran didn't spring this morning's surprise visit on us, I doubt Abby and I would be here together tonight."

"I do what I can, but feel free to name a daughter after me," she said with a wink followed by a cackle.

The roots of her hair as inflamed as her face, Abby said, "Aunt Sara you can't say things like that out loud. Remember how we talked about having an inner monologue...you know, thoughts you keep to yourself." By the time she'd finished, Abby's eyebrows had risen to an alarming height.

"Keep looking at me like that and you'll give yourself wrinkles, baby girl."

Abby didn't know why she bothered to try and reign her aunt in. The woman was downright impossible sometimes.

"Actually, I think it's a great idea. I've always liked the name Sara. Maybe Jane for a middle name?" Matt asked with a twinkle in his green eyes.

After swatting him with her cloth napkin, Abby did a mental fist pump, the words to the song, "We're going to the chapel and we're gonna get married" flitting through her mushy, love-induced brain.

Matt grinned as though he could hear her thoughts, and Aunt Sara sniggered while Nancy beamed as though she'd been handed a winning scratch ticket.

They worked together to clean up; Matt washed while Abby dried, and Aunt Sara loaded the dishwasher with anything that wasn't china or silver.

"Let's head to the living room to open gifts. Everything else can wait until tomorrow and the lovebirds can sit on the floor and canoodle some more," said Nancy as she shooed them all into the hallway with a dishtowel, Sara leading the way past the stairs.

With a rare gift for faith, Nancy had purchased gifts for everyone. A few minutes later, they were all gathered around the fire, filled to the brim with gifts, warmth, and joy.

"Oh Nancy, they're exactly what I've been looking for. Wherever did you find them?" asked Sara, hugging her friend. The women chattered about antique cookie cutters and sugar cookie recipes while Matt and Abby gazed into each other's eyes, smitten beyond reason.

"Abby's next," announced Nancy, as she motioned for Matt to hand Abby a bundle from under the tree.

Packaged in a stamped burlap sack and tied with a red ribbon Abby slowly pulled opened her gift to reveal the folded fabric inside.

"Mrs. Dixon, it's beautiful!"

"Please, call me Gran. Something tells me it won't be long before you need this blanket. Do you recognize it?"

Nodding her head in the affirmative, Abby buried her face in the soft cotton quilt, smelling of cedar and vanilla, its wedding ring design in pastel shades of blue, pink, and yellow, just as she remembered from the Fourth of July picnic.

"When Gran asked if I would mind, I told her that I couldn't think of a more appropriate gift under the circumstances," Matt smiled in her direction.

Abby looked at Matt where he sat next to her on the rug, tears clouding her vision. She sniffed and did her best to keep them at bay.

Once Gran and Matt had exchanged gifts, Aunt Sara yawned and said, "Well, I don't know about y'all, but I'm exhausted after such a full day. Matt, would you mind driving Abby home so I can take my leave now?"

"Happy to oblige."

Gran saw Aunt Sara out before taking herself off to bed. She waved and headed for the stairs quoting, 'But I heard him exclaim, ere he drove out of sight—Happy Christmas to all, and to all a good night!'

"Merry Christmas, Gran," they replied.

"Those two aren't very subtle, are they?" asked Matt.

"Not a lick, but in this case, I don't mind."

"Good, because I think we have some mistletoe around here somewhere."

Abby laughed and leaned in to kiss him softly on the lips. "I don't think we need the mistletoe," she said, breathless.

"Me too, but before we get carried away again, I have something for you." He reached for Abby's hand and placed the small box he'd stashed under the tree into her open palm.

"But I don't have anything for you."

"I couldn't have asked for anything more this Christmas than getting to spend it with you."

Abby slowly peeled away the silver ribbon and gold wrapping paper, lifting the lid of a brown paper box with a gasp. There on a bed of white tissue paper lay a small silver, rectangular box with tiny legs. Engraved filigree adorned the top and a delicate clasp on the front guarded the contents within.

"It's beautiful," she whispered.

"You sure are."

Abby smiled and promptly forgot the gift in her hands.

"Well, go on, open it up," he said, eyes dancing with excitement.

Careful not to exert too much pressure, Abby undid the clasp and opened the lid. Inside was a small silver heart with the same filigree as the box etched on top.

Leaning forward Matt asked, "May I?"

When Abby silently turned around and lifted her hair, he grasped the delicate chain in his capable hands and clasped it behind her neck. The pendant sat in the center of her chest close to her own heart, a symbol of Matt's loving devotion.

Hand on the heart at her neck, Abby looked at Matt in wide-eyed disbelief. "When did you buy this?"

"A month ago. The chest is from an antique store in Georgia and dates back to Victorian England, but I bought the necklace here in town and had the engraving done to match."

"But we broke up…"

"I know, but I believed we were supposed to be together. Don't get me wrong, I was angry and hurt before I realized God was ultimately in charge of the outcome. My feelings for you didn't change, so I bought the gift and hoped someday I'd have a reason to give it to you." Matt took her hands in his. "I love you, Abigail Jane Hart. No matter what your past holds or what our future brings, I love you."

"We still haven't talked about my mama," Abby said, her voice tight with nerves.

"And it's about time we did," he said looking her directly in the eye and making sure he had her full attention. "But nothing you tell me will change who you are or my feelings for you."

He drew her close to him in front of the fire and placed their quilt around her shoulders in comfort. Her voice hovered just above a whisper and at times she struggled not to cry as she shared some of the more difficult details of her mama's story. Matt just held her tighter and wiped away her tears. When she was finished, he turned a tender gaze upon her and waited patiently.

"All this time I was afraid she didn't love me. Or that maybe there was something wrong with me. Instead, she loved me so much she gave me Aunt Sara."

"Sweetheart, I'm glad you know the truth. None of us are perfect, and we all make mistakes. Thankfully, God provided his son to atone for those. His grace means we can stand before him without guilt or shame. Our Heavenly Father loves you no matter what, and I, for one, would never want you to be anyone but who you are, Abby."

Resting her head on his shoulder, Abby said the words she'd held back for far too long.

"I love you, Matthew Lee Dixon."

"I know you do, sweetheart. It's why you pushed me away to begin with. You were afraid to love me in return."

"Well, my plan backfired, because pushing you away didn't make me love you any less. It only made me realize my love for you wasn't dependent on you returning the sentiment." She said the words quietly and dropped her gaze to her lap.

Matt placed his finger beneath her chin, raising it until he'd captured her eyes. "God's love is like that too. Neither determined by our actions or lack thereof, it is abiding and faithful. With his help, I plan to love you like that, Abby. No more holding back, agreed?"

"Agreed," she said, nodding emphatically.

"Now that we've got that settled, we should probably seal our deal with a kiss." He leaned in, anticipating her response. Abby slid her hands to his chest while he cupped her face and drew her in. Sweet and tender, the kiss reflected the promises they'd spoken until passion ignited and burned at the edges.

"I don't think Gran intended for us to use this quilt tonight, so it's probably time I took you home," he admitted, slowly dousing their desire with a little distance.

Abby placed her hands in his and let him pull her up, only to find herself in his embrace again. She thought back to all those months earlier when she'd first come back to Homily, and a hospital waiting room where she'd felt more scared and alone than she could remember at the time. She never imagined Aunt Sara's heart attack would lead to falling in love, or that the man she loved would lead her back to her mama.

Maybe God does work in mysterious ways.

Matt

By the time Matt arrived on Christmas Day, the snow had been shoveled from the sidewalks and the neighbor's snowman looked more like a dog with droopy ears. Surprise in hand, Matt knocked on Abby's door only to have Sara open it. Sheepishly, he stepped into the house, the mistletoe he'd pilfered from the bandstand's gazebo on his way over hidden behind his back. Abby came gliding down the stairs, looking fresh and radiant in jeans and his favorite hoodie. It was nice to know she'd kept it, despite their time apart, and the kiss she placed on his cheek in greeting reminded him how far they'd come since yesterday morning.

"Hello, gorgeous. Hope I'm not too late for dessert. I had an important stop to make on my way over."

With a flourish, he pulled the mistletoe from behind his back, and though it didn't produce the expected result, it did have Abby giggling.

Close enough.

Waggling his brows, he said, "I'll save it for the porch swing later."

"Don't you think that's a little presumptuous of you?" She quirked an eyebrow and gave him her best scowl, to no avail. He was entirely unrepentant and only grinned until he dimpled, and she melted.

"No, not at all. After all, I have it on good authority that you happen to like mistletoe and kissing."

"True," she conceded, simultaneously grabbing his hand.

Matt let her pull him back out the door he'd entered not three minutes before. They settled onto the porch swing, sitting close to ward off the cold, and because he could never be close enough to her. It was becoming an addiction, craving her touch.

"I should have grabbed a coat or a blanket," she said with a shiver as she tried to get even closer to him.

He pulled her onto his lap and wrapped her in his arms while she buried her nose in the warmth of his neck, asking in a muffled voice, "How was the hospital?"

"Busy. Christmas Day is merry and bright with a little crazy thrown in for the fun of it. Tomorrow will be calmer, and then New Year's Eve will be all-hands-on-deck. Alcohol and driving never mixes, yet people continue to do it. How was your morning?"

"Like yours, merry and bright but with a whole lot of crazy."

Matt laughed, a deep rumble in his chest. "Let me guess: Sara is being difficult. How was dinner?"

"I made every effort to change the menu this year. Turkey breast instead of ham. Nope. A spinach and kale salad in place of green bean casserole. Nada. Roasted sweet potatoes drizzled with honey rather than brown sugar and enough butter to kill a horse. Zilch. And then there were the mashed potatoes made with heavy whipping cream, brioche rolls, and a cheese ball to top it all off." Abby groaned in frustration. "I'm going to die of clogged arteries, let alone the woman who's already had bypass surgery."

"What's for dessert?"

"Triple Cherry Crumble and Southern White Cake, because celebrating the birth of Jesus Christ requires a birthday cake," she said in a mocking tone that carried enough sarcasm to level a small city.

"Perfect, I'll have both."

Abby swatted his arm. "Not helpful *Doctor* Dixon."

"No need to get your socks in a knot, sweetheart. I'll have Dr. Shultz call and check in with Sara later this week. I'm sure it will help her get back on track. Of course, you could challenge her ability to make anything healthy taste good. I'm fairly certain she'll do everything within her power to prove otherwise."

"That's brilliant!"

"Don't you mean I'm brilliant?"

"No, I do not. The idea is brilliant, but one such instance doesn't change the entire package. Aunt Sara is definitely not the kind of woman to back down from a challenge."

He was glad to see the defiant gleam back in her eyes. "I think this brilliant idea deserves to be celebrated with a kiss, Miss Hart."

"It's a good thing you brought some mistletoe then."

"I told you I was brilliant," said Matt, eyes filled with mirth.

"Maybe just for today," she acquiesced.

"Deal. I love you, Abby."

"I know you do," she said and grabbed his coat to pull him in.

"Oh yeah?" He asked, breath mingling with hers and heart rate increasing by the second.

"Yeah, you said so yourself. You. Are. Brilliant."

"And you're all mine."

Intent clear in the shining pools of her eyes, she replied, "Uh-huh. Now stop talkin' and kiss me."

"Yes, ma'am," he said, taking her lips in a fervent kiss. Mistletoe tossed to the side, he held her close, kissing her until it felt like they had almost become one person.

Abby leaned back just enough to meet his glazed eyes. "We should probably go in soon. Aunt Sara will have dessert ready by now."

"Who needs dessert, when I have you?" Matt asked, picking up the mistletoe to hold above her head. Abby laughed exactly the way he knew she would, and he grinned as he listened to the sound of his future ring through the air.

Twenty
Eight

Abby looked up from the table she'd been prepping for tea.

"Aunt Sara should be here any minute," she said, placing the last cloth napkin on the table as her mama sat down.

"It's not like Sara to be late. Is she out with Abe again?"

"She didn't say, but I'm almost positive she is. Matt and I have a bet going on how long it will take Aunt Sara to exchange her single days for the last name Wilson."

"What are the stakes?" asked Grace with an intrigued smile.

"Winner gets a kiss. Either way, we both win," replied Abby, wiggling her brows up and down.

Grace was still laughing when the Michaelson twins came through the shop door at exactly five minutes to three to indulge in free tea and gossip. Abby allowed herself an eye roll when they insisted the décor still lacked Aunt Sara's finesse for tradition. She'd won the battle for the awning, but the war might be a lost cause, not that Abby would ever surrender completely. Bribery, on the other hand, was a distinct possibility.

"Another truffle, Miss Faunella?"

"Don't mind if I do, thank you."

"Did you hear about Shelby's son, Franklin?" asked Miss Florence, leaning in to share.

Abby was almost certain the older woman wasn't referring to the business association's move into the twenty-first century. Determination, paired with a cup of grace on Franklin's part, had helped breathe new life into Homily's downtown. Abby and Aunt Sara could hardly wait until the theatre reopened.

"No, but I'm sure you're going to tell us anyway," replied Abby and Grace in unison.

"I heard from the receptionist at my doctor's office, who heard it from her hair stylist, that Franklin has his hands full with some woman from the Big Apple."

"If that's true, I'm sure she's very nice," said Abby, trying not to get caught up in someone else's business.

"They say she's spicey," said the twins together, their drawn-on eyebrows disappearing into the lines on their forehead.

When they started talking about Anna Mae Thorne, Abby tuned them out. According to the rumor she'd overheard yesterday,

Miss Fourth of July had run off with a plumber in the next county over who specialized in bidets. The mayor was conspicuously absent from public life, but Abby thought a woman could do a lot worse than marry a man with a steady job. Not to mention clean nether regions.

Cue Maggie's cackle, over and over again.

At least Homily's grapevine never fails to amuse, thought Abby.

Aunt Sara arrived shortly after, flushed and grinning.

"Yep," whispered Abby to her mama. "Aunt Sara looks like a thoroughly kissed woman if I've ever seen one."

"You mean, she looks like you every time you look in the mirror."

"Exactly," beamed Abby.

Aunt Sara had encouraged the budding relationship between mother and daughter with the same love and support she'd always given them, though they'd been quick to reassure her that no one could ever take her place.

"Well, of course not," Aunt Sara had said. "You brought your mama back into my life, and I knew when the time was right, I'd return y'all to each other. The circle's simply complete; it was only a matter of time. Lord knows he took long enough."

Abby and her mama had looked at each other and burst into a fit of giggles, but Aunt Sara was right. Everything had come full circle, and where her heart had been filled with hurt, grace and hope now resided.

"What on earth is so funny?" Aunt Sara asked from the doorway as she surveyed their grinning faces.

Grace immediately jumped in to take the brunt of her brusque tone. "Nothin' much, sissy. You just look flushed."

"And late," added Abby. "Must have been an important errand," she needled.

Sara's left brow shot towards the ceiling while her eyes looked down the length of her nose. "It was," she stated and promptly marched from the dining room into the shop's kitchen.

Abby and Grace started giggling all over again.

With a radiant smile, Aunt Sara called over her shoulder, "If y'all are done carrying on, it's time for tea."

Abby wrapped her arms around her aunt from behind, squeezing gently. "'Cause any time is a perfect time for tea."

Epilogue

....

Christmas Day, one year later.

"Are you ready, sugar?" asked Aunt Sara, a sniffle threatening to sneak out.

"More than. How's my makeup, Mags?" replied Abby, spinning in her matron of honor's direction.

"Perfect. I have to admit Reese really does have a gift. She even covered up my pizza face," Maggie replied, smoothing her high-waisted dress over her growing belly. "I swear this one's a girl," she finished with a sulk.

"You're glowing, and Tuck can't keep his hands off you," said Abby sincerely.

"True," smirked Maggie.

Grace poked her head into the kitchen as Abby made a last-minute adjustment to the short veil held in place with pearl-beaded hairpins. "There's a fidgeting groom on the other side of this door. Ready to put him out of his misery, baby girl?"

Abby nodded, picked up her bouquet of peonies and daisies, and almost barreled through the door, eager to join the man she loved.

Abby surveyed The Christmas Tea Shoppe decorated yet again for the holidays. Boughs of fresh greens wrapped in cranberry garland draped the doors, windows, and top of the fireplace mantel, with a real fir tree covered in silver and gold ornaments, the occasional red-breasted robin perched on its branches, and a gold star shining on top. White twinkle lights left a soft glow over every surface while candles swam inside pools of dainty teacups throughout the room, the smell of bergamot, cinnamon, and a touch of Christmas magic permeated the air.

She and Matt had decided to keep the ceremony short and the guest list small. Aunt Sara planned to host an open reception at the church when they returned from their honeymoon, so the rest of Homily could celebrate their union in style.

Matt's mom and dad sat with his gran, the women discreetly dabbing beneath their eyes, while Tucker wrestled his mini-me grizzly into submission at his wife's glare. Reese and John held hands and beamed at one another wistfully, no doubt remembering their own vows, while Aunt Sara and Mama kissed her cheeks before placing Abby's hand in Matt's.

His breath caught when their eyes met, a wide grin spreading into an impish dimple as he took her in from head to toe. Antique lace found stashed in her nana's hope chest overlaid the top half to create capped sleeves on her silk ivory cocktail dress from Buttons in Blue, cinched at the waist with a thin, patent-leather belt, leaving the bottom to flow over her slender hips to the knee. A gift of pearl drop earrings from Gran and a pair of baby-blue heels bought by her mama for the occasion completed her ensemble.

"Do you, Abby, take Matthew Lee Dixon to be your lover, best friend, and partner through life's ups and downs, never withholding yourself and giving grace daily until eternity?"

"I do."

"Matt, do you take Abigail Jane Hart to be your—"

"I do! Can I kiss the bride yet?"

Everyone laughed good-naturedly as Pastor Kirk shook his head of gray hair. "It's always the groom," he chuckled. "I now pronounce you husband and wife. You may kiss your bride, son."

Matt lifted her veil with trembling fingers and watched her every expression. Abby smiled coyly and rose up on her toes to meet him halfway, completely forgetting their audience as Matt seared her lips and made her toes curl.

Married life might not always be as perfect as this moment; every relationship has its share of strife and struggle. But Abby was confident they would work through it together, giving and receiving grace along the way, because sometimes the best endings are born from difficult beginnings.

Acknowledgments

....

Precious Heavenly Father, I am who I am because of your grace and unfailing love.

Mark, thank you for choosing me that fateful night, and for choosing us every day since then. Thank you for the sacrifices you've made to help me get to this point, and for always wishing for me whatever I wish for myself. Until the day God calls me home, I am adoringly yours.

Henry, Grant, and Alice, you are shining lights in a dark world. I marvel at your capacity for empathy, kindness, and forgiveness. Especially when it comes to me. Love you, to the stars and back.

My clan on both sides, for your encouragement and support of my crazy midlife dream. I count myself blessed to have each of you in my corner. And yes, I will probably use each of your names in a book at some point. I know you can hardly wait.

Brianna Showalter, I am eternally grateful for your friendship and inspiration. The cover, inside art, and layout are beautiful, just like you.

Sanity Group, thank you for the countless cups of tea, faithful encouragement, prayers, and acceptance.

Arlyn Lawrence and Kerry Wade, I literally could not have done this without you. Thank you for your time, hard work, and encouragement. Praise the Lord for editors!

And last but most definitely not least, my readers. Thank you for reading *The Christmas Tea Shoppe*. I hope you enjoyed Abby's story, but most of all, I hope you experience grace. You are loved beyond measure by your Heavenly Father. No matter what. Every. Single. Day.

Special Note: For those of you who understand Grace's story all too well, I hope you tell someone you trust, if you haven't already. It is not your fault.

National Sexual Assault Hotline: 24/7, confidential support @ 1-800-656-4673

Playlist

....

Small Town State Of Mind by Niko Moon

American Honey by Lady A

All On Me by Devin Dawson

Rumor by Lee Brice

Do I Make You Wanna by Billy Carrington

Good Girl by Dustin Lynch

10,000 Hours by Dan + Shay, Justin Bieber

Just the Way by Blanco Brown and Parmalee

God, Your Mama, and Me by Florida Georgia Line

Here Tonight by Brett Young

Born To Love You by Lanco

My Jesus by Annie Wilson

About the Author

Jaclyn E. Robinson lives in the beautiful Pacific Northwest with her husband, three children, and a wee dragon—aka cairn terrier—named Mungo. She drinks copious amounts of tea, but welcomes coffee drinkers as friends, and adores caramels with her scotch. Neat and smooth, please. One can never have enough books—borrowed, owned, paper, or electronic. And, if she had her way, Ms. Robinson would be buried in an incredibly old and famous library someday. (Shh, don't tell anyone.)

Made in United States
Troutdale, OR
11/21/2023

14810468R00224